GREE

Kalpana Swaminathan is a pe
her detective Lalli, she finds her city an endless source of curiosities. The Lalli novels have been translated into Marathi, French, Italian, Spanish and Japanese. Kalpana's work includes *Ambrosia for Afters, Bougainvillea House* and *Venus Crossing*, which won the Crossword Fiction Prize in 2010. And, with Ishrat Syed, she shares the avatar **Kalpish Ratna**.

Other Books by Kalpana Swaminathan

Ambrosia for Afters
Bougainvillea House
Venus Crossing

Lalli Novels

The Page Three Murders
The Gardener's Song
The Monochrome Madonna
I Never Knew It Was You
The Secret Gardener

For Children

The True adventures of Prince Teentang
Dattatray's Dinosaur
The Weekday Sisters
Gavial Avial
Ordinary MrPai
Jaldi's Friends

Kalpana also writes with Ishrat Syed as Kalpish Ratna.

GREENLIGHT

Kalpana Swaminathan

B L O O M S B U R Y

NEW DELHI • LONDON • OXFORD • NEW YORK • SYDNEY

First published in India 2017
This export edition published 2018

ISBN 978 93 86349 70 5
2 4 6 8 10 9 7 5 3 1

Bloomsbury Publishing India Pvt. Ltd
Second Floor, LSC Building No.4
DDA Complex, Pocket C – 6 & 7, Vasant Kunj
New Delhi 110070
www.bloomsbury.com

Typeset by Manipal Digital Systems
Printed and bound in India by Replika Press Pvt. Ltd.

To find out more about our authors and books visit www.bloomsbury.com. Here you will find extracts, author interviews, details of forthcoming events and the option to sign up for our newsletters.

for my mother *Savithri*, in devotion

Prologue

Pinki was the first to go.

It was past six when her mother noticed Pinki was missing. The older children, just home from school, were clamoring over chai-chapatti. She gave them each a dollop of mango chhunda to keep them quiet, and went out looking for Pinki.

Somebody remembered seeing Pinki an hour ago, playing by herself near the pump. But she wasn't there now. The older children darted through the slum's labyrinth calling out to her. Other kids joined them, yelling out her name.

Pinki's father came home at seven. They searched the slum once more, turned the place inside out.

Nothing.

Pinki was five, too young to cross the main road. Her mother couldn't believe she had ventured out on her own.

At nine they went to the Police Chowki. The police promised to look, and perhaps, they even did.

They were still looking for Pinki three days later, when Jamila's mother sent her to the store for a bar of soap.

A-1 General Store on the main road had a side entrance where they sold goods at cut price. That's where Jamila was supposed to go, but she never got there.

Jamila was six.

They were still looking for Jamila two days later, when Pinki's parents found a parcel on their threshold at 6 a.m.

It had been left propped against the door. Pinky's father had to give the door a hefty push to open it, the parcel was that heavy. It fell with a soft thwock that made Picky's mother scream.

It was a parcel, done in newspaper, trussed with string.

A parcel, as big as a large pillow.

Or, a small child.

By that time, Mary was missing.

By that time too, all the children were prisoners. Their parents kept them close, watched them like hawks, snapped if they complained.

Every house bristled with suspicion.

In the midst of such surveillance it was incredible that Mary should vanish, but vanish she did.

Mary's mother took her to the golawalla. Mary was a long time picking a flavour and her mother stopped to chat with a friend.

Mary skipped about, sassing the golawalla. She chose a lime green gola and walked back to her mother, sucking intently on the deliciously acid treat.

When her mother turned around, Mary wasn't there.

The next morning, they found Jamila.

By now, everybody was on the lookout for big newspaper parcels.

It took them two more days to find Mary.

By then, Sindhu had disappeared.

A constable had patrolled the place ever since Jamila disappeared, but he saw nothing, or did nothing.

At Miravli Police Chowki, the paperwork went really fast.

The police were considerate and sympathetic. They assured the parents they would manage matters without an autopsy. The bodies were cleaned up and sent back by afternoon. The police even helped with last rites.

Children stopped going to school. All day they sat cramped in small dark rooms listlessly watching TV, quarrelling or crying till they fell asleep.

Eventually, when Sindhu went missing, Inspector Tambe of Miravli Chowki spoke to the press.

Tuesday, 21 March

March was not meant for murder. Not March, flirting a pink froth of blossom on newly green trees. Never March, busy with birdsong, brisk mornings, close afternoons and a swift swoon into night, adrift on a tide of stars. Not this March, so tender with unexpected love, not now.

But this was March, and here was murder, and I in the midst of it.

It happened at Kandewadi.

At *our* Kandewadi.

I can say it now. Even before murder, there was chaos. It burned in me, a slow fever I could not localize. Nothing had changed—except that I was in love. It skewed everything. Unhinged, the days swung and rattled past, leaving me clueless. The others didn't seem to notice, not even Lalli. They only noticed my happiness and didn't enquire into it. And then the call came, plunging us all into chaos.

The call interrupted dinner. I had agonized over that dinner for nearly a month.

Savio, still on the phone, caught my eye and said 'Kandewadi.'

'Our Kandewadi?' I asked.

He didn't reply. His face changed, and he looked away. The next moment, muttering an apology, he was gone.

Did I imagine it, or was the air relieved?

Certainly, with Savio gone, conversation became easier. The company, liberated from some unspoken constraint, grew intent on our guest. Nobody commented on Savio's abrupt departure. The food vanished with amazing docility. Arun was telling his Siachen story, and they were listening, spellbound.

I should have been relieved, but the look on Savio's face haunted me.

Arun finished his story to a flurry of questions.

Dr Q, whose idea of action sports is wrestling his umbrella open in a shower, wanted to know about skiing. And as for Shukla, whom I had invited in a moment of wild generosity, Shukla clamored for pictures. Even Lalli asked about the highway through the Karakoram.

It was as if Arun, like Arda Viraf, had toured heaven and hell and returned to tell the story.

Now and then they threw me a bone, but I was quite content to watch them silently.

They adored Arun.

And what a relief that was.

Or should have been.

I realized I was distracted. I needed to know what had happened at Kandewadi.

I went to the kitchen for the dessert and made a sneak call.

'You don't want to know, not now,' Savio growled.

'Just tell me it isn't those kids.'

He didn't answer.

I needn't have sweated over the darned dessert. Walnut fudge ice-cream. They would have scoffed those walnuts whole, shell and all, listening to Arun yarn about the Great Wall of China.

It was only to be expected, I suppose. I had been talking Arun nonstop for a month. They mentioned him frequently too, as in: That Guy (Savio), Our Mathematician (Dr Q), Ek-Do-Teen-Char (Shukla). Only Lalli referred to him by name.

I hadn't realised they were expecting something weedy and retiring.

Lalli's eyes widened when Arun entered, and a morose silence overtook the rest of the company.

Then Dr Q quickly got courteous and Savio made a few polite remarks. It was left to Lalli to draw Arun out, and that didn't take very long.

Shukla became attentive when Arun mentioned his Siachen adventure, and then Savio got that phone call.

Past the Great Wall, Arun had them hooked on a numbers game, and Shukla, who's a Sudoku addict, settled down to really enjoy himself. Suddenly, I wished them all gone. I was glad they were all so madly enthusiastic about Arun, but I wasn't planning on having them crowd me out of his life.

Finally, it was over. Farewells were said, and I picked up the car keys, eager to romance the moon.

'Oh, Shukla's going my way,' Arun said, with a consoling squeeze, but he seemed glad enough of the company. I heard Shukla's asinine bray all the way down to the gate.

'What did he say?' Lalli asked, as I shut the door and came in bleakly.

'Eh? That—that Shukla was going his way.'

'Yes—they seemed simpatico. But I meant Savio. What did he say it was?'

Back it came hurtling, that rush of doom.

Kandewadi.

Our Kandewadi is not the big one at Girgaum that everyone knows. Our Kandewadi is a small slum sunk off the Andheri-Kurla Road, a maze of tin shacks and lean-tos, winding in and out of a sputter of small industries. Metal works, mostly. These factories were all you ever heard in Kandewadi. Their jagged metallic clangour was the white noise that mapped most of the day.

Every morning, at precisely eleven o'clock, these sounds stopped.

Workmen laid down their tools and came out of their sheds. In little shops and kiosks, tradesmen dawdled, making customers wait.

For ten minutes, everything stopped, everyone bided time.

Savio and I had watched this curious pause a few months ago.

We were on our way to Ghatkopar when Savio looked at his watch and pulled up, saying there was something he wanted me to see. I followed him into the galli that branched into Kandewadi—and walked right into the caesura.

The stillness was near absolute.

'What are they waiting for?'

'Here they come.'

Children dressed for school oozed out of the pores of Kandewadi. It was time for the afternoon shift. Some had parents to chaperone them, but most were unescorted, the older girls keeping an eye on the little ones.

One thing set them apart from children elsewhere. They didn't rush out. They walked with a sedate air of enjoyment, almost a sense of occasion.

They were all extremely spruce, the girls particularly, their hair ribbons in crisp bows.

The workmen stared as they passed.

The children took no notice. They didn't smile or wave or call out to their dads. They walked past, their chatter subdued till they reached the main road.

Once they had crossed the road, they erupted, running and frolicking the rest of the way to school.

The men relaxed too. Laughter loosened the air. The radio blared. Men strolled over to the kiosk. Someone called out to the chaiwallah for a cutting. A general ease settled in as work resumed. Even the machines sounded more harmonious now.

'The first time I saw this I thought they were waiting for a religious procession,' Savio said. 'Afterwards, I realised it *is* a religious procession for each of these guys. Kandewadi is this whole area, but this slum's called MiniIndia. The name's recent. Second generation. It was settled after the '93 riots. Survivors—nobody cared whether they were Hindu, Muslim, Christian. They were people who had lost everything. And look at them now. Look how they *hoard* life, every drop of it. How do people live, Sita, despite everything? When it all gets past bearing, I come here at eleven to watch these men watching their kids.'

The air was acrid with chemical fumes, the heat intolerable. Men worked in these claustrophobic sheds for close on eighteen hours. And in the huts hidden between the factories, women ran homes, fed children, and sent them out shining into the world because, somehow, it's got to be done.

That was the Kandewadi I knew.

And I knew too, from Savio's silence, that something terrible had happened there.

I felt curiously excluded from everything. It didn't console me to learn Lalli was charmed by Arun.

I'd planned this dinner for so long, its unqualified success was a bit of a letdown. Everything was crowded, there was too much noise.

I craved Arun, the way I crave the blank page.

So when the phone rang and Arun asked me if I'd spend the weekend with him, driving to Chiplun, I agreed.

It was just what I needed. The open road and just—us.

Wednesday, 22 March

I didn't sleep well that night. The phone woke me at six. I heard Lalli pick it up. That was unusual, Lalli never returned from her run before half past.

I blundered bleary-eyed into the kitchen to start the coffee.

Lalli was still on the phone. Ten minutes later, when I carried our steaming mugs into the balcony, she intercepted me.

She was dressed to go out. Something had come up, then.

'Kandewadi?'

She hesitated.

'I'll be ready by the time you finish your coffee—'

'Sita. Savio asked me to keep you away.'

'He can tell me that himself when I get there. Unless you don't want me, either, Lalli?'

'No, no, I'd rather you came along.'

That put the lid on conversation.

I drove through the sleeping streets not registering anything except the same feeling of exclusion that had oppressed me last night. The thought of what awaited us at Kandewadi dislocated me even more.

I caught sight of Savio on the main road, and pulled up.

He looked sheepish when he saw me.

'You want me to go away?'

'Yes, I do.'

'I'm not going.'

'Yeah. I can see that. Let me tell you about it before we go into Kandewadi. This isn't our case, Lalli.'

'Miravli jurisdiction. Their time's taken up by something important at the airport? They'll ignore the apocalypse if there's a chance of chicken feed at the airport.'

'Airport it is. Diamond heist. They've screwed up here, and now the press has the story, so they've called me in to take the heat.'

'You have to do it?'

'Yeah, he has to do it,' I butted in. 'It's Kandewadi.'

'Don't, Sita,' Savio muttered. I disregarded that and quickly told Lalli what I'd seen that morning.

'So what's happened to those children, Savio?'

He couldn't get the words out for a minute or two—it felt like an hour. A train thudded within my skin, tunneling me, rattling my bones, getting ready to shatter my skull with unbearable tension.

Savio spoke with slow distinctness. 'Four little girls have gone missing over the last month. Their bodies were found. Raped. Mutilated. Strangled. Each child was found three or four days after she disappeared. Their bodies were returned to their homes in newspaper parcels. Delivered at the doorstep in the early hours. Miravli Chowki called me over last night—that's why I left—sorry about that, Sita. It was good to meet Arun at last.' He got that out with nice mechanical precision, even tried a watery smile.

'Never mind Arun. Go on.'

'Right. I took the file home with me—but they had next to nothing. Four bodies, and they've done nothing beyond a KD roundup.'

'What's happened this morning? One more?' Lalli demanded.

'Yes. Tambe called me at half-past five. It's my case now, officially. And we haven't seen a thing yet. The mother's got the body, and she's not letting go.'

'You've tried?'

'P.C. Sunaina tried—Lalli you must talk to these new kids. The girls all think they have to be toughs. This one brandished her lathi at the mother.'

'Nothing I can teach her then. Either you're born with compassion or you're not. Why didn't you try, Savio?'

'The usual—the child may have been raped and the mother will resent any man touching her.'

'This job's beyond gender, Savio.'

'Easy for you to say that. You don't have a penis,' Savio retorted.

'Okay, I'll go, but I'm not through with that argument.'

Lalli got out and we followed Savio into Kandewadi.

The place was very different at this hour.

At my earlier visit the houses were hidden. I realised now the tumult and noise of the factories had concealed them. This morning the factories had effaced themselves behind shutters. They were borders now, nothing more. Lanes opened between their blank outlines, and houses jostled on either side.

As usual, a tree marked the axle of this carousel of lanes. A cement platform ringed the tree. People crowded at a remove, watchful, silent.

A stern young policewoman, swishing her lathi, kept them at bay. Police Constable Sunaina.

They were all watching the woman crouched against the platform. She had her back to us, shielding her lap from the world. A dog came whining up and settled itself against her bowed back. Its appearance drew a gasp of horror from the crowd.

P.C. Sunaina picked up a stone and hurled it at the dog. It yelped indignantly, but stayed.

'What do you want?' P.C. Sunaina barred Lalli's way with her lathi. 'Police case. You're not allowed.'

Lalli stopped equably. She took the lathi from Sunaina and broke it across her knee.

It was done in a flash, and the policewoman's mouth worked soundlessly as Lalli tossed the pieces away.

Lalli walked up to the platform and sat down on the ground. I followed.

The mother took no notice of us.

She had pulled her sari over the bundle in her lap. It was blood soaked. Her hands, tirelessly soothing her burden, were bloodstained.

Not once had she raised her eyes.

The dog had got up to make room for Lalli. He joined me now, whimpering uneasily.

Lalli touched the woman's arm lightly. She said, 'You've been holding her a long while now. Let me hold her for some time.'

The mother turned to Lalli, her eyes focusing slowly.

Lalli held out her arms.

The woman let go of the child, still bundled in her bloodsoaked sari.

Lalli did not attempt to free the child, but took her as she was, still hidden, still connected to her mother's body.

Somebody came forward with a sheet. It was a white sheet, one of those crisp new sheets the police keep ready for homicide.

The mother said, 'Why didn't I hear her cry? She couldn't bear any pain. Yesterday when she grazed her knee she cried for so long—why didn't I hear her cry?'

Lalli said, 'She didn't cry.'

'It was—so quick?'

'Yes. It happened in a flash.'

'She felt no pain?'

'No.'

'Who did this to her?'

'I will find out.'

'You? Why?'

'Because that's my job.'

She was some time digesting that. Then she said, almost pleading, 'Be careful with her.'

'Yes.'

'Don't let them do anything to her.'

'I will take care of her.'

'You must be gentle—I never said a harsh word to her. I just wanted her to live happy. But she fell ill, you know?'

'Is that so?'

'I took her to the hospital, but I couldn't make enough for the medicines, just couldn't, so I took care of her at home.'

'You took good care of her.'

'No. I'm not a good woman. I'm on the job. They don't know my name here, though I've lived here since she was born. They just call me randi.'

'What is your name?'

'Tara.'

'And hers?'

'Deepika.'

'It's a sweet name.'

'You think it's like sleep?'

'Death? Perhaps.'

'I locked the door when I went out. She was fast asleep. Maybe she never woke up. It was quick, you say, maybe it was over before she knew.'

'Very likely.'

'Do you think they frightened her? But she was not a timid child, she was very brave.'

'She was brave because you are brave. You braved the world to raise her, didn't you?' Lalli spread the sheet on her lap and restored the stained pallu to the mother's shoulder. 'Is there anybody with you?'

Tara shut her eyes and shook her head.

The crowd had begun to thin. Most of the women had left. Tara looked around desperately, but nobody would meet her eye.

'Let's go home,' I said.

Leaving Lalli to carry the dead child to the jeep, I walked Tara to her house.

The tin door of the miserable shack gaped open. I followed Tara inside. She pointed with a trembling finger to the bed on the floor. A thin quilt folded down, a small cushion, a sheet stitched from a sari. Caught heartbreakingly in its folds, a battered doll.

Tara picked up the doll. 'She only had this old thing. All the other kids had new dolls—'

She fell down on the bed, and crammed her face into the pillow, sobbing.

The place darkened. There were people at the door, three women.

I walked up to them.

They backed off.

I stepped out, and shut the door.

These were older women. Late forties, fifties. Grandmothers.

'What's she making such a natak about?' one demanded.

'Like she's the only one who's lost a daughter here,' the second added.

'At least, in her case it's understandable. What about the others?' the last one said.

'Understandable? Why?' I asked.

'She left her kid alone at night, didn't she, enjoying her dhandha? Serves her right for her wickedness. What about the other mothers? Sindhu's mother, Jamila's, Mary's, Pinki's—those were all good mothers, what did they do to deserve such grief? Every day I prayed, God if you need one more child, take that randi's and leave us good folk in peace. So this is God's justice today.'

I was about to answer that when Savio arrived.

The three women lost their sanctimony very quickly and turned on looks of concern.

'We only looked in to see if we could help the poor thing,' one of them whined.

'Say the word and we'll get you breakfast, Sahib.'

'Nothing for me, thanks, but the poor girl inside could use some tea. Will you look in on her then, later? See she gets a meal.' Money passed hands.

'We'll see she gets something to eat, but as for company, she won't lack that in the dark,' the fat one said, and they walked off laughing.

Tara was still flat on the floor, sobbing into the child's pillow. Savio went out and returned with a kettle of tea.

We got her calm gradually, and made her sip some tea. In a while she managed to give us a coherent story.

It had been a difficult night for Tara. She didn't get to her spot till after eleven.

Tara's spot was at the naka, she was careful to keep far away from home. She had given Deepika her dinner at eight, and played with her till she fell asleep around nine.

She didn't feel like going out, but she had to make some money soon. So she stretched out for a bit, then took her time getting ready. It was a few minutes short of eleven when she left.

'How do you know?' Savio asked.

'There's a clock near the petrol pump, haven't you seen it? It was eleven when I passed it.'

She had only one customer last night, a no-good loafer who wouldn't pay, as if she were to blame for his misfortune.

She really was very tired, so she sat down in a doorway and fell asleep. When she woke up it was still dark, but she thought she'd call it a night and go home.

It was five when she passed the clock. She had just entered Kandewadi when she heard the shout.

A little after five that morning Kandewadi was shaken awake by a roar of outrage.

Everybody counted their children. Then slowly, door after door opened, and people filled their doorways, silent, anticipant. Somebody had stumbled over a newspaper bundle. Soon somebody else would wail, and claim it as their own.

The air held its breath, waiting for the wail which would come presently. That wail would rip trees out by their roots, blow away the roofs. If they looked its way, the wail would gouge out their eyeballs and scorch the sockets to cinders, so that all they ever saw again was ash.

They had heard that wail before. They would hear it now.

They waited, but no wail came.

Each man examined his neighbor, trying to judge who would be the one to step out and stake his claim.

Nobody stepped out.

And then, they saw Tara.

She came running, running, she dived into her hut and then—they knew.

Kandewadi exhaled. There was congratulation in that relief, a sense of achievement even, in having escaped this time. This time it didn't matter.

Doors and windows crowded with avid faces.

'It's that randi!' somebody said excitedly. 'Serves her right for leaving her child alone at night.'

'Women like her don't deserve children.'

'Shh. Here she comes.'

Tara staggered out into the mist. She stood in the middle of the road as if she had given up any intention of moving.

'It's at the peepal,' somebody said.

Tara heard that and started off towards the tree.

Nobody walked with her.

A few men stepped out of their houses and followed at a distance.

As Tara neared the tree, they stopped. Women joined them. Teenagers, young men and women. All jostling and elbowing for a view.

Tara cried out once, a short harsh cry like a crow's, and then she collapsed over the bundle.

The crowd stayed, watching.

And, useless though they knew it was, somebody thought to call the police.

'What about the other children?' I asked Savio.

He named them: Pinki, Mary, Jamila, Sindhu.

Unlike Deepika, they had all disappeared in broad daylight.

'What have the Miravli police done so far?'

'Nothing at all. The forensics was botched. No autopsy. They gave the bodies back immediately to the families to hush things up. Clamped curfew on the place and hoped it would all die down.'

'Die down!'

'Don't even go there, Sita, or I'll kill somebody. I can't afford to lose it now.'

Savio's voice trembled. Every part of his huge frame was in a clench. Sweat poured down his tense face.

He looked gaunt. I realised he had lost weight. That couldn't have happened over the last twenty-four hours. I hadn't noticed a great deal about Savio of late.

This case could be bad for him. Savio was the guy they called in when cover-ups couldn't camouflage the mess, and this was a spectacular mess. Four—now five—children raped and murdered and they didn't have a single lead? They couldn't possibly be such idiots. They had been ordered to kill the case after the first murder, and the murders had continued. It seemed to me the first thing we needed to know was–who had gagged the police, and whom was he protecting?

'A politician?' I asked. 'But whom is he shielding?'

''Tambe has no idea,' Savio shrugged. 'These netas won't show their hand, they have innumerable chamchas waiting around to do their muscle work. And there's money. All the guys at Miravli Chowki, other than Tambe, were paid to look the other way.'

'How do you know Tambe wasn't paid?'

'He went to the press, didn't he? He was threatened, his kids were threatened. He's gone on leave now.'

'So we'll never learn who's being protected.'

Savio looked surprised. 'Why, of course we will.'

'When?'

'When we get the guy, of course!'

'Can't you just swagger up to the politico and force his hand?'

Savio laughed. 'The only person who can do that is Lalli—and not this time.'

'Why not?'

'I won't let her get killed. The builder-politician nexus is very nasty in this area.'

'They can't touch you, huh?'

We were still in Kandewadi.

Tara sat in a corner of her hut, holding her head in wordless misery.

A man approached Savio.

Dagdu More, Pinki's father. He offered to come to the morgue with us, and claim the body for Tara. 'She doesn't have any family, I'll do what needs to be done.'

It was the first sign of kindness I had seen that morning.

The second was not long in coming.

Two women hesitated some distance away, waiting for some sign from Savio to advance.

They looked wretched. Their hands linked, they took a step forward. Turbulence came off them in waves.

'Mothers,' I whispered.

'Yeah. Must be.'

Magnetised by their distress, I walked towards them. For a moment we stood in stunned confrontation.

'I'm Pinki's mother,' the younger of them said, her face crumpling as she pronounced the name.

'And I, Jamila's.'

I didn't know what to say, I could only hold out my hands. Their touch restored me. We walked hand in hand to Tara's hut.

At the door, I stayed back.

After a while, Jamila's mother came out. She transfixed Savio with a fierce look and hissed, 'This woman says her daughter died at once. She didn't suffer like my Jamila. Is that true? How does she know?'

I remembered Lalli's reassuring words. I didn't think Tara had registered them.

'Why didn't her daughter suffer? Why wasn't she tormented like the rest? What was so special about her daughter?'

Savio, who hadn't heard Lalli's words, cast about for a reply.

'She was sick. Her daughter died at once because she was very sick,' I said in a low voice. 'She had been ill for a long time.'

Jamila's mother considered that slowly, weighing my words against her own injury.

'She said the other lady will catch him. You bring him here, Sahib, when she gets him. Don't worry about court and such, he will find justice right here. You're new here. We heard yesterday they'd sent for you. Tambe Sahib told us.'

'Yes. I'm in charge now. Anything you hear, anything anybody wants to tell me, this is my number, just phone me immediately. I'll be back in the evening.'

'You will have a havaldar here then, for the night?'

'No.'

'Why not? You don't think we deserve it?'

I couldn't bear the look in Savio's eyes as he mustered control, so I said, 'He won't have a havaldar here because this place needs more than a patrol. You've had a havaldar here, didn't you? Did it work?'

She shook her head. 'Nothing worked.'

Savio said, 'Tara needs someone around. Look after her—what's your name?'

'Kulsum.'

'Is your husband at home?'

'Where else? He sits with his head in his hands like a statue. Not a word from him. I put food before him, after an hour he'll maybe eat a morsel, then push it away.'

'Go home, Kulsum, and send him to me. Tell him to get the other fathers.'

'Hah. They're all the same. They have become our children now.'

'Time they did some work, then.'

'Is that what you mean to do?' I asked Savio when Kulsum had left. 'Round up vigilantes?'

'It's an inside job, Sita.'

Inside job.

Savio was saying the predator was right here, amidst us. Amidst the adoring parents who watched the daily procession of school children. One of those parents, perhaps. Watching prey.

It seemed the worst treachery imaginable, the foulest offence, one I was not prepared to consider. 'That's impossible. You can't possibly believe that, Savio. He can't belong to Kandewadi.'

'No? Then how come nobody saw him come or go? How come the kids disappeared in broad daylight? Why didn't Deepika raise hell last night? Sita, the kids knew him. They trusted him.'

'If I believe that, I'll never believe anything again.'

'Yeah, I thought so. Now go home.'

My phone rang, cutting short my protest.

It was Arun. 'Lunch?'

'No—I'll have to get home first.'

'Where are you?'

Why couldn't I answer?

Savio had wandered off the moment I picked up the phone.

'Hello?'

'I'm on my way home, I'll call you when I get in. It was the best I could manage right then.

The phone call had jolted me, and I couldn't concede why. For a moment, for just perhaps the nanosecond after I heard Arun's voice, I had no idea who he was. I had responded mechanically, lying, prevaricating.

'Now you know why I didn't want you here,' Savio said. 'Come on, I'll walk you to the car.'

Lalli wasn't back yet.

I showered, set the house to rights, got the day going, and called her. She was still at the morgue.

'I'm coming there,' I said and rang off before she could stop me.

The phone rang almost immediately. It was Ramona, my favourite YA, twenty-three, going on eighteen.

'Guess whom I bumped into? Omigod, he's gorgeous.'

'Really? I hadn't noticed.'

'You're not letting this one go, Sita! Promise me. It's not like you've got forever.'

'Ramona, you sound like your aunt.'

'Sita, wait! You sure he's not gay?'

I laughed.

'Oh great, if you're sure. I mean there's got to be a snag somewhere, right? They're never this perfect—dreamy, smart *and* loaded. Hilla told me you're head over heels—'

'Cartwheels.'

'Can I come over now, like we've got to get you organised.'

'Ramona, I'm on my way to the morgue.'

'Aren't you always?' she retorted.

With that still ringing in my ears, I couldn't bring myself to tell Arun why I couldn't meet him for lunch. I merely said I had to meet Lalli and thought I might get free by six.

'Shopping?'

'This and that.'

All this made for a very thoughtful voyage morgue-wards and I was there before I knew it. I always drive better on autopilot.

I expected to find Lalli in Dr Q's office. At this hour, Dr Q, our police surgeon, is neck deep in cadavers. He usually leaves a macabre puzzle on his desk for Lalli to solve while he finishes his autopsies. A broken tooth, a fragment of rib, a sliver of brain, any detritus of human decay—Lalli always rises to the bait, and they quarrel over the trophy for the rest of the day. Today, though, I found her frowning over nothing more grisly than a file. She looked up absently as I entered and asked, 'How is Tara? Is someone with her?'

"Pinki's mother, and Jamila's. Lalli, why did you try to console Tara by saying her child died instantly? The other moms are livid because they're daughters suffered so horribly. I covered up by saying Deepika was ill, and died of shock.'

'You're right.'

'You set off a lot of rage by that bit of kindness, Lalli. Tara believes it's the truth.'

'It is.'

'But the other moms have their knife in Tara now for it. Lalli, I don't understand how you risked saying that—you hadn't even looked at the body then—Tara still had her—it—on her lap.'

'It's obvious this murder's different. A quick, convenient abduction, and the corpse returned to Kandewadi within two or three hours. There was no time for gratuitous cruelty. The purpose was different.'

'Purpose?'

'Yes. The earlier murders—I'm reading about them now—had a different motive.'

'A different murderer?'

'No. Just a different reason.'

The file she was reading looked too slender to contain the history of four tragic lives.

'Short on detail?'

She grimaced. 'No autopsies. Just an overview. All four reports use practically the same words: *Death by strangulation, multiple injuries with sharp instrument to face and private parts.* The truth was very much more bizarre, I hear from Deepak Tambe. The injuries were brutal. But that's as far as his technical knowledge goes. Now we've lost the evidence—two bodies cremated, two buried, and we can't dig those up or all hell will break loose. Anyway, I'm keeping that option as a last resort.'

'And Deepika?'

'Poor little thing. Strangled with a scarf, probably. But her body was riddled with tuberculosis.'

'Strangled in her sleep?'

'No. She was abducted.'

'Why didn't she cry out?'

'She wasn't alarmed. She went willingly, with someone she trusted.'

Inside job.

'Can't be an inside job, Lalli,' I said. 'It's impossible.'

'That's precisely why it happened, Sita. Because it's impossible.'

Dr Q came in, looking very different from his usual dapper self. He slumped in his chair in gloomy silence before he said, 'Apart from tuberculosis, I've found nothing. Death was instantaneous. I've given you nothing to work with Lalli. What are you going to do?''

'Think.'

'The first four were truly sadistic murders. This one's different,' Dr Q said. 'Almost an accident.'

Lalli agreed. 'Yes. Those earlier children were gone for days. That meant careful planning. The murderer made repeated forays into Kandewadi despite knowing about the police patrol. That didn't change his M.O. But it changed for this murder. This was a last minute decision—hurriedly planned, the easiest victim chosen. It was a show of might. So what new challenge triggered that defiance? It's obvious, isn't it?'

'No,' I said.

'No? We were at dinner last evening, when Savio was called to take over the case. The news travelled fast. Within a few hours, the murderer struck again. He was making a statement.'

'How did he know Savio had been called in?' I asked.

'He may not have known about Savio, but he did know that Miravli had been taken off the case.'

'So his protection was withdrawn?'

'Probably. Savio got his orders from the Commissioner because Tambe leaked the story to the press. By tomorrow Kandewadi will be on national television 24/7, and you know what that means.'

'More confusion.'

'No. More murders.'

It was most unlike Lalli to make so cynical a comment. I did not then realize it was prophesy.

Something else was not right. A detail I had noticed, and which Lalli, surprisingly, chose to ignore.

'Lalli, you can't be right about the child's injuries—Tara's sari was bloodstained—soaked, actually. Where did all that blood come from if there was no wound? It was fresh, wet, and there was plenty of it.'

'Ah, I was wondering when you'd ask. Deepika had been dead a couple of hours when I took her body from her mother, but the blood was much more recent. The body was wrapped in newspaper, trussed with thin coir. The bundle was besmirched with blood.'

It seemed a horribly ritualistic touch, to soak the victim in someone else's blood. What did it mean?

Lalli shrugged. 'I'd go with something more prosaic.'

'Like?'

'Somebody bled all over the package. A gastric bleed. I smelt alcohol, so I can guess here—the man who bled is an out of work alcoholic, well known in Kandewadi. He's probably missing now.'

'May turn up dead,' Dr Q said quietly. 'That was a big bleed.'

'Yes.'

They fell silent, not yet ready to explain.

'The murderer wouldn't be so stupid as to leave his blood at the site of murder,' I said.

'Not stupid, just ignorant,' Lalli countered. 'He may know nothing of blood groups or DNA. And don't forget the peepal was *not* the site of murder.'

So she too thought the murderer belonged to the fringe, the drifters and losers who made up the rogue element of Kandewadi.

'Still, Dr Q, I won't call the earlier murders sadistic killings. In all five cases, the children were killed elsewhere and dumped next to their homes,' Lalli said. 'That's an important feature. Most sadistic killers, especially child killers, are careful to conceal the body. The motive's very different here. These are murders of arrogance.'

Arrogance seemed a strange motive for murder, but we were miles away from motive. We had to still explain the blood to begin with.

'So this could still be the murderer's blood?' I persisted. 'He bled as he was dumping the body?'

'That seems likely. Savio will tell us more about the crime scene.'

'What about the earlier murders?' I asked.

'All the earlier bodies were wrapped in newspaper too. All the bodies were discovered between 5 and 6 in the morning. They too were dumped close to the victim's home, in every instance in the middle of a path usually frequented in the mornings. Again, you see, a show of might, a gesture of contempt, to despoil and throw the remains right back, like garbage.'

It was a horrible thought. The kind of barbaric vengeance wars were all about.

'Did the police at least save the newspaper wrappings even if they got rid of the bodies?' I asked.

'No. All I could get out of Tambe was that the papers were "mixed",' Lalli said.

A mélange of languages? I had two explanations for that. 'Then the murderer either has a large multilingual and well-read family—or else he raided a raddi shop.'

'That's somewhere to start at least,' Dr Q said. 'The police must have found the raddi shop by now.'

Lalli's derisive laugh dismissed that.

'Dr Q, slowness and stupidity in the police is always intentional. Kandewadi has been ignored so far—but that's only because the Miravli guys buckled under pressure. And now Savio will have to bear the brunt of that ignorance, and resist that pressure.'

As we walked back to the car, I noticed Dagdu More talking to a woman who seemed vaguely familiar. She turned, caught sight of me, and waved.

I responded—without placing her.

'Oh she's a journalist,' Lalli said. 'She caught me when I got out of the jeep with the body. She seems to know you.'

'Seema Aggarwal.'

The name popped up out of nowhere. College probably. Ah yes— she ran with the brat pack for a while, got dumped, and abruptly turned left. Not my kind of person.

'No, didn't think she was, but she'll try to be now,' Lalli murmured. She was growing more cynical by the minute. Something about the case—something more than even the visceral horror of it—had wrung her bitterly. Perhaps it was the memory of an earlier experience.

'You've seen something like this before, haven't you?' I asked.

'Yes. Yes! I thought I would never have to again. Once in a lifetime was more than I could bear. And the worst was to leave it unsolved—it wasn't my case, I just happened to see one of the victims.'

'And this is similar—so there's precedent—'

'No. I know in my bones it's not the same. As yet, I can't back that intuition with reason. I'm going back to Kandewadi now. I suppose you have other plans?'

'I don't see why you should suppose that,' I retorted. 'I'm only meeting Arun at six.'

'Don't you want to—'

'No. I'm driving.'

She tossed me the keys with a look of relief.

I knew she wouldn't want to talk, so I let my mind wander and switched to autopilot.

An alcoholic, they said. An alcoholic bled white. Savio should have found him by now.

Savio hadn't. The mohalla drunk, one Vilas Godambe, was right there, proclaiming innocence. He swore by his mother that he hadn't touched a drop since last Ganapati.

'No wonder your mother's curse won't let up,' the tubby woman with him said. 'His tank has been full last two days, Sahib. He's been sleeping it off all yesterday, snoring like a pond full of toads, can't hear anything else even with the TV turned on full. Now the money's all gone, and payday still ten days away.'

'That so, Godambe? Show me your hands, hold them out,' Lalli ordered.

It isn't often she sounds so cold.

Godambe stuck out a pair of flabby hands.

'What's your line of work?'

'Clerk.'

'He's educated, Bai, what can I tell you? Now he tells the kids don't bother about studying, no college for you, look at your father and you'll know where a degree gets you.'

'So what are the children doing now?'

'This and that. They only want to be like the kids in the Tower, talking on the mobile all day.'

'Shut up, Kamala. They earn their money don't they? They're good children. They do small jobs, give their mother some money now and then.'

'And their father the price of a drink, I suppose? Savio, there must be a few cases of cirrhosis in the Municipal Hospital down the road. Get a havaldar to take Godambe there.'

'What for? I'm not sick!' Godambe protested.

'You will be, very soon. So you might as well know what's going to happen to you.'

'What? What'll happen to me?'

'You'll see. Now get out.'

Lalli sat down abruptly. The lean-to was full of sacks bulging with foam bits from a nearby shed. They made good beanbags. Godambe and his scolding wife shuffled out.

Savio looked strained. 'The word's out in all the hospitals around this area, but I doubt if it will do much good in locating our bleeder.'

'No, he wouldn't go to a hospital. He'd lie low till he felt strong enough to crawl home. Or else he's dead by now. That was a large bleed. He may not have stopped bleeding.'

'That's the first thing I checked, no other bloodstains at the crime scene—'

'Which was not the site of murder,' I said. 'Perhaps he crawled back to the murder site. It's his hideout, isn't it?'

A tense silence greeted my comment.

I wondered if I had spoken out of turn, the air had turned so hostile.

'That place, Sita,' Lalli's voice was almost a whisper, 'where do you think it might be?'

'Anywhere but inside Kandewadi.'

My words, based on no apparent logic, were out before I even understood them.

Savio looked thoughtful. 'How were the bodies returned? Nobody was seen entering or leaving Kandewadi on any of those mornings. There's been a police patrol on since the second murder.'

'Paid to look the other way,' Lalli said.

'Not in a crime of this sort,' Savio protested. 'We haven't sunk so low yet, Lalli.'

'I object to that "yet" Savio,' Lalli said. 'I've seen it happen all my life.'

Lalli is the only elder I know who doesn't think the past was a moral place.

'Look at everything Tambe told us. Cursory questioning, No forensic evidence. No autopsy. Quick cremation. Why should the patrol have been any more honest? There's more going on here than these five murders, Savio. Godambe is the public drunk—what about other losers?'

'I'm questioning them now—but not a sick one in the lot, Lalli. Are you sure he's an alcoholic? A gastric bleed's possible in other conditions as well—'

'Certainly. But two facts here suggest he's an alcoholic. First, the blood reeked of alcohol. Second, it was a large amount of very dark blood—but not tarry, which happens when blood is mixed with gastric acid. I'd say bleeding varices—that could be a guess if it hadn't been for the smell.'

'It might have been his first drink. With the stress, that brought on a gastric bleed.'

'Possible. Is there a doctor nearby?'

'Only a quack. He's shut up shop since the police patrol. Most go to the hospital in Miravli when they're really ill. Otherwise, it's the chemist.'

Lalli said it was time she looked in on Tara, and no, she didn't want us with her. That left Savio glaring at me across the sacks. 'You're off to meet that guy now, I guess. You shouldn't have come here in the first place.'

'So you keep telling me.'

'It's just that—I can't bear for you to be sad when you should be happy. You don't want this messing things up.'

'It won't,' I assured him. And left.

'I'd prefer to not talk about that,' Arun said, a trifle pedantically, I thought, when I told him about Kandewadi.

'Why don't you tell me about Fermat's Theorem instead?' I retorted. And, irony not being one of his joys, he actually did.

Of course, the convenient thing about being in love is that one can always switch to nonverbal mode, which tided me nicely over the math.

'You haven't been listening, have you?'

'I was, I did, but—'

'Time I rescued you from your sordid existence, Sita.'

I laughed, but the guy was dead serious.

'You think my life's sordid?'

'Isn't it? All these horrors thrown your way. Nobody but an old aunt, and brutish policemen for company. I said as much to Vasu last night.'

'I don't like you.'

I almost said that, but I didn't. There was the weekend ahead, and would I be so excited if I weren't madly in love?

But he was still talking.

'Your brother's just as bad. He said, "Sita knows what she wants." So what do you want, Sita?'

What did I want?

It was growing dark. A breeze seized the trees and tossed an early star high over the moon. A curl of perfume from a jasmine bush unravelled me. Arun's fingers entwined mine. There was nothing more I could want.

Then somewhere in the crowd a child called out gleefully. Her laugh lilted and was lost. I felt ice in my belly, ash on my tongue.

'I want to go home,' I said.

Lalli was still away when I got back. The empty house seemed unfamiliar. I thought of Tara's bewilderment when her neighbors had exhausted their curiosity and kindness, and gone away, leaving her alone with the cleared floor, the abandoned doll, the purpose of life put away.

I thought of the other kids of Kandewadi, of how they would never again walk the eleven o'clock parade with pride. The sounds all around them would still stop, but it would be a different silence.

Watchful.

The kids would drag their feet, not understanding how it had all gone so wrong. They would keep their eyes down, their voices low. They would walk afraid, panting to cut free and race across the road and gulp down the world for what it was. They were jailed now. Questioned, warned, menaced and scolded by adults crazed with dread.

I sat at the table, my notebook blank, my thoughts benumbed, knowing and not knowing the other things that were at that moment, happening elsewhere.

The wordlessness of the moment stretched for hours. Even the questions that besieged me were without the familiar crutches of logic and event. I just wanted the day to be over, and then, somehow, it was.

Thursday, 23 March

When I woke, Lalli and Savio were almost through breakfast—a gloomy and desultory meal by the looks of it. Lalli silently pushed the toast in my direction. Savio looked haunted. The paper lay between them, face down.

I picked it up.

'What was I supposed to say?' Savio groaned. 'All I said to her was that one word—no.'

'And all she asked you was one question—if the child had been raped?'

'Yeah. And she's got two columns from that.'

I went on to read Seema Aggarwal's exclusive:

KANDEWADI SLAUGHTER. VICTIM WAS NOT RAPED, SAY POLICE.

Despite this being the fifth murder of a child in the Andheri slum of Kandewadi, the police are far from apprehending the criminal. The body of six-year-old Deepika was found at 5 a.m. on Wednesday, barely twenty-four hours after the case was handed over to Inspector Savio D'Sa of Homicide. Since then the police patrol in and around Kandewadi has been withdrawn, on his orders.

When contacted on this issue, Inspector D'Sa declined to comment.

This paper broke the story of the Kandewadi murders last week.

Reliable sources have since revealed the shocking brutalities inflicted on the victims, all of whom were below the age of five. The children were raped and tortured before being strangled to death.

When asked about the latest victim, Inspector D'Sa refuted earlier reports and denied that the victim had indeed been raped.

'You can't deny indeed,' I muttered. 'Full story on page 6.'

'I'm off,' Savio rose abruptly.

A month ago, I would have walked him to his bike. Now, Arun got in the way.

Savio looked up once at the balcony as he started off, and I waved. He didn't wave back.

'Read it,' Lalli said.

'The full story? Okay, here goes—'

And then, I couldn't.

I set down the paper, trembling.

'Oh God, Lalli, where did she get all this? *The gruesome injuries sustained by the victims included penetration with sharp objects. Sticks or pieces of glass may have been used, said a witness, whose name has been witheld on request. In one case the child's body was wrapped in her own intestines, and a glass bottle—*'

'Leave it, Sita. It's probably all true.'

'Lalli, how did she know? Tambe didn't tell you any of this, did he?'

'No. I think Tambe told us all he knew.'

'Then who told her? The parents?'

'No. Tambe told me the bodies were "cleaned up"—restituted, and made decent, as much as possible before they were handed over to the parents. She's written things the police didn't know. Besides, Tambe's her only police contact.'

I said angrily, 'Every time someone reads this, these children will be brutalized all over again.'

'Very few will agree with you, Sita.'

'Don't you?'

'Of course I do. Violence is pornography—and not just for the criminal.'

'Lalli!'

'Did I shock you? The true purpose of the media is to get noticed. What better than a direct appeal to the pelvis?'

'Is the brain wired in parallel for sex and violence? What's it then, a neuronal tangle that fires willy-nilly?'

'Simplistic, but true. Savio can tell you more about it. But it's not as new as it sounds. Back in the 1950s, behaviorists like Tinbergen and Lorenz spotted the connection between sex and violence.'

'In rapists?'

'In fish! But the idea's the same.'

'So which is true? Is every human being a potential sex maniac? Or do all sex maniacs have screwed up brains?'

'To me, both questions are irrelevant.'

'Irrelevant? Why?'

'Because these crimes are acts of free will.'

'You mean there are no criminal compulsions at all?'

'Look around you. Most people in our city are compelled by poverty and misery. And yet—how many of the impoverished are criminals? Misery hasn't robbed them of free will.'

'What about insanity then? Criminal insanity?'

'All crime is insane. Certainly, there are psychopaths, and certainly, there's the occasional brain tumor.'

'But?'

'That's no more than one percent. The rest commit violent crimes with complete responsibility.'

'And you think reading about violence turns on the reader?'

'Not all readers. But yes, it does. It puts that bit of the brain on high alert, gives a jolt to the hypothalamus. Reading is imagining, don't forget. Let me tell you an anecdote from my undergraduate days.'

Lalli seldom spoke about her early life. About her days in medical college, not at all. Savio once mentioned that she had solved her first case when she was eighteen, but he knew nothing beyond that.

There was an angry flash in her eyes, as she continued.

'Forensic medicine lectures were usually a bore, but on this afternoon, the hall was packed to the rafters because there was to be a slide show. Real cases, mind you, not textbook pictures.

'Five minutes into the lecture, I sensed a difference in the air. Pin-drop silence, tense, brittle. I looked around. Quite a few men and women wore a glazed look. By the end of the lecture, the atmosphere was positively feral. Had you been there, you would have said the room reeked of sex—my sense of smell is not as acute. But it was more than sex—the audience had become a mob, alert, aroused, quivering. And yet—what were we watching? Really sad stuff. Pictures of apparent suicides. They were actually accidental deaths during auto-erotic strangulation. That sad and pitiful act of loneliness had turned on the audience.'

'What set you apart?'

Lalli laughed. 'My insufferable urge to observe others.'

She'd started young, then.

Watching a film with Lalli *is* insufferable—she's more interested in the audience than in the screen. Plays are even worse because she can actually see the audience.

'Yeah I took that for granted,' I said. 'But there's another reason. *You felt sad.* You engaged with the victim emotionally. The others didn't.'

'That's a thought.'

'To push that further, you saw the victims as people. The act was circumstantial. The others noticed nothing but the graphic details of the act—and turned savage.'

'Savage? As in disinhibited?'

'And also plain subhuman. They were watching a slide show, certainly more graphic than newsprint. Do you think Seema's story could provoke that savage rush?'

'I'm sure of it.'

'Then you think everybody's a potential criminal.'

'Not at all. Everybody has the capacity for crime, but very few have the will.'

'If you think Seema Aggarwal didn't invent these facts, I'd better find out who her source is—there's an email ID in the paper, but perhaps I can talk to someone who knows her.'

'Don't bother,' Lalli yawned. 'She'll come looking for you.'

Lalli had spent the night at Kandewadi with Savio. She looked completely worn out.

'Why don't you lie down for a bit?' I suggested.

'What does Arun think of all this?' she asked.

'He doesn't want to.'

'And?'

'He thinks I have a sordid life.'

'Sordid!'

'Yeah, strange word, eh? He's not big on words. Maybe he meant morbid.'

'What's the difference?'

'Sex and death again. Wires entangled in the brain.'

We laughed, but it didn't ring true.

Arun phoned to say he had a friend who wanted to meet me and could she come over right now?

'What's this about?' I asked.

He made an impatient sound, a furry semi-growl I rather liked.

I don't like strangers sprung on me when I want to write, but, oh well.

'Twelve o'clock?' I said, and prayed she wouldn't stay for lunch.

Lalli placed something next to me. I picked it up without looking—and then dropped it with a cry.

It was the doll I had seen in Tara's hut, Deepika's battered doll.

Plastic dolls come in two categories. The bloated baby-faced staple of yesteryears is still going strong in shades of peach and beige. This is the sort that parents choose.

The other sort is the leggy Barbie clone with precocious breasts and detachable wardrobe. Her spidery limbs and taut torso are unyielding and brittle. These dolls have sharp pixie features and are big on hair. Little girls lust after them.

Deepika's doll was of the first sort.

It wore a pink net dress. Tara had evidently made it as apology—she had stitched on sequins lavishly. Many now hung loose, but many more had been ripped away.

The doll's face had been improved with some detailing in blue ballpoint. Besides ambitious eyebrows, a pair of spectacles had been inked in. Narrow ovals, elegantly angled, they gave the face a cat-like allure. A tentative moustache had been attempted, then, earnestly rubbed away, leaving a blue stain around the bubblegum pink pout.

'So what do you think?' Lalli asked.

'It's a two-way guilt trip. Mom's guilty because she chose the wrong doll. She stitched the dress to make up. Kid's guilty because she hates the doll, but feels bad about hurting her mother.'

'Tara tell you about it?'

'No, I deduced it.'

'Thanks, Sherlock. I meant to ask if Tara told you about the new doll.'

I remembered Tara's words then.

'Yes, she said all the other girls had new dolls, but this old thing was all she'd given her daughter.'

'Exactly. So I asked to see those new dolls, and guess what, none of the little girls in Kandewadi has had a new doll recently. Deepika's life was a little different from the others. She didn't go to school, Tara taught her at home. Tara's educated—eighth standard. Tara spent all day making piece jewellery, those pretty trinkets sold on trains. She made earrings, mostly, and Deepika helped her. In the evenings she played around the house under Tara's eye. So the only kids she knew were those in the immediate vicinity, and for certain, none of them had a new doll. But that's just what their mothers say.'

'Meaning?'

'The children might have a different tale to tell. Are you free later today? Around three? We should have set up everything by then.'

'Set up what? A trap for the killer?'

'I wish! A safe-house for the kids between school and dinner time. TV, games, drawing, books, that sort of thing. Parents can pick them up when they're back from work.'

'You'll need a huge space. There must be a hundred kids—more.'

'Fifty girls and thirty boys below ten. I've spoken with the older ones already. I think only the little ones are in danger. Can you come?'

It hurt that she thought to ask. I nodded and went back to the doll.

The doll had one game arm. It was held in place by the net sleeve, but worked itself loose at first touch. Funny. This kind of doll did not have detachable limbs.

It wasn't easy to slip off the sleeve. It had been sewn very tight on the inner side with large uneven stitches, ugly but effective. Deepika's handiwork probably.

I unpicked the stitches with misgiving,

I almost felt her anxiety to keep the deed from her mother.

I won't tell, I whispered to her, to myself, I'll sew it back again.

The arm hadn't come detached. It had been cut—sliced was more apt—with a very sharp blade and then the blade had been twisted to widen the gap. That hadn't worked well, so the rest of the circumference had been tediously clipped with short bladed scissors, leaving a small fraying stalk attached to the shoulder.

Lalli had silently joined me. We peered into the gaping aditus to the doll's hollow torso.

'It's her treasure trove,' Lalli said in a low voice.

I couldn't bring myself to look and pushed the doll across to her.

She slid in a cautious finger and drew out a bit of pale blue fluff. More emerged, and finally a silky powder puff toppled out.

There was more. A green satin ribbon with silver dots. Three long feathers dyed yellow, pink and purple. A pair of sparkly earrings.

And saddest of all, a small school tie, grey with two crimson bars. The tie was faded and worn with washing and its tip had been chewed to a frazzle.

Lalli went to the cupboard and returned with needle and thread. We didn't put back the treasures immediately.

'She pinched them.' I felt a traitor saying it.

'Not all of it. She only pinched the tie and the earrings,' Lalli said. She stuffed in the tie and the earrings and stitched the sleeve back over the restituted arm. 'Somebody gave her these things over a period of time.'

'What makes you say that?'

'Notice the escalation in luxury. The feathers are from a dyed feather duster, many local shops still stock them. Or maybe it's from a household fixture. The silver dotted satin ribbon is the new Chinese merchandize flooding all the shops. But the puff's different.'

She was right. An elusive fragrance rose from the pale blue fluff, and wrung me with pain.

Lalli had disappeared into her room. She returned dressed in a soft cotton sari, a deep shade of mustard I hadn't seen before.

'I'll expect you at four,' she said as she left.

I was still staring at the doll when the doorbell rang.

I was startled to find it was nearly twelve. I had recently returned Mr Mistry's grandfather clock to its rightful owner, and without its reverend bass to warn me, I often found myself in a time warp. The timepiece on the bookshelf was as sneaky as an hourglass, always half an hour ahead of whatever I was doing. I ignored it unless I needed something from the shelf.

Darn—if it was noon already, this must be Arun's friend.

But it was Seema Aggarwal.

My surprise obvious, she said, 'I hope this isn't inconvenient, Seeta.'

'Sita,' I corrected mechanically.

'Yeah, I remember you made a big thing of that in college. What's it? Numerology?'

I didn't get that, but explained awkwardly 'Seema, come in, but I have another appointment any moment – '

'Oops! Arun said it was okay for you around twelve, I'm a little early.'

'You're Arun's friend?'

It sounded rude, but I'd said it already.

She shrugged. 'Ex. Whatever. We're still friends.'

'He didn't mention the name—come on in and let me get you something to cool off.'

Ex *what*? Oh well, he'd tell me by and by.

'Thanks,' she took the glass of sharbat from me and settled down with a couple of cushions. 'Oooh. This is cozy. You do live. But this isn't your place is it?'

'No. I live with my aunt.'

'Tall lady I met at the mortuary? I was surprised to see her, really.'

'Oh? Why?'

'She carried the body into the morgue, you know. Actually physically carried it in her arms.'

Did she expect Lalli to swing it about in a bag?

I kept silent, taking in Seema Aggarwal.

She had changed, of course. Who hasn't, in ten years? *Then* she had been what we called flashy–trashy before her trophy boyfriend dumped her. On the rebound she turned feminist, forswore low-rise jeans and cropped tops and went about saving the world in baggy shalwars. That phase too, had apparently worn off.

She was dressed in khaki cutoffs and a checked shirt unbuttoned over a black lace vest stretched very thin. Journalism was her thing now, and a very good thing, too, apparently. The bag was Fendi, the shoes definitely not Linking Road. She took out a small recorder from the bag and set it ostentatiously between us.

'What's that for?'

'I want an exclusive—didn't Arun tell you?'

'He just said a friend wanted to meet me.'

'As vague as that? And you agreed? You must be smitten.'

'An exclusive what?' I asked with some irritation.

'You found the body in Kandewadi, didn't you? You and your aunt? I tried talking to her, but it was hardly the right time— Perhaps I could meet her too, Seeta?'

'Sita.'

'Yeah. You said. Numerology. You really think it will change your luck?'

'That's the second time you've mentioned it. What does Numerology have to do with my name?'

'Seeta becomes Sita and it's not Numerology?'

'It never was Seeta. I was born Sita. Different word. Different meaning.'

'Sure. Whatever works for you.'

Nothing gets me as mad as hearing my name mangled. I was furious now, but considering her provenance, all I could do was scowl.

'So tell me—how did you find the body?'

'I didn't. And I have nothing to say,' I blurted out. 'You're wasting your time here, Seema. I got all my information from your story this morning.'

'But how come you and your aunt landed up with the body then? Do you know people in Kandewadi?'

I decided to lie. 'Yeah. We heard of what happened, and went there.'

'To help, I suppose. You knew of the earlier murders?'

'Now we do, from your story.'

'But how did your aunt end up carrying the body in the police jeep?'

'She told the child's mother she would accompany the body.'

'Why?'

'Why not? Somebody had to.'

'Your aunt's done this kind of thing before?'

'Maybe.'

'You came in much later. Where were you? Still in Kandewadi?'

'No. I had stuff to do. I got to the mortuary later to pick up my aunt.'

'She seemed to know her way around. She has contacts in the police?'

'You have contacts in the police don't you? All those details in your story—'

'I have my sources, yes. Okay tell me, Seeta—sorry Sita—you saw the body, you know the child had been brutalized, raped, mutilated—can you tell me what you saw exactly?'

I stopped her. 'I did not see the body.'

'No? That's too bad. But your aunt has. When can I meet her? Where?'

'You can't. She's gone to Delhi.'

And Lalli, my untrustworthy aunt, chose that very moment to walk into the flat.

I glared at her. 'You missed your flight? Again?'

Lalli played up. She threw her hands up ruefully. 'I'm sorry!'

'Have you called Delhi?'

'I didn't dare—'

'They'll kill you, that's my only comfort,' I said. 'Seema, meet my aunt who makes it a habit to run away from airports. Lalli, this is the friend whose story you read on page six. Now excuse me while I take off to straighten your life.'

Phone in hand, I dived into the kitchen and made convincing noises. I could hear them clearly.

'So you were on your way to Delhi? A family visit?'

'Distant.'.

'You remember we met yesterday, very briefly.'

'Did we? Oh. Where?'

'At the mortuary.'

'Ah yes.'

'You brought the body.'

'So I did.'

'Why?'

'Somebody had to.'

'Surely the police were there.'

'True.'

'The less said about them the better, eh?'

'That's what your story says.'

'But you carried the body, you know the truth.'

'About what?"

'The murder.'

'I don't.'

'But what about the injuries? Was the child raped?'

'Not to my knowledge, but you should contact the Police Surgeon for details.'

'Dr Qureshi, right? He's never available.'

'Right.'

'Which NGO do you work for?"

Lalli laughed. 'Oh I don't work for anybody. '

'Retired?'

I didn't hear Lalli's answer.

Seema said, 'So what's it like on Ground Zero?'

'Sorry?'

'Kandewadi. What's it like? What was the feeling you got this morning?'

It was time for me to move in. I held out the phone to Lalli. 'They won't take no for a answer, they have you on the two o'clock flight. And this time I'm driving you to the airport. Sorry Seema, got to run. We'll catch up later.'

'Okay, listen, I'm counting on you for tomorrow—'

'What's tomorrow?'

'Follow us on Twitter.'

I remembered then the paper had exhorted me much the same way: follow us on Twitter@kandewadi.com

The door had barely shut on Seema when Lalli picked up the car keys.

'That was only pretend,' I protested.

'That charade's over, but another beckons. I returned to ask if you'd come along.'

'Where to?'

But she had charged ahead of me. I grabbed my bag and followed.

We were driving to the mortuary—Lalli was driving, I was listening.

'This morning the police found a body in a nallah, a few streets away from Kandewadi. A young man in his twenties. The body was nude. They also found clothes stuck in the castor bushes along the nallah bank some distance away. The clothes were bloodstained.'

'It's him!'

'Maybe, maybe not.'

'But why not? He died proclaiming his guilt!' I protested. 'Why would he strip otherwise? Guilt, stronger than the fear of death, overcame him.'

'Irrefutable. Certainly, he was guilty—but of what? If he's the guy who brought the dead child back, does it also mean he murdered her?'

'How can you tell anymore?

'For starters, we should identify him. Then trace his last hours. Shouldn't be too difficult. Savio doesn't think this is the murderer. He's fighting the ACP over it. The Commissioner asked me to sit in. They're in a great hurry to close the case.'

'Why?'

'That's what I want to find out. Also, the autopsy must be over by now. Dr Q asked me to bring you along.'

'Me? Whatever for?'

'For the joy of it.'

So it was over, and without any effort or skill on the part of the police. The murderer, if that's what he was, had bled to death in a nallah, and the children of Kandewadi were safe again.

No wonder Savio felt cheated—but that peeve wasn't enough for him to insist it was the wrong man. He must have another reason.

'Which reminds me, we never did ask Seema who her reliable source was,' I said.

'Nobody in the police. She wouldn't have asked me if I worked for an NGO, otherwise.'

'True.'

'Whatever's the party planned for tomorrow, do please go, Sita. Check out Twitter@kandewadi.com.'

'Pressure group for police action, probably.'

'That would make sense, but somehow I don't think it's a pressure group.'

'Then what would she need me for?'

'You'll find out.'

A welcome committee awaited Lalli at the mortuary. The uniforms whisked her away, leaving me to cool my heels in the corridor.

Not for long. Shukla's Cheshire cat grin lit up the horizon.

'What Sita, back to morgue? I was thinking you must be in Siachen by now,' he observed.

'No reason why I can't be both places.'

'Reason is there in physics. Ask Ek-Do-Teen-Char, he will explain.'

'Savio's in there with them?'

He nodded gloomily. He seemed to have run out of wisecracks, a first for Shukla.

'Big trouble. Savio should have refused this case.'

'No.'

'Easy for you to say that, Sita. But I'm not blaming you. It's your job.'

'My job?'

'Suppose, for purpose of argument, two minutes only, you are usual mistake, Seeta not Sita. Why for you need golden deer? Forest is full of brown deer, spotted, chital, sambar, all types freely available, but no, you will ask for golden deer. First you want leather for fashion, then quickly because of activists you become pc and say don't kill it, I want it for a pet. So double trouble. If he kills deer, he is terrorist. If he lets deer escape, he is idiot.'

'That's just the male viewpoint. Anyway, what's that got to do with Kandewadi?'

'Nothing. Only showing logic of your point of view.'

'Savio's not one to dodge a difficult case.'

'Listen, Sita. This is not about a difficult case. It is about Savio. But if I have to explain that to you, it's too late.'

'Too late for what?'

'Too late for you. Better pack up and run to Great Wall of China.'

And the irritating man turned on his heel and walked away.

I sat down gloomily in the anteroom.

In a little while Savio came out. We walked to the canteen. The waiter plonked down two milky coffees and abandoned us.

'Lalli said you don't think he's the guy,' I said after I'd watched him twirl the spoon in his coffee, setting off an eddy of grounds.

'The body? Yeah. It isn't him. But they want it to be. Dr Q's not sure, so he sent for Lalli.'

'But you're sure?'

'Yep.'

'Why?'

'No motive.'

'Motive! Wasn't the act motive in itself?'

'Crime for crime's sake? No. Here's this twenty-year-old kid—dead from a big bleed from the stomach. No alcohol in the stomach now, but there was in the earlier bleed, both on the newspaper packaging and on the clothes. But the body shows no other signs of alcohol abuse. So I'd agree with Dr Q, it is a stress-induced gastric bleed.

'That's all we have. Once we match the blood, we'll know for sure if this is the man who bled over the packaged body. That's all we'll know.'

'I agree,' Lalli joined us. 'There's nothing to connect this boy with the murders except circumstantial evidence. There's nothing to connect him with the previous murders at all. I had quite a fight in there, Savio. I could only get them to listen by threatening to make them look silly. One week. The Commissioner's willing to hold off for a week, no more. After that, he's making a statement. I've got the ACP to shut up for the time being, but he's likely to erupt. This is make or break for you, Savio.'

'A week, you said. May not be enough. What do you want me to do?'

'You know what to do.'

'Sita?'

'Don't drink that coffee.'

'That's all you have to say?'

'Yeah.'

'Sita, Dr Q wants you to view the body,' Lalli said. 'I haven't yet, so we might as well.'

She walked on ahead, leaving us to trail her.

'Savio, why are they so eager to close the case?'

'They've wanted it gagged from the beginning. Tambe said the pressure was something frightful. In the first murder things moved quickly for 24 hours, then the men were taken off the job, diverted to the Airport, and substitutes sent in. Then the second murder made Shahani—he's the guy in charge—sit up in alarm and he put up a patrol—'

'Of substitutes?'

'Exactly. Eyewash. Third case, and everyone panicked. Tambe did what he could, which, frankly, wasn't much, but he used all the pull he had to get Shahani in line, and when that didn't work, he leaked the story to the press. Apart from your friend, the press hasn't been all that interested.'

'She's not my friend. Still, if her story's caught public attention, I suppose that's all for the good.'

'You wouldn't sound so gloomy if you thought so.'

'Oh, it's just vile, writing up all those horrors with relish. Voyeuristic. Lalli thinks it's porn.'

He nodded, but he was far away.

'Who wants to kill the case? Did you find out?" I decided to be blunt about it.

'No. I got my orders from the Commissioner, which was strange enough. Shukla's not with me on this one.'

'No? What's he doing here then?'

But we were entering Autopsy now, and Savio found no need to reply.

Besides, Shukla was there with Lalli, standing respectfully behind Dr Q.

Dr Q isn't so much doctor as high priest to the dead, and the autopsy room is his sanctum. In here, you wait till he notices you. My visits here were rare—I had perhaps entered the room twice in all. I had never watched an autopsy.

Why had I been summoned?

'Sita, I need your help,' Dr Q had his back to me. 'Stop right there at the door. Now close your eyes, and let Savio lead you to me. When I ask you to open your eyes, say the first word that comes to mind. *Now.*'

I shut my eyes with alacrity, perhaps to escape the ambience.

Savio's fingers trembled on my arm as though my skin might singe him. He stayed a step behind me, close, a cocoon of warmth.

As I took a step forward, the mortuary with its ghastly occupant vanished from consciousness. I was lifted into another dimension.

Where was I? The air pooled, soft and still. Delicious tendrils of coolness caressed my neck. I leaned back in luxury, bridging the gap between us. I was laved by languor, unfurled, anticipant—

'Open your eyes please.'

'*Kanaka.*'

I turned to Savio. His deep eyes mirrored mine.

And then the trance broke. I realized where Savio had led me—right to the last slab in the mortuary. I tried not to look at what lay on it.

Dr Q was waiting.

'Kanaka. *Cananga odorata*. Ylang-ylang. There was a tree in my grandmother's house. Greenish yellow flowers like delicate banana skins.'

That was what I had smelt. The scent had turned the room of death into paradise.

'Ah. I knew I could depend on you,' Dr Q sounded smug. 'I thought I smelt something on the body, but it was elusive. The clothes are gamey—this scent is quite different. So what is it, Sita, a perfume?'

Perfume? Ylang-ylang's sweet peppery note lends shimmer to some greats, Chanel 5 for one. But this was so much more. Pure. Intense. Then, gone with the next breath, just as the petals of the flower wilt at first touch.

'No, not a perfume,' I decided. 'It smells more like the fresh flower.'

Now that the scent had completely ebbed away, I was jolted into confronting the slab.

Next to me was the body of a young man. That's all I saw. In death, youth was his only identity.

Stitches from neck to pelvis laced him shut, like a complicated boot. Various bits and pieces of him dotted the adjoining bench. Deprived of them he was yet complete and beautiful, like an untenanted shoe.

As I turned away, I smelt the perfume again.

No. I *remembered* it.

I had smelt it before I entered the autopsy room. I had smelt it very recently.

I felt Lalli's eyes question me and I shook my head impatiently. I couldn't recall any more just then.

I heard Dr Q say, 'All I can find is bleeding from lower end of the esophagus, a classic Mallory-Weiss tear. No gastric ulcer, no gastritis. The bleed was probably caused by stress, although there was alcohol in the stomach. Is this the man who brought in the dead child? I'll have to match the blood before I can tell. But yes, he probably was.'

Lalli picked up a filthy T-shirt from the pile of clothes on the bench.

'Look at the bloodstains on the shirt. There's a clean area where the package was in contact with his body. There's blood around it. Spatter marks at the sides, a drip below. He bled over the package. I won't wait for the blood match. This is the man who delivered the parcel that contained Deepika.'

'Agreed,' Savio said. 'If he's a Kandewadi man, he wouldn't have picked up the package out of curiosity. By now everybody knows what a package like that contains. If he's a Kandewadi man, he was holding the package with full knowledge of its contents. But he could have been just a passerby. He picks up the package on impulse. Perhaps he's a regular thief, or else decides to take his chance on something big and carefully packed. A minute later, he remembers having read or heard what it could be. The sheer terror of the moment brings on the bleed. Then he drops the package and flees.'

'No, you're wrong!'

I was startled to recognize the voice as my own.

'Savio, he was no passerby. He knew what the parcel was. He knew who it was. *He knew Deepika.*'

Why did I say that?

They were waiting for me to explain, but I couldn't.

And then, perhaps the air stirred, awakening a current of perfume, and I remembered where I had smelt kanaka, earlier—

'Lalli, *he* gave Deepika those treasures. The pale blue puff inside her doll smelt of kanaka too.'

Lalli sighed. The room grew quiet, waiting for her to explain. She told them about the doll and its hidden treasures.

About the pale blue powder puff, scented with ylang-ylang.

'Tree is growing in backyard. Banana-skin tree. Find tree, find murderer.'

Shukla's incisive logic as usual cut to the chase.

'Does it flower in March?' Lalli asked.

'All summer. Maybe March isn't too early.'

'Trees are not keeping to schedule,' Shukla rebuked.

Silently, I agreed.

Not anymore, they weren't.

23rd February used to mark the first scarlet flags on our coral trees, but I hadn't seen a single coral flower the last five years. Plumes of lagerstroemia and generous copper-pod still coloured April, but I could seldom find a golden lantern of cassia by the 14th to light up Vishu. Startling cups of flame of the forest showed now and then on very young trees that didn't know any better. And the gulmohar, which should have been properly reticent till the monsoon broke, bled all over pavements in March. Trees were definitely not keeping to schedule.

'Ok, look for a tree,' Lalli shrugged. 'Sita, which was the more intense—the scent you smelt here, or the one on the puff?'

They were both the same, really.

When I said so, Lalli's face cleared, a faint flush brightened her, and she seemed impatient to be gone.

'That's it, then, Dr Q? Bleed from the lower esophagus, classic Mallory-Weiss tear, hypovolemic shock. And you'll let me know about blood levels of alcohol and heroin.'

'Not enough?' Dr Q grimaced.

'Not enough, not nearly enough.'

Dr Q's eyes followed Lalli as she left. He turned to me, 'Get me a flower when you find the tree.'

'If,' Shukla corrected him. 'Outside Jijamata Udyan, where to look?'

'That's easy—look within a kilometer radius of Kandewadi. The scent disappears real fast,' I told him.

Shukla left too, and Savio and I and Dr Q stayed deadlocked with the corpse.

'Can't trust this new fellow to do the decent thing,' Dr Q muttered and shuffled away. He returned with a suit of clothes draped on his arm. He keeps a small unisex stash for unclaimed bodies, standard issue white pyjamas and shirt.

The surly man in tow seemed to be the new attendant.

'Watch while we do this, next time I won't be telling you how,' Dr Q growled at the attendant, and handed Savio a towel.

I watched as they hosed down the body, wrapped the towel around it, and moved it to the next slab.

The surly man had lost some of his surliness by now and came forward to help Dr Q pull on the pyjamas, while Savio dried off the hair and passed a comb through it. By the time they got him on the trolley, the dead man looked spruce enough for a job interview.

The attendant hesitated over the green sheet meant to cover the body.

Dr Q raised a forbidding eyebrow.

The attendant let the sheet fall and pushed the trolley out, looking unhappy.

People didn't understand Dr Q's ways very often, and he never bothered to explain his courtesies towards the homeless dead. Savio and Shukla compacted silently with him, as Lalli had, earlier.

But this body, I thought, might not need them. A small knot of frightened faces had gathered in the corridor, waiting to put a name to the dead man.

They didn't know him.

Savio mumbled he didn't expect they would, not after Dr Q's ministrations.

The corpse had never looked this comely in life.

Savio wheeled away the trolley and returned in a few minutes with the passenger looking considerably changed.

He was a mess now, but he looked more comfortable. With his hair ruffled and the bloodstained T-shirt tucked over his shoulders, he didn't look so dead now, merely tired, a boy fast asleep. The onlookers remained thoughtful. Then a voice said hesitantly, 'Looks a bit like that kid from the store, doesn't it? What's his name—Daya?'

Daya it was.

An hour later, A-I General's proprietor Jaggu Gala, brought post haste to the morgue in a police jeep, made the identification unwillingly.

'All my boys come to me from the village. This one came from somewhere close to Rajkot, sent by a previous employee. What more can I tell you? They come to me and beg for a place to sleep, a meal, a few rupees. I'm a fool to open my heart to them, but it's my nature. I feed pigeons, stray dogs, even ants sometimes, how can I say no to these kids? If once in a while there is a rotten mango in the lot, is that my fault?'

'I know your brand of charity,' Savio growled. 'Twenty boys living in the loft—'

'Thirty.'

'How many draw salaries?'

'Six.'

'And the rest?'

'That's upto the salaried boys. If they want to help their friends, who am I to stop them? This is a difficult city.'

It was nearly three. Lalli must have got the party going at the crèche. She'd taken the car, so I told Savio I'd find my way back.

'I'll drop you,' he frowned. And because I didn't reply immediately, he said he'd ride pillion.

We hadn't done that in a while, and I thought it would be like old times, but it wasn't. I was too careful, and Savio too reticent.

Was this the man who had led me blindfold an hour ago?

That must have just been the ylang-ylang.

Kandewadi was quiet. The news of Daya the store boy hadn't percolated through yet. Jaggu Gala had been dropped home after questioning. The bewildered men who had hazarded the identification were still in the mortuary corridor when Savio and I left.

I turned the bike over to Savio, and found Lalli.

A shed had been requisitioned for the crèche. It was small, but that was an advantage here, it made it easier to keep an eye on the kids. There were five women besides Lalli, and about fifty kids, presently mesmerized by the large table laden with goodies—a big squelchy cake, chips, bhel and a thermocol tub of ice cream. Even more exciting was the mountain of gifts piled in one corner, glittering with iridescent wrapping.

'There are prizes for everybody in this competition,' I heard Lalli say, 'and I'm going to put all your drawings up on the walls outside, so that everybody can enjoy them. So are you ready?'

'Yes!'

'I know everybody wants to draw different things, but in today's competition, I want a special drawing—and I want you to draw a new doll.'

'Whose new doll?' one girl asked.

'Anybody's. Or nobody's! It could be a doll you've seen or a doll that you want to see or a doll that someone told you about—anything will do as long as it's a new doll.'

'Boys don't play with dolls,' one wise guy piped up.

'That's because they're stupid,' his pigtailed neighbour said.

Lalli intervened. 'Oh, I didn't ask you to play with a new doll, just to draw one. Even boys, I think, can manage that. If you make a good drawing, we girls will show you how to bowl a googly.'

'Girls don't play cricket.'

'Shall we show them, girls?'

'Yaaay!'

'So let's draw a new doll, and don't forget to write your name beneath your drawing!'

And so they got down to it.

They wouldn't have been that quick without the inducements on the table, but in half an hour each kid handed Lalli a drawing.

Then the floodgates were opened, and leaving the other women to manage the mob, we sneaked away with the drawings.

The police had their station set up in an adjoining hut. We made ourselves comfortable there to examine the art.

All the drawings were vibrant, but before I could revel in them, Lalli had picked out two.

One was almost a duplicate of the cat-face Deepika had inked on her chubby doll. This one had triangular, up-slanted spectacles, light blue lenses with green eyes showing through. She had a small heart-shaped pink mouth. Her hair was drop dead gorgeous, and colored purple. She was dressed in a red lampshade. The neckline bisected her breasts into yellow and red hemispheres. Her legs were about a mile long and her feet stuck out in red glitter platforms. Bumping their heads against those glorious shoes were five straggling letters:

ANITA.

The second painting was a watercolour.

Lalli's hand trembled as she held it. I watched her face grow intent.

She laid it down gently and we looked at it together.

By any measure, it was a remarkable picture. The artist had used watercolours, and restricted the palette to two colors, black and green.

There was no doll in this picture.

Instead, the artist had painted two converging banks of trees in dense black. The white background between their trunks had been left untouched, but above the trees, a grey wadding of cloud enclosed a white sky. It was very easy to imagine a moon. The foreground repeated the pattern: the divergent shadows parted around the unpainted ground which dazzled with its whiteness, reflecting the moonlit sky.

At first glance the picture looked like a white hourglass on a black background.

The stem of the hourglass was marked with a bright green dot.

It would have been easier to make that dot with a green felt-tipped sketch pen—all the children used those pens—but this child had chosen not to. Instead he had painted the viridian dot with the brush loaded with water and the effect was blotchy.

That hardly mattered, though, the rhythm of the painting was spellbinding. The black trees and their shadows converged and diverged from the green focus and the wheeling sky and moonlit ground gave the scintilla an unexpected effulgence.

'Pity about the blotch,' I sighed and noticed the name for the first time:

ASIF.

Lalli disagreed about the blotch.

'It's a deliberate effect,' she stated flatly. 'He meant it to blur.'

'Meant what to blur?'

'Let's find out.'

We gave them half an hour to settle down and then the artists came in one by one.

Lalli asked each child about his or her drawing before handing it over to be pasted on the wall outside. Then they collected their gifts and went home.

Anita turned out to be a feisty eight-year old.

Lalli asked her if she'd seen a doll like this one.

'No, I didn't, but *she* did.'

'Who?'

Anita's face shut stubbornly.

'Did she get this new doll?' Lalli asked.

Anita shook her head vigorously. 'She never got it. I told her there are no dolls with glasses, but she said she'd seen it and she'd be getting it.'

'From where?'

Anita counted her toes.

'It was a secret?'

Anita nodded.

'Don't worry then, you needn't tell me. It's a very nice picture, Anita, but I don't think you want this doll.'

'It's a bad doll.'

'Yes, it is.'

'That's why I said no. I knew it was bad, so I said no and ran away.'

'You're a sharp girl alright! Do you stand first in class?'

'Second.'

'You must be first next time.'

'Why?'

'Because you have brains. You said no to the doll, didn't you? You should say no to many pretty things. Ribbons. Earrings. Bangles. Your parents will buy all those things for you by and by.'

'But I want them now.'

'True. But we have to wait for nice things, don't we?'

Anita nodded solemnly.

'You should tell your friends that too.'

'I told them already.'

'Good! Who offered to show you the doll, Anita?'

'Daya. He's from the store. He has so many pretty things.'

'Here's your drawing, Anita, but I'm not going to put it up on the wall because it's secret, right? I'm going to keep it for myself. You can make another drawing instead. '

'Can I draw you?'

'Of course.'

She walked away importantly.

Eventually, Asif turned up.

He was a small bony kid of five. His grave eyes were heartbreaking.

'Asif, this is a very beautiful picture. You love drawing, don't you?'

He nodded and drew a little closer to Lalli and whispered something.

'Okay, I won't,' Lalli said. 'It can be our secret if you like.'

She picked up Asif and seated him on her lap. The child was trembling. A tear slid down his cheek.

'Sita, see if there's any cake left, Asif didn't have any.'

'I don't want cake.'

'You don't like it?'

His small face crumpled in misery and he buried his face in Lalli shoulder.

'You don't want to eat alone?'

'Aapa will be angry with me.'

'No, Asif! She'll want you to eat an extra piece. One for her too.'

'Ice cream?'

'Ice cream too. But not if you don't want to.'

'I want to, but it's finished.'

'We'll get some more. Shall we look at your picture first? '

He detached himself from Lalli and hurriedly aligned the paper on the table.

'Don't look at it crooked. Now it's straight.'

'It's night,' Lalli said.

'Eleven o'clock.'

'You saw the time?'

'We have a clock. Digital.'

'Right. So it was eleven o'clock. Aapa was with you?'

'No.'

He spoke so low we could barely hear him.

'She wasn't there. It was before Aapa came back. I woke up. It was eleven o' clock.'

'And you saw this from the window?'

'No. From the gutter. I went out to pee.'

'And this?' Lalli pointed to the green splotch. 'What's this, Asif?'

'Green light.'

'You saw this green light?'

'Yes. My eyes hurt.'

'It was very bright?'

'Yes.'

'What did you do then?'

'I went back to sleep. And in the morning they brought Aapa home.'

'Whom did you tell about the green light, Asif?'

Asif hung his head. His fists were balled tight.

'You saw it again, didn't you?'

He nodded miserably.

'Once more?'

'Yes—I had to go.'

'Of course.'

'And in the morning they brought Mary.'

'I see. Asif, your picture is very, very good, but I'm not going to put it on the wall. Instead, I want you to paint a lovely picture of your Aapa for me, and we will get it framed and you can put it next to the clock. Would you like to do that? You can paint here. You needn't paint at home.'

'Ammi will be angry.'

'No, no, she will listen to me.'

'Because you're old?'

'Yes. Asif, why did Aapa go away?'

'To get a new doll. We were playing, when they called her.'

'Who called her, Asif?'

'I didn't see them. We were playing. It was my turn and then Aapa said, they were calling her to come get her new doll, and she ran away.'

'Okay, let's get that ice cream now, shall we?'

I stayed back, fighting tears, reliving Asif's painting.

Asif woke up between his parents. There was not much space for him there, not like before, when he and Aapa had a bed on one side of the room. Now he had her special pink cushion with the squirrel on it, but he didn't like it anymore.

He had to pee, and pee fast.

Asif wasn't afraid of the dark.

Everything looked friendlier at night, even his parents did.

The clock winked as if it knew where Aapa had gone. It said 11:00:00.

He knew that meant just 11, it wasn't one hundred ten thousand as he'd thought at first. Aapa said zeroes didn't count.

It was just eleven.

Asif slid out of bed and went to the door. His heart thudded as the latch moved—but they didn't wake up. If they caught him now, they'd yell and he would definitely pee in his pants.

But they didn't stir.

He hurried out to the gutter, it was just at the end of the wall.

There!

Now he was safe, Asif could look around.

Everything was different at night outside, too.

It was bright tonight, but he couldn't find the moon. It was hiding behind those big clouds, and he wasn't going to let it get away. The clouds scudded like big balloons, it wouldn't take very long to find the moon—

Everything was different at night, you saw things that stayed hidden all day.

Those trees, for instance. They were way past the mohalla, too far to be noticed by daylight, but here they were now, like black curtains tied back to let in the moonlight.

It was soft and peaceful and Asif felt happy just standing there waiting to catch the moon.

Then suddenly a green light sprang up between the trees. It flashed like a torch right in his eyes.

Asif shut his eyes tight, but when he opened them, the green light was still flashing. There was nothing there between the trees, just this light.

Asif rubbed his eyes.

It was still there—a blur of green.

Asif forgot the moon.

He ran back, and slipped indoors, his heart thudding

He climbed into bed and clutched Aapa's cushion till he felt safe again.

They quarreled in the morning over the door.

'You left the door open again,' Abbu roared. 'You've lost my daughter, now do you want to lose my son too?'

'My daughter would have been found safe and sound if you were more of a man. Why didn't you latch the door?' Ammi retorted.

And so it went on the whole day, back and forth till their anger dissolved in tears.

Asif crept to his corner and played quietly with Aapa's dolls till he fell asleep again.

I was jolted out of my reverie by the growing murmur outside. It swelled angrily, like an enraged hive, subsided, then welled up again with periodic infusions of energy.

Kandewadi had just learned about Daya.

I stayed where I was, decoding the sound. It had passed from horror to jubilation to a seethe of frustration. Very soon it was all one sound: voices, wails, protests, all subsumed in a throaty growl of menace.

The lanes of Kandewadi were choked with people. I caught sight of Savio arguing earnestly with two men who carried flaming torches. Lalli was nowhere in sight.

'We must have justice,' the torchbearers kept insisting.

'Burning down the store isn't going to get you justice.'

'It's all Jaggu Gala's fault. He shouldn't have employed such a monster.'

'He didn't know the boy was a monster. Did you?'

'We trusted him. How can we trust the other boys from that store?' Their voices faltered. They knew their arguments were weak, but this was beyond reason. Death had cheated them of justice and somehow, they had to get even.

'Leave it, if he's dead, he's dead, our children are safe now,' a woman's voice rang out.

'Easily said when your daughter's never been harmed. What about mine?'

Harsh, bitter, low, Sindhu's mother's voice silenced them all. She plucked the torches from the men's hands and dashed them to the ground. 'Go home!' she hissed. 'Go home and leave us to our grief! Go! Go!' Her husband led her away and the crowd melted, muttering its derision.

'I'm having a hard time explaining why we're still here now the killer's dead' Savio remarked. 'I don't dare tell them it wasn't Daya.'

'It was Daya,' I said and told him what Anita had told us.

'So what's new? We know he lured Deepika, and now he seems to have lured all of them. We still don't know that he killed them.'

'What makes you so sure he didn't?'

'Oh, I'm not sure at all. But I won't damn him just yet.'

Lalli joined us.

'Savio's unconvinced,' I reported.

'About Daya being the killer? I agree. Take a look at this.'

We followed Lalli into the police shed.

To my surprise, she placed Asif's drawing before Savio. 'Asif saw this when he went for a pee in the gutter. He saw it twice—on the night before Jamila's body was found, and on the night before Mary was found. The first time, it was eleven o'clock. The second time, he didn't notice. But this is what he saw.'

Savio whistled.

'Exactly.'

'Meaning?' I demanded.

'It couldn't have been a coincidence,' Savio said.

'Why not?" I countered. 'Maybe that green light's there every night. Asif may not have gone out on any other night. He made the connect between the green flash and his sister's body being found because everything he saw that night would have seemed terribly significant. That's just the kind of connection children make. The next time he goes out he sees the green light again, and the morning after brings Mary's dead body home. That would make the green light seem portentous. But maybe he would have seen it had he gone out any other night as well. Maybe it's just there.'

'Only one way to find out,' Savio said.

The door opened hesitantly and a small face peeped in.

'Come on in, Anita,' Lalli smiled.

Anita threw an uncertain look at Savio and sidled up to Lalli. Savio strolled out taking no notice of Anita.

'Daya's dead,' she said flatly.

'Yes, I heard.'

'Who killed him?'

'He got sick.'

'He was okay, he wasn't sick!'

'When did you see him?'

'In the evening? Before.'

'I see. What did he say?'

'He said he was going to get his tempo and would I like a ride, but I said no. He said he'd show me the doll if I went with him in the tempo. I said if the doll is in your tempo you can bring it here, why should I go with you to see the doll? So he laughed and ran away.'

'This was before dinner or after?'

'After. Everybody was watching TV, but I was looking out of the window.'

'What program were they watching?'

'Serial, I don't know the name. Everybody shouts and cries in it.'

'Do they watch it every night?'

'Yes, that's why we have to eat dinner really fast. Daya wasn't sick.'

'Sometimes people get sick suddenly, Anita.'

'Then he would have been sleeping, no? Why would he want to go in his tempo then?'

'Maybe he got sick after.'

She considered that. Then she said delicately, 'Did Daya hurt them?'

'Do you think he did?'

'No. Daya was our friend.' Her luminous eyes were very stern. 'If he was sick, we would have got medicine for him.'

'I'm sure you would have. Daya was foolish.'

'That he was,' Anita agreed. 'But we all knew that was not his fault. He was just born that way.'

Lalli said, 'Anita, you'll hear a lot of stories about Daya, now that he's dead—'

'Because now he can't tell us they're all lies?'

'Yes. That's what they are—just stories, not the truth.'

'Will you tell me the truth?'

'If I find out.'

'You'll find out, easy,' Anita said. 'But you've got to tell me first.'

'I will. Now go home before they start worrying.'

She hugged Lalli impulsively and ran away.

'You can't still think Daya was innocent,' I protested.

'Hardly innocent! But I don't think he murdered the children. Yes, he lured them. And he brought Deepika's body back. Perhaps he brought all the bodies back. And even if that's all he did, he did it with the full knowledge of what had happened to those children. That makes him just as culpable as if he raped and murdered the children. But did he? I'm not sure, and how can I afford not to be!'

I hadn't seen Lalli so anguished in a long while.

'Where did he take those children? From where did he bring them back?' Lalli ground her palms into her eyes as though to erase the horror her brain replayed.

Suddenly, the answers to her questions seemed ridiculously easy.

'All you have to do is find the ylang-ylang tree,' I said.

But there was no tree.

Shukla had surprisingly taken on that quest, and had spent the evening checking out the one kilometer radius. He phoned to give me the bad news with evil triumph.

'Banana-skin flowers do not exist. That is my full and frank opinion after examining every tree within one km radius.'

'One km radius is a dumb idea,' Lalli murmured. 'Think time, not distance. So Sita, and what does twitter@kandewadi have for you?'

I'd forgotten all about Seema and her social media. There was an email inviting me to join the protest at 10 a.m. at Sachivalaya. If I found that inconvenient, I could show up at the Writers for Change reading at 6 p.m., ending in a candlelight vigil.

'Go be a Writer for Change,' Lalli advised.

'Oh if you want to know what the world's saying, #kandewadi will get you the latest. 45 tweets in the last hour.'

'Let's see them.'

@cowgirl:
OMG there's a lunatic at large.

@deshbhakt;
Teenagers are setting dangerous eg western clothing like jeans and tops

@ikidyounot;
Like jeans and Ts make you a rapist LOL

@makemyday:
What are you talking of jeans and Ts when children have been murdered

@lightofislam:
Parents should look after kids and not allow them to roam the streets. This is a crime of poverty and ignorance.

@fashionista:
Is it true the kids were strangled with their own intestines?

@bambaiyya33:
Eeww! Can that even be done?

@jaimaharashtra:
Bhaiyyas and goonda elements are spoiling good name of Marathi manoos

@sanskriti:
Purity is basis of Indian culture

@worriedmom
I try my best to keep my kids from mixing with slum people, but there's too much contamination in school.

@salsaqueen
How could they even? I mean these were children

@radicalrani
Men are beasts. Except what kind of beast will wrap its prey in intestines.

@surrealdream
Can't get over the horror of it

@BGOE:
Horrified? You should feel pity, not revulsion.

@Glider:
Why focus on trivia and ignore the main event

@Blade:
Too distracting. Shouldn't be repeated.

@Chocolate:
Scary, huh? And all you're doing is imagine it. What if you could actually see it?

@Marketman:
See it? It would strike me blind.

@Blade@marketman:
Dazzle you?

@marketman;
Nothing so dark can dazzle

@Blade@reply:
A bright darkness can

@Chocolate:
reminds me of an old song: raindrops on roses, whiskers on kittens

@Sexygirl;
duh what's sound of music got to do with it?

@chocolate@reply don't you know the last line

@sexygirl:
Youre a perv, @Chocolate, these are some of your favourite things?

@chocolate@reply:
No, the line before

@sexygirl @reply:
YAWN

@angryjangri:
What's the police doing?

@Glider:
getting rich

@Blade@reply:
getting it wrong as usual

@superdad:
How can any man even think of such violence? A child is the very essence of purity

@BGOE @superdad:
Exactly.

@superdad:
Glad you agree @BGOE. I pity the murderer

@BGOE:
I don't think he wants your pity @superdad

@superdad:
Really? Why not?

BGOE @ superdad:
because he pities you.

@superdad:
Why@BGOE?

@Glider:
because youre a loser

@vaginawarrior:
I agree with Glider, only losers pity rapists, they should be castrated

@Blade:
Who? Losers or rapists

@vaginawarrior:
Both

It was just endless blather. I left her to it.

We hadn't eaten since breakfast, and the desolation that oppressed me was probably just hunger. I fixed a light hot meal and when I took her plate out to Lalli, she thanked me absently and went back to the screen.

I wondered what, among all those inane tweets, had caught her attention.

Surprisingly, Kandewadi was not on television, not even on the reality channels that bristled with scandal. Apparently, Seema's source was exclusive after all.

It was still dark when I awoke, the window a black void.

Something had woken me urgently. I was taut with alertness.

The house was noiseless. Something was missing—the gusty billow of the fan in Lalli's room that lent a breathy quality to the house at night. The fan in my room was noiseless and no comfort at all, but I had got used to the amphoric tidal waft from Lalli's room.

I got out of bed. Lalli's room was empty. She wasn't reading in the living room either. It was a little past two—too early for her walk.

The car keys were in the ceramic bowl next to the phone. I tried her mobile. It was switched off. Worried, I called Savio.

He answered on the first ring.

'Sita?'

'Lalli's gone out, she hasn't taken the car, her mobile's switched off.'

'She'll be alright. Go back to sleep.'

'I'm awake. You too.'

'Yeah. This place spooks me at night—they're all asleep as though nothing ever happened here. Or maybe they're all awake huddled behind locked doors.'

'You're at the station—that shack where we looked at the pictures?'

'No, I'm outside. I'm sitting at the tree.'

'Where Tara was?'

'Yes. '

'The dog's there with you?'

'Kaliya. How did you know?'

Suddenly I wished myself there too, sitting with Savio, at that tree. I could sense Savio's hesitation in the hiatus.

'What?'

'What what?'

'What is it you're not telling me?'

'Nothing.'

'Something's bothering you.'

'Not bothering exactly. Arun called me, we had quite a long chat.'

'Oh? About what?'

'The case, actually.'

'Really? Arun couldn't bear to hear about it yesterday.'

'That's the impression I got earlier, not a man for messy stuff. But he wanted to know all about Daya—sorry, Sita, but I couldn't very well tell him—'

'I should think not! How did he know about Daya, anyway?'

'I thought you had told him.'

'And then put him up to pump you? Savio, what's wrong with you?' My outrage surprised me. 'What have I ever done to deserve that?'

'Nothing. Mea culpa. Forget it.'

'Easily said. Do you really think I'd repeat what I see when I'm with you and Lalli anywhere?'

'No. Not anywhere or to anybody. But Arun isn't just anybody.'

'Even so, I wouldn't. Not now, not ever.'

Savio sighed. 'Let it go, Sita. It doesn't matter.'

Usually, those words consoled me. But they didn't now.

'Here's Lalli now,' Savio said. 'See? I said she'd be okay. Now get some sleep.'

Surprisingly, despite my disquiet, I did.

Friday, 24 March

There were voices in the kitchen when I woke. The air was nervy with coffee.

I jumped out of bed, rejoicing.

The very next moment it all rushed back, crumpling my soul. It wasn't just Kandewadi. It was Arun.

He hadn't called. No texts, no emails.

I was committed to spending the weekend with him—hey wait a moment, I wanted to spend the weekend with him, I positively ached for it. But it wasn't going to happen now, was it?

I dragged myself out of my misery and sleepwalked to the kitchen which was pretty crowded for 7 a.m. In addition to the home team, there was Shukla.

'Here she is!'

Evidently they had been talking about me, for their voices held equal degrees of warmth and embarrassment.

'Sorry I worried you last night,' Lalli hugged me impulsively and I clung to her, almost like Asif. Shukla offered me a biscuit.

'So what do we have?' Lalli asked. 'Five dead children, one dead young man.'

'Sex maniac,' Shukla put in.

'Which one?' Lalli asked. 'Which one's the sex maniac? The man who killed the first four girls? Or Daya?'

'You're not connecting Daya to those murders then?' Savio asked.

'Daya is connected with Deepika's murder—and we don't know how. There's nothing to tell us he was connected with the earlier killings.'

'Oh, there is, there definitely is. He lured the girls.'

'But did he kill them? Savio, if we hadn't found Daya, what was your profile of the murderer?'

Savio hesitated. 'I'd say the killer's a man easy to ignore. He just doesn't cut it in terms of confidence and personality. He's probably a drudge, used to taking orders. His rage is sublimated only by total domination and possession. He might be any age—early twenties to sixties, but

I'll put my money on early twenties. If he's older, he should have killed before. These things run to pattern, and I'm not seeing one here. That's the Kandewadi Killer—but was that Daya? I don't know.'

'I don't agree with your profiling, Savio,' Lalli said. 'Before I tell you why, let's take a closer look at this dead boy. Daya lured the children. He didn't take them by force. The kids trusted him. Why? I think that's the central question. Look at Anita's response. She made the connect between the new doll and the disappearance of her friends. She knew that Daya had shown them the doll and other pretty things. And yet she didn't blame Daya for what happened to her friends. She wasn't scared of Daya, but she was scared of the new doll. Somehow Daya escaped the loop, and I need to know why.'

'Anita didn't tell parents,' Shukla scowled.

'It was a secret. You don't tell on your friends before puberty, Shukla,' I said.

'Even after puberty I am not telling their secrets, or by now it will be all over with you, Sita. But, own parents, own child must tell own secrets.'

'Well they didn't, Shukla,' Lalli said crisply.

'New generation.'

'Old one was worse. Don't you see what I'm getting at? Sita just said it, but I don't think she noticed it herself.'

They looked at me expecting another pearl, but my inner oyster had shut shop.

'You don't tell on your friends, Sita said. The children looked on Daya as a peer. He was in his twenties, yet these little ones thought he was one of them. Kids do that with adults only under a few special circumstances. That degree of acceptance implies equality. You'll find, very likely, that Daya was simple-minded. I prefer that term to the many labels that mean nothing at all. Daya had a mental age of about ten, I'd say. The children, sadly, thought he could be trusted to do no harm.'

No harm?

The idea was terrifying. The children thought of this monster as one of their own. But was he a monster?

'Low intelligence doesn't necessarily mean criminal intelligence,' Lalli said. 'I think Daya did as told, without much understanding.'

'But why would he do as told?' Savio asked.

'Such people can be patao-ed easily,' Shukla said. 'You give, they take. No machinery inside.'

'What do you mean?'

'See how wheels are turning in your brain all the time, Sita? Always asking what this means, what that means? No wheels in Daya's brain. His actions are without reason or consequence. He has escaped good or bad. He just exists. Sanyasis are striving full lifetime for this only, but with Daya, it is natural.'

'That doesn't mean he lacked free will,' I objected.

'Free will—yes. The ability to tell right from wrong—no,' Savio said. 'But who manipulated him?'

Savio's question led to a gloomy silence.

Calories were definitely called for. I hustled up breakfast. The second round of cinnamon toast got us back into the case.

'So why do you disagree with my profiling, Lalli?' Savio asked.

'First, these are not the usual lust murders. True, the children were raped and tortured before being killed. But there's a strange element here. The bodies were returned—you could say delivered back where they belonged. It tells me the crime was incomplete without this step. In the last case, Deepika's, that's all that happened. To the murderer, this was the most important step. Without this last act of restitution, there was no release. That overturns your argument that total domination and possession was necessary to him.'

'Why he is doing this last step, Lalli? I am thinking he wants to show Kandewadi people they are nothing, less than nothing. It is hate crime.'

'No, he brings the body back as a dog brings a tribute to his master,' Savio said. 'He's obeying instructions. He was not on his own.'

'How do you know that?' I demanded.

'You told us, Sita,' Savio grinned.

'I?'

'You asked us to check on Asif's green light.'

'And?'

'There was no green light last night, so perhaps Asif was right. The green light was connected to the return of the bodies. We know Daya returned at least one of the bodies. Perhaps the green light was meant for him,' Lalli said.

'A signal?'

'Yes. Somebody besides Daya knew about the murders—accomplice or murderer, I can't tell. But definitely Daya wasn't acting alone.'

'So it's not over?' I suppose I'd known that all along, but it was still a harsh truth to confront. 'The kids of Kandewadi are still at risk, then?'

'Yes,' Savio and Shukla said.

Lalli shook her head. 'I don't think so. Not because Daya was the killer, but because he fulfilled the most vital step—returning the corpse. Without someone to do that, there was no point to the exercise. Daya was uniquely qualified to lure and restitute—to the children of Kandewadi, he was one of them. Is there someone else who can fit that role now? I doubt it. The killings at Kandewadi will stop, but they might begin elsewhere.'

'Where? In another slum?' It seemed too vague, too general a prediction to have any practical value.

'How can I tell? We need to find Daya's partner. To do that, we need to find Daya. Who he was, how he lived, whom he befriended. No family, Jaggu Gala said. Right now, he's just a corpse with no backstory.'

'He is corpse with full knowledge,' Shukla snarled. 'Even if he was buddhoo, he was not innocent. But he was without fear. To bring that parcel, so boldly without slightest fear. How do you explain that?'

Savio answered. 'First, he was protected—he was certain he wouldn't be caught, despite the very public way in which the bodies were returned. He was so secure in this belief either because he was actually protected by a powerful master, or, he had the illusion of protection. Paranoia is a common feature of criminal insanity. Maybe that was it, Lalli. The man was delusional.'

'Perhaps. But I think his delusion lifted, Savio. He would have had that bleed even without alcohol. The realization hit him when he was delivering Deepika's body. He had a breakdown. Perhaps the entire sequence of his actions rose up in his mind, and he could no longer escape or deny them. That was a stress bleed, Savio. The alcohol was just incidental.'

Nobody contradicted her. Lalli got up. 'Let's go find Daya's life,' she said.

Lalli and I got to A-1 General Stores at ten.

Savio had warned us that the staff on duty today were all police plants. The real employees had been taken to the chowki where Shukla would question them.

The store was open and Jaggu Gala was at the counter. He greeted us with unctuous familiarity, and said he was keeping the side door shut today. The side door was meant for customers from Kandewadi.

'What to do, they are poor people, I sell them necessities at reduced prices. Everybody must live. I am a religious man. But where has that put me today? I am the target of their anger. I am shocked at what happened to these innocents. I am terrified to think that all the time it was Daya, working here, eating and sleeping here. But how am I to blame? Was it my fault? My only fault is that I opened my heart to a poor boy from the village.'

'No doubt. Show me where you house your boys.' When Lalli used that voice, it precluded argument.

Jaggu gloomily let us in behind the counter and yanked one of his shelves.

A partition swung open and we found ourselves in a narrow cell. From a height of three feet upwards the wall had a number of kadapa platforms that served as bunks. There was a bare two-foot interval between them. Each was littered with clothes, bedding, bags.

Behind us, Jaggu sighed. 'I keep telling them to tidy up. But do they listen?'

Thirty boys, he'd said. Even with two to the bunk, the place wouldn't hold more than ten.

'How many to the bunk?' I asked.

He looked shocked. 'They adjust. Sometimes they grumble, but they adjust.'

'Which is Daya's bed?' Lalli asked.

'He slept on the floor—his stuff's there.'

Jaggu pointed to a bag with a folded mattress placed over it. The mattress was thin, ragged. The bag was the usual rexine holdall, battered and patched, clearly a hand-me-down. Daya could never have sat upright in his corner. From the dent in the bag it was evident he used it as a pillow.

The room—or recess—had a skylight, a ventilator that had been nailed shut to keep out the rain. The light it transmitted through a thick coating of grime was weak and wavering.

Lalli's powerful flash darted about that sad corner pitilessly. I noticed now the rolled up clothes stacked beneath the mattress and the bag. Here was his whole life, compacted.

There was nothing much in Daya's bag. A towel, a cracked plastic wallet containing a hundred rupee note, and a driving license issued two years ago. A flat tin box that had, till very recently, contained chocolate. The brand was a reputed Swiss one, and the luxuriously moulded interior smelt delectable. There were a few specks of chocolate, miniscule slivers on the surface between the wells. Lalli dabbed them up with a fingertip.

'He shared them,' she said. The needles of chocolate on her fingertip, scarcely thicker than a hair were blurring already with the warmth of her skin. 'He divided them with a very thin blade. That's hard to find these days, nobody uses razor blades. Perhaps the store has some, let's check.'

But there was no need to.

We found it almost immediately. Stuck in a slender oval of soap was a narrow triangular blade with a wicked edge to it.

Lalli said it was a surgical blade, but it looked too delicate to incise skin.

There was little else.

The bedding and the rolled up clothes were either ragged or worn and faded from repeated washing. As the only furniture of an anonymous life, these things too would pass to a new owner before the week was out—if not his roommates, then someone out on the street would claim them. Nothing would remain of Daya's life but the horrific finish of it.

Lalli surprised me by refuting that thought. 'The life he led here was anonymous, so we must look for the other.'

'You're not suggesting he led a double life?'

'Yes, I am.'

'In imagination, you mean.'

'He didn't lure those girls in imagination, Sita. He didn't bring back Deepika's body in imagination. He didn't have that first and last drink in imagination, he didn't bleed to death in imagination. Everything happened, but it happened elsewhere.'

Lalli requisitioned the lot and one of the men carried it to the car.

'Lets look at it again at the chowki. Shukla won't be finished with the boys as yet.'

On an impulse she returned to Jaggu and asked him about the kind of jobs he had allotted Daya.

'He was only, may be, eight annas to the rupee, but customers didn't mind that. The boy always had a pleasant smile, enjoyed being teased by the women, no harm in that, he was a pretty fellow, but innocent. God help me what am I saying, innocent! Now we know that's the last word we can use for the devil, but that's the impression all of us had of Daya—innocent. But it's not as if he was completely stupid, nobody could cheat Daya.'

'Did the other boys tease him? Bully him?'

'No. That surprised me sometimes, knowing what boys are. He didn't join in all their schemes and tricks, but they let him be. They were kind to him. Not one of us suspected he was such a serpent.'

'And you—you trusted him. You were quite confident in sending him out on deliveries, pickup from wholesalers, that sort of thing?'

'Without question. He used to drive my tempo till it got messed up. After that I switched to hiring a truck once a month, less headache.'

'Why, what happened to your tempo?'

'Broke down, suspension gone, tyres gone, no use anymore. Sell it for scrap, I told Daya, but he never did. It's still sitting in the scrap yard in the next lot, covered with filth.'

Lalli, promised to let him know when his boys could return to work, and shaking off his slimy sanctimony, hurried me to the car.

Of the twenty odd boys the police had picked up from A-1 General Stores at 6 a.m., Shukla had retained five.

Lalli picked up the chocolate box from Daya's bag before we went in.

All five boys were between sixteen and twenty, stunted and un-healthy. They could be excused for looking dirty and unkempt—they had been harried out of bed.

Shukla's badgering hadn't helped. They stared at Lalli with sullen belligerence.

Ignoring them, Lalli addressed Shukla. 'I've got some things to show you, Shukla, let's go.'

She practically shooed Shukla out.

As we were leaving, she noticed the five angry faces for the first time. 'Breakfast's on its way, bathroom's down the corridor—with a havaldar outside. Make yourselves comfortable. I'll be back in half an hour.'

Shukla awaited us impatiently. 'No need to feed those rogues. Couldn't get a word out of them, and I've been at it since seven.'

'Naturally. They're starving, their bladders are bursting and they're scared shitless. What do you expect? I'll deal with them, you've got more important work.'

Shukla's brief was simple. He had to find that tempo. And Lalli want-ed it found within the hour.

He muttered a bit. 'First banana-skin tree, then tempo, what next? Urine of kite?'

'No, milk of tiger,' Lalli retorted. 'You get me the tempo and I'll get you the tree, Shukla.'

'You will?' I asked when Shukla had left.

'Certainly!'

'I thought you were going to show him that surgical blade.'

Her eyes glittered wickedly. 'All in good time.'

The boys looked almost human now. They shuffled to their feet when we entered, a rare courtesy these days. Amenities over, Lalli came straight to the point.

'You know that Daya is dead. You'll hear many stories about him now, and some of them may even be true. But they're all stories from people who didn't know Daya. You, on the other hand, knew him. You were his friends—'

'But we didn't know he was a murderer,' one boy burst out. 'He was just time-pass.'

'So how did you pass your time with Daya?' Lalli asked.

'We kidded him, a little bit, not much—'

'Lucky, or he might have murdered us too!'

'Yeah, how are we going to know next time?'

'Next time what?' Lalli asked.

'The next time there's a new boy in our room. Maybe he'll murder us in our sleep.'

Lalli said coldly, 'Stop kidding around, or I'll conclude you're hiding something. If you're going to waste my time you can cool your heels in the lockup till you're ready to talk sense. Answer me straight and you'll be out of here in ten minutes. Which is it going to be?'

They hadn't expected this of Lalli. Their brains changed gear almost audibly.

'What do you want to know?'

'Was Daya friends with you?'

'Yeah, he was nice. Didn't fight or argue.'

'What do you know about his family?'

'He didn't have anybody back in the village except an uncle who kicked him out because he was only baarah anna.'

His friends were a bit more generous than his employer who had granted him just 50 paise to the rupee.

'What about here? Who were his friends, apart from you fellows?'

'He didn't have any.'

'He never went out for movies and stuff. Sometimes we took him along, but he was no fun.'

'Why not?'

'He didn't seem to like it. He didn't like songs, didn't like dance, didn't like dhishum-dhishum. What's left to enjoy in a movie then?'

'What about girls?'

They looked innocent to the point of imbecility.

'What about little girls? Ever seen him hanging around them?'

Here they were very definite—no they'd never seen Daya with any of the little girls in Kandewadi, or the bigger ones either. But that's not to say he didn't talk to them, they all did.

'What did Daya have to say when you learned that little girls had been raped and murdered in Kandewadi?'

They were quiet for a long moment. They exchanged glances. Then the tallest among them said almost in a whisper, 'He said there was nothing to cry about.'

A plump boy, Prakash, said after a beat of silence, 'He didn't mean it that way.'

'How can you say that now?' three or four voices burst out.

Prakash nodded unhappily. 'Yeah, we can't say that now. But then—' His voice trailed off and all of them fell quiet.

'Then, at the moment when he said it, how did it seem to you? Why did you think he said it?' Lalli's voice was very low, very calm.

'He was just trying to console Mangesh,' Prakash said. 'Mangesh started crying when we heard Pinki's body had been found. Of course, we knew Pinki and Jamila were missing. We helped look for them. All the children from Kandewadi came to our shop. We knew all of them. Mangesh has two small sisters, so he got very scared when he heard what had happened to Pinki. Then we went to see Pinki's body, Mangesh and us five, some Kandewadi people called us to help.'

'Did you see the body?'

They nodded miserably.

'What did you see?'

'It was wrapped in newspaper. There was a lot of newspaper, they had removed it from the body. We could only see Pinki's face, it was horrible. Her dress was drenched in blood. That's all we saw. We ran away, scared.'

'Daya came with you?'

'No, no. We told him the news when he came into the room because he asked why Mangesh was crying. That's when he said—that's nothing to cry about, Pinki could not feel any pain anymore, she was happy, she was with God. So we thought then he was just consoling Mangesh.'

'He was a sant,' Prakash said suddenly. 'He was going to be a sant. He told me that. In a few years, he said.'

'Daya was going to be a sant? Like a Baba, like a fakir?' Lalli asked.

'No, not like that common stuff. He said Babas and fakirs were frauds, cheating people of their money, fooling around with women. He was quite angry about them. He said when he became a sant neither joy or sorrow could touch him and all his pain would go away.'

'What pain?' another boy demanded. 'He was healthy, he couldn't have felt any pain.'

'But he was only barah anna! You don't think that hurt?' Prakash demanded.

The protestor subsided and Prakash went on with his story. 'Yes, he was in a lot of pain. He was looking to end it. He tried by being nice to people, doing kind things for them, helping them, but that only made it worse. They took advantage of him and laughed at his simplicity.'

'That got him angry?'

'No. Daya couldn't get angry, he just got sad.'

'Did he tell you that?'

'No. He didn't talk much. I often saw him crying. But that was before. Afterwards, I think he tried to control it.'

'After what?'

'After he met Master.'

'Who's Master?'

'He's the one who told Daya if he became a sant he wouldn't feel pain anymore.'

'And did Daya tell you how he planned on becoming a sant?'

'He said Master would teach him.'

'When did he tell you this?'

'About six months ago. Before Diwali. All of us went back to the village for Diwali, but Daya didn't. He said he'd be okay here. He didn't want to go home. We told him he could come with us, our folks wouldn't mind, but he refused.'

'And when you returned from the village?'

'He looked happy. Laughed a lot. Didn't cry so much. Yes, Daya was happy. He was happy right till the last time we met.'

'When was that?'

'Wednesday night.'

'At bed time?'

'Before. He took his bedding and climbed out on the roof. He often did that when it was hot.'

'Many of you do that?'

'No. Just Daya. The roof's only patra, and it won't take the weight of even two boys.'

This bit of wisdom started off an argument. Lalli quelled it by producing the chocolate box.

'That's Daya's,' three or four voices spoke in unison.

'He shared the chocolates with us,' Prakash said. 'There were only two, but he divided them between the six of us.'

'You each had a bite?' Lalli asked.

'No, he cut them with a blade. Very sharp blade, it nicked his finger. He couldn't have enjoyed his share, it had a bit of blood on it. We teased him, saying he was a *preit*, but he grinned and said his blood didn't taste so bad. It was a dangerous blade, so I told him to stick it in a bar of soap to keep it from injuring him.'

'Was it this blade?' Lalli slid the blade on the table.

They drew back slightly as they nodded.

'So he divided two chocolates between the six of you—what about the rest of the box? Did he eat them all?'

'No. He said there were only two in the box when he got it.'

'Who gave it to him?'

'He didn't say. Customer, probably. People do that some times.'

'So this happened after Diwali?'

'No, it was recent. Maybe a month ago.'

After a short silence, Lalli said, 'You can go now, but I need to know immediately if anybody comes looking for Daya. Just slip across to the control room in MiniIndia, okay?'

They assured her they would and made a rush for the door.

But Lalli got there first. 'What about Daya's tempo?' she asked.

'That old thing? The boss got rid of it long ago,' Prakash looked puzzled.

'That's all you know,' the tall boy said. 'It looks a goner but Daya used to sputter around now and then. It's in running condition. You can check it out.'

'It's in the scrapyard behind the shop?' Lalli asked.

'No. That's where the boss left it, but Daya rescued it long ago. Is this all about the tempo then?'

'Could be. Where did Daya keep it?'

'No fixed place. Parked where he could.'

'So he took you guys on joy rides?'

'No chance. He said he only used it when he had to make deliveries too far to walk. He never used it for fun or for himself. Daya was like that.'

'Yeah, he was like that, but now he turned out a murderer. How are we to tell?'

They looked at Lalli, awaiting an answer.

'I don't know if Daya was a murderer,' Lalli said. 'But I'm going to find out. Once I do, I'll answer your question. But no matter what that answer might be, you've already told me the truth about Daya. You've done well.'

Their faces relaxed, and grinning sheepishly, they left.

Shukla found the tempo that afternoon.

Savio had been missing in action all morning, and there was a hurried phone call from him asking Lalli to be there when Shukla examined the tempo. He was with Dr Q, and couldn't get away.

Why was Dr Q keeping Savio from this case? One week. The Commissioner had given him, just one week, to prove his case. What if Savio was wrong? What if it was Daya?

'We haven't heard anything that tells us it wasn't Daya,' I told Lalli. 'All this talk of being a sant. Maybe he heard voices tell him to go and murder little girls.'

'Maybe. But where did he do it? Why? How?'

'He had the tempo, didn't he? He drove them someplace—'

'Yes, but where?'

'I don't know. You'll find out when you find the tree.'

'Ah.'

'You told Shukla if he found the tempo you'd find the tree—'

'And he's found the tempo, so let's go find the tree.'

Shukla had had the tempo towed into the chowki before we got there. He'd found it in Sahar, about half a mile away, parked between two derelict lorries.

Nobody around knew a thing about it.

They hadn't noticed it drive in, they hadn't noticed the driver, they had never seen it before. They hardly saw it now. It was practically invisible to them.

They answered Shukla's questions because he had found the tempo and it was bad form to contradict a police officer.

I could imagine the scene, Shukla roaring, 'What is this in front of you? Is it or is it not a tempo?' And the aam janata answering quietly, 'You say it is a tempo, Sah'b, who are we to argue with you?' There was something about Shukla that made stonewalling the universally appropriate response.

'Backside locked,' he told Lalli almost accusingly.

It was a closed vehicle, with a tin hood fitted on the back. The letters A-1 were barely discernable and GENERAL STORES had peeled off. The tin was cracked and rusty. The shiny brass lock on the bolt was at complete variance with the general decrepitude.

As we neared the tempo, I stopped, weak-kneed, dizzied by a tender drift of ylang-ylang.

Lalli, who had noticed nothing, walked ahead. I called out to her, 'It's here. I can smell it.'

Lalli yanked open the cab door and reached beneath the driver's seat.

I had joined her by now. She found the usual tin toolbox secured with a string knotted through the simple latch.

It flew open at her touch. There was a white plastic bag inside, stamped Duty Free. Lalli drew it out carefully.

As she opened the bag, it exhaled a powerful gust of scent. Lalli laughed out, 'Shukla, I've found your tree!'

The ylang-ylang was not a kanaka tree. It was a slender flute of glass stamped with the monogram of a distinguished Parisian perfumer, but with no other label. To ease open the stopper would be to swoon with pleasure.

Wrong place, wrong time, definitely wrong company.

'Ylang ylang absolute, or else a parfum prive too expensive to even imagine,' Lalli said.

She should know. She has one of those—the flacon is a wicked twist of black and gold that she very seldom opens.

Shukla looked disbelieving. 'This is your bananaskin flower, Sita? See how you confused the case. Normal person is smelling perfume. What perfume? Two minutes in mall and Mrs Shukla can tell. But that is too simple for our Sita. You are wanting the urine of eagles, many eagles—'

'Or the milk of many tigers,' Lalli broke in. 'Shukla, Sita was spot on. If she had said perfume instead of tree, we would have been misled, and as you say, gone racing to the nearest mall.'

'So where has this led us?' Shukla was far from convinced.

'We must let it lead before we can follow. Patience, Shukla. You found the tempo, and see what it's given us!'

We had been distracted by the perfume. There was something more in that packet. Lalli pulled it out with a conjuror's flourish.

It was a large, rather flashy doll.

More, it was *the* doll: the cat-faced, bespectacled siren that had lured five little girls to their deaths. A vapid creature with masses of golden hair, pink plastic spectacles iridescent with glitter, and feline green eyes.

I realised Anita had actually seen the doll.

Its gorgeous costume was very like the lampshade she had painted—red silky fluff simply silly with sequins. But her glimpse had been fleeting.

The doll's astonishing cleavage was coyly veiled by a frill of yellow net. Anita's impressionist transcription had that down as the equator bisecting the globes into red and yellow hemispheres. But the shoes were dead right—the kid had these shoes down to the last speck of glitter.

'Anita actually saw the doll—and didn't succumb,' I said.

'Maybe she wasn't supposed to,' Lalli murmured. 'All Anita had to do was verify the rumour. You see, everybody knew about the doll, but only those who hadn't seen the doll were chosen.'

She laid the doll down on a sheet of newspaper. Shukla grabbed it and shook it violently. If Lalli hadn't laid a restraining hand on his shoulder, I think he would have torn it limb from limb. Now he let it fall muttering, 'For this? For this?' on an ascending scale of incredulity.

'Dr Q has Deepika's prints. At least those we can check,' Lalli said.

There was nothing else in the cab.

But once they had dusted for fingerprints, Forensics would go over it inch by inch. If there was evidence, they'd find it.

We went around to the back.

Shukla broke the lock and opened the doors, and shone a torch into the tempo's interior.

It was almost completely occupied by a roll of carpet bound with coir. Shukla cut the cord.

A thick expensive Kashmir carpet unrolled, a rich blue weave, embellished with arabesques in red, brown and yellow. It was about 6 feet by four in dimension. Lalli's finger hovered over a brown interruption in the red and yellow sequence of design.

'Blood.'

There was no longer any doubt that the tempo had been used to transport the victims. A crushed carton of fruit juice and a straw were recovered beneath the seat and whisked away to be analysed. The sweepings also turned up, heartbreakingly, a blue hair scrunchie with a small tinsel daisy.

'This time you are wrong Lalli,' Shukla said heavily. 'This Daya is complete shaitan. It is common for shaitan to behave like sant, very common. I am surprised he fooled you.'

'What makes you so certain I'm wrong?'

'First, type of trap. Too much cunning plan. Show doll to only one child, bossy child who controls group. Plan depends on her telling everyone. There is paw of cat element in this.'

'Agreed.' Lalli disappeared into the tempo's dark maw. The doors banged shut after her.

Shukla tuned to me. 'Second, hidden personality. Maybe this Daya is split, like very famous story told to me by Savio. Outside personality is bhola. Inside personality is shaukeen. Too much shaukeen, not fifty-fifty. That carpet is twenty thousand, easy. Maybe stolen. Perfume also may be stolen—'

'Shukla!' Lalli's voice rang out like a cheer. Her eyes were brilliant, her face flushed. She hurried, almost running, into the chowki.

'Thanks God, at last mera number lag gaya,' Shukla sighed. 'Lalli has seen that Shukla is genius, that is enough.'

If I knew my aunt, that was definitely not what she had seen.

Shukla went on with his exposition, but I was no longer listening. I was puzzling over the picture the tempo had summoned up. Could it have happened like this?

Deepika was fast asleep when Tara left, locking the door. She was still sleeping when the door opened.

A light touch woke her.

Her eyes widened. She sat up excitedly.

'Baby, chalo! The doll is waiting for you. Let's go get it.'

'Now?'

'Sssh! We have to be very quiet. It's a secret, I told you!'

'But it's night! My mother will be angry if I go out at night.'

'How will she know? It's our secret, not hers!'

Deepika giggled. She loved secrets.

'Even Suman doesn't know? And Lily?'

'Nobody knows, except you and me.'

It was great fun stealing out of the house in the middle of the night.

Once they were out of the house, Daya picked her up in his arms and ran.

Deepika clutched him, her eyes big with excitement as she noticed the tempo.

'In with you. We're going to take a ride.'

'Really? In your tempo?'

'Yeah, you'd like that?'

'Can I ride in front with you?'

'Sure.'

Deepika climbed in. None of the other girls would believe her adventure tomorrow, but then she'd have the doll to show them, wouldn't she?

'Here, Baby, enjoy.' Daya stuck a straw in the carton of fruit juice and handed it to Deepika. 'It's guava. You like guava, don't you?'

'It's my best thing. Don't you want some, Daya?'

'I finished mine. Now we're off!'

Deepika settled down in her seat, sucking contentedly at the straw.

Everything was turning out to be so exciting.

She tumbled heavily against Daya, fast asleep.

Daya stopped.

What then? What did he do after Deepika was doped?

'Newspaper,' I said. 'He did it where there's newspaper. Raddi shop.'

'Now after banana-skin tree you want me to find raddi shop?' Shukla was indignant.

'He needed newspaper, didn't he, to package the bodies? Besides only Deepika's body was returned immediately. He kept the others for three, maybe four or five, days. Where? Couldn't have kept them in the tempo could he?'

'Depends. Was he keeping them dead or alive? If alive, you are right. If dead, I'm correct. He is half and half. What is the name of Savio's story?'

'Dr Jekyll and Mr Hyde. Jekyll's good, Hyde's wicked.'

'Exactly. Everyday Daya is Jekyll, then one day he becomes Hyde, kidnaps, rapes, kills, cuts them up and locks up tempo. Immediately, Hyde-Daya becomes Jekyll again. But a thorn keeps poking, poking, and then after a few days Jekyll-Daya remembers. Rushes back to tempo, becomes Hyde-Daya, packages bodies, delivers parcel, becomes again Jekyll-Daya. Cycle is complete.'

Lalli's appearance put an end to Shukla's theory. Something had come up, she said, and we had to leave at once.

'But stick at it, Shukla, and get the carpet seen to.'

'I was just telling Sita about Jekyll-Daya and Hyde-Daya—'

'Sita will tell me on the way, I must run, Shukla, this is urgent.'

'Personal?'

'Very personal.'

She slid in behind the wheel and took off even before I had shut the door.

'Where's the fire? One thing I can tell—it isn't personal. You got a lead, didn't you?'

'Right. I do have a lead, but it's personal as hell. What was Shukla going on about Jekyll and Hyde for?'

'That was just blather, but he had another more important question—how long had the children been dead? Or as you'd put it, what was the PMI?"

The PMI or post mortem interval is the period between discovery and death. It's critical to reconstructing the murder.

'That's pretty tardy of Shukla if he's thinking of it only now. In all the cases PMI was within few hours: rigor had set in, but wasn't complete—that was Tambe's assessment. Only Deepika's body was found before rigor had set in, within two hours of death. That's all I know at present. Why was Shukla worried about PMI?"

'He said if the children had been kept alive all the time they were missing, it couldn't have been in the tempo.'

'Definitely not. There was a hideout.'

She drove towards Kurla, branching off near Bel Bazar. It was no longer a cattle market now, but the dairies had made a comeback. The place made me shudder. In the 2005 flood, many owners had abandoned their cattle, leaving the animals still tethered in their barns. For weeks afterwards, the swollen river was jammed with bloating corpses of buffalo. I could have sworn the air still held a mephitic reek.

Lalli parked outside a tabela and asked for Lilavati.

The two men lounging on the string cot didn't respond. They stared and continued chewing, very like one of their own buffalo.

'I really don't want to do it this way,' Lalli murmured as she got out.

'When was your last inspection?' she asked the men. 'I think it's about due now. I'll send the inspector this afternoon and if his report is unsatisfactory, I will be here to inspect your cattle myself.'

She flashed her badge, but she needn't have.

The men bounded up, smiling ingratiatingly. True, an inspection was due, but that was only because they were having the sheds renovated.

'Till then, I suppose those are your cows lunching at the garbage dump down the road?'

'Cows! Madam knows what cows are, they have minds of their own. I'll send my boy immediately to round them up. You were looking for Lilavati?'

'Yes.'

'If you don't mind the charpoy, please wait here, I will bring her to you at once.' He caught my eye and leered. 'Pappu fetch two glasses of lassi, extra malai ... for madam and Babyji.'

'No lassi for us, thank you.'

'It's no trouble. Our very best—'

'I will wait in my car. Send Lilavati to me.'

Lilavati was a stony-faced woman of about forty in a white sari worn the Gujerati way.

'What is it?' she demanded. 'Birth or death?'

'Death.'

'Five hundred. Extra, if there's a mess.'

'Get in.'

'How far? Rickshaw fare extra.'

'Get in.'

Lalli drove out of Bel Bazar, out of the maze of Kurla, into Kalina. She parked in the shade of a banyan outside a small park.

'So where's your house, then? And who is dead?' Lilavata asked.

'Let's sit here, Lilavati.'

'Here? In the park?'

'Why not? Better than the chowki, I thought,' Lalli said. 'But if you'd rather go back to Miravli Chowki just say the word.'

Her eyes widened with intelligence. 'I would rather die than go back there. So it's that business, eh?'

'Yes.'

'Who are you?'

'Lalli.'

'Acchha? I've heard of you. Aren't you the one who found Salima?'

'Yes.'

'And this is your daughter? Also police?'

'Yes. What do you know of the business at Miravli Chowki?'

'Those children?'

'Yes.'

'I've never seen anything like that before, I hope I never see anything like that again. In my job, you see all sorts of things; rapes, abortions, murders. They call me when there's a mess. I fix it. Same thing in Miravli Chowki. They called me to fix it. First time, it was not so messy. Second was very bad, the third one was the worst. The doctor had put bandages all over. I thought I should leave the bandages untouched, but Tambe Sahib, he told me to open up the bandages and check the body completely. I know there are post mortem doctors, so I asked why not send the body there, but Tambe said there were orders against a post mortem.'

Lilavati stopped. Her features contorted in a grimace of revulsion.

'What did you see? Describe it completely.'

Lilavati spoke as if in a trance. 'She was so little. Light as a feather. Skin wrinkled like a hag's. Raped? She was split like an orange, with the torn shreds hanging out. She was so little.'

'What was beneath the bandages, Lilavati?'

'Nothing. Nothing! Those bandages were a sham. The doctor put them so that her family would think her legs and arms had been injured and not notice the rest.'

'What was the rest?'

'Everything inside had been pulled out through the tear. But that was not all of it. Her stomach was cut open. Guts were pulled out and looped around her like rope. Liver was missing.'

'Lilavati you know sometimes kaleji can mean different organs—'

'Not to me, I'm a butcher's daughter. Left side spleen, right side liver. Liver was missing.'

'All of it?'

'Whole thing.'

'What did you do?'

'I packed in everything, taped it. I asked them to bring me a small banian and after I bathed and cleaned up the body, I pulled that on so that nothing showed. I asked Tambe what I should do about the bandages. He said put them on, and so I did. That was the third one. There was one more.'

'Tell me about that one.'

'Each one was terrible, the last was no different, torn and broken. This one had many fractures, legs, arms, fingers. I saw the last body as soon as it was brought in. By then they knew whom to call, they made no attempt to send for the doctor. All three girls had been raped, but that had not killed them. They were killed only when he had no further use for them.'

'How could you tell?'

'The injuries were not all inflicted on the same day. Some wounds were two or three days old, others fresh. There were burn marks and bruises everywhere on the skin. Bite marks too. But all the children did not have their stomachs cut open. Only the second one did. They were not easy to clean. Blood and stool had dried on them like scabs, but after I had bathed the bodies and I looked at them—'

Without warning, Lilavati broke down. She wept helplessly, giving in to the torment that kept lashing her with every word she had spoken. Lalli shot me a warning glance when I moved to comfort her.

When she resumed, her voice was very calm, her eyes blank.

'What's left for me to tell? I did what was asked of me. The police paid me well.'

'How much did the reporter pay you?'

'What reporter? I haven't spoken to anybody till today, and that's God's truth. You want to know why? I'm scared. Never thought I'd live to say that. I'm not scared of what this shaitan can do to me. I'm scared of looking into his eyes. What will I see there? What kind of madness? When you work the brothels you know that men are mad, but that is an animal you're familiar with. What kind of madness is there in a man who can do these things to a child?'

'I'll catch him, and then I will look in his eyes.'

'No. Don't do that. If you look in his eyes, you will kill him. You don't want blood on your hands.'

My aunt's response shocked me. She held out her hands.

'I already have blood on my hands. A little more won't hurt me.'

As we drove home, Lalli told me a little about Lilavati. She was one of the vanishing tribe of midwives who nursed, aborted, delivered, laid out and also occasionally suffocated inconvenient babies and kidnapped convenient ones. Women of her ilk were experts in treating sexual injuries common in the flesh trade, often turning a minor injury into life-threatening septicaemia.

Like most trades, Lilavati's too was fast becoming outdated. The flesh trade now called for a different set of skills—piercing, tattooing, cut-rate vaginal tightening, hymen reconstructions and genital mutilation. The last was the most lucrative as parents living in countries where FGM was outlawed brought their little girls to Bombay to be cut. And doctors were fast robbing Lilavati of that livelihood.

'Hospitals drive a dark trade in FGM,' Lalli said grimly. 'I've had the pleasure of arresting one gynecologist, but that public shaming only worked for a very little while. Women like Lilavati are a shade more ethical.'

Lilavati had discovered what the book trade knew all too well—lust has no market, unless coupled with cruelty and pain.

Mangesh lit a bidi and settled down for a breather on a convenient sack in the shade. He had been on his feet since seven, unloading sacks, stowing and packing before getting behind the counter to help the new guys out. Every second boy at A-1 now was police. It made the rest of them nervous and they got out when they could. Mangesh's bidi fell from his trembling hands. He let it go, morosely ground it out with his heel.

Daya! He had butchered those little girls, every one of them. It was—impossible. Why had he done it? They knew these kids, they played with them, looked after them, Daya took them on rides in his tempo when Jaggubhai wasn't around—and all that while, this, this had been going on in Daya's brain.

What had Daya done all this for? He had fooled them all by talking like a sant. 'Don't shed tears over Pinki, Mangesh,' he had said. 'She's free now, gone to a place where there's only happiness. Nobody to scold her or scare her, think of that!' And Mangesh—all of them—had thought those words of wisdom. They had believed Daya, because Daya, unlike them, was innocent. He shut his eyes when they showed him dirty pictures, he didn't like it when they ogled girls at the bus stop. When Prakash's mother had fallen ill, Daya had paid for his bus ticket home. It just didn't make sense. But there was no getting away from the truth— Daya had brought those mangled bodies back to their parents.

Mangesh had a glimpse of his little sister's happy grin. How she had wept when she lost her first tooth! Nothing would console her. She had clung to him the whole day. What if something were to happen to his Meena—

A sob broke from him and he got up, smashing his fist against the sack in rage. He punched and pummeled it till he was tired out. He'd been out here too long, Jaggubhai would have his throat. He was just entering the shop when Prakash called out, 'Mangesh, that guy was asking for you.'

He caught sight of an elderly man leaving the shop. He didn't look like a familiar customer, but Mangesh hurried to catch up with him.

'You were looking for me, Uncle?'

The man stopped and considered Mangesh for a long moment.

'You're Mangesh?'

'Yes.'

'Where's Daya today?'

Mangesh shook his head. 'He isn't here. I can get you what you want though.'

'No. Will he be in tomorrow?'

'No. He's—he's left,' Mangesh brought that out with difficulty.

'Gone back to the village?'

'He's dead.' There! It was out now.

'Dead?" The man's voice had gone all tight. 'What happened? Accident?'

So Mangesh told him. He didn't mean to, but it burst from him in a torrent.

The man staggered to the wall for support. He was looking really ill now. Mangesh asked him if he was alright.

'It's the heat,' the man gasped and began to retch.

Mangesh hurried into the shop for a glass of water.

When he returned, the man was gone.

Later, when the police questioned him, Mangesh couldn't remember what the man looked like.

I got to the meeting early.

There were about ten women pecking at potato chips and swilling masala chai. The literati here fuels on masala chai when they're not knocking back whiskey neat. My abstinence marks me immediately as a pre-FOXP2 hominid.

I'm usually greeted with—'You ... er ... write?'—on a rising note of incredulity, and I always hasten to assure them I can read too.

And of course they always get my name wrong.

It was no different this evening. I had chosen to speak last because, as yet, I had no idea of what I wanted to say or read.

I had brought along *The Triangular Hour* anyway. If the audience was tame, I could maybe inflict a page on them.

The audience was women between 16 and 70, all edgy. With distress, I thought.

Seema was there to introduce the speakers, but well ahead of that, she introduced Kandewadi.

'Five children were murdered,' she began. 'Five girls were raped and murdered. Little girls, children. Terrible things were done to their bodies, terrible terrible things. Their stomachs were cut. Their intestines were pulled out. We are here this evening to talk about this. To talk about your views, to give vent to your outrage. What does this say about Indian men? Are we safe from them? Are our children safe? These children were not just raped. They were brutalized.'

I felt like shouting that rape was brutal in itself, and *just* trivialized the crime—but I kept quiet.

'What was done to them, exactly?' a voice enquired. 'I read somewhere they were also sodomized.'

'I'm not very clear.' A young woman got up. 'I mean is it even possible? I mean isn't that what men do, like, to other men?'

It took ten minutes of fervent discussion, much of it anecdotal, to set her right on this. Sodomy 101 stopped just short of drawing diagrams, and at the end of it the naïve young thing said, 'But how disgusting! I really hope he wore a condom.'

'Somebody said,' a deep reverberant voice began, commanding silence from us all.

This was an elderly woman with School Principal written all over her. She acknowledged our attention with a gracious tilt of her noble head.

'Somebody once said, I forget who, but he said every man has a beast inside and it is upto every woman to tame it. I tell this to my girls as they leave us—face the beast with courage and you will succeed in taming it.'

There was mild applause and then the audience hurried back to brutalities. They wanted to know if all five children had their stomachs cut open and their intestines ripped out. It seemed important for them to know this, as if they were grading the victims.

'Was only the organ used?' one free spirit demanded. 'I seem to have read sticks and rods and glass pieces. Am I right?'

Ten women agreed about the rods. There were very few takers for glass pieces.

Could this be really happening? I couldn't believe any of these women actually had a grasp on the reality of what had been done to the children. They didn't think of them as children, but as bodies. No, not bodies either—mere receptacles for a sexual voiding that was fascinating because it was unusual and perverse. Nobody asked about the children's suffering. But they were avid as hell to discuss the act.

Seema was asked to explain the injuries and she dodged that neatly by throwing a question at the house.

'Most rapes are committed by men known to the victim. Why have the police not investigated the men of Kandewadi yet? Fathers, uncles, brothers, grandfathers even, of the victims? Why has this simple first line of enquiry not been opened up?'

Certainly that line of enquiry opened up the floodgates here. Everybody had a story to tell about horrors in the family.

One woman burst into tears, and revealed she had been raped by her brother for most of her life. This shocking interlude of reality disciplined the audience. She was perfunctorily congratulated on her courage, several visiting cards were pushed her way, and she was coaxed to have some refreshment before she went home. Someone would find her a cab. With perfect tact and understanding, she was all but dragged away. I caught sight of her sobbing into her dupatta as she nervously gathered up her things.

With her departure, order was restored, and we returned to Kandewadi.

'We should realise how far reaching this is,' one woman said. 'Maybe it happened in a slum, but how far are we from slums? There are slums everywhere. There are Kandewadis everywhere. These people are everywhere. Nobody is safe.'

I noticed for the first time, several very young women taking notes. One of them announced, 'I'm a journalist, I work late. What advice do you have for me? Yesterday when I was walking home from Mira Road Station at two a.m., a guy followed me. What should I do?"

'What did you do?'

'I asked him why he was following me and he said he wanted to be sure I was safe. How could I trust him?'

This asinine discussion went on for ten minutes. Finally, unable to stand it any longer, I asked, 'Why didn't you ask one of the guys at work to drop you home? You say you live a long way from the station.'

Of course I realised immediately I had said the fatal thing. That was the whole point, wasn't it, of all of us being here, to take back the night and walk without fear?

Absolutely. Still, if you must walk a deserted road at two a.m., surely one of the guys at work would have offered his company?

'How do I know I can trust him?' she shot back.

The audience agreed wholeheartedly. Every man was a suspect. At two a.m. the guys at work could be just as dangerous as roadside mavaalis. There followed the predictable rush of anecdote.

'But what should I do?' The girl's plaintive voice persisted. 'How do I know whom to trust?' And she shot terrified glances at us all, like an ingénue from a period piece.

'Nobody's safe,' the School Principal pronounced. 'And you, least of all, my dear.'

Seema stepped into the breach by grabbing the mike.

'Let's not forget this evening's all about Writers for Change. We've all been reading the brave Indian writers who have come out with their own painful stories of rape, molestation, abuse. These are our heroes, our true saviours, standing up fearlessly for the Kandewadi victims, sharing their anguish by relating their own experiences. They have broken the taboo of silence. Their courage compels other Kandewadis to speak up. Although I'm a member of the press, I know not all our papers will print these stories. But our writers have been courageous, they have approached countries where the press has greater freedom, countries that stand up against misogyny—'

'Which country is against misogyny?' I interrupted.

'Certainly the American press has been printing their stories—'

'America? The USA has more rapes per minute than any other country. What about the way their press writes about sportswomen, or haven't you been reading? Did I hear you say Australia? They had a woman prime minister—and every potshot the press took at her was vile and sexist.'

There was a shocked silence. Then someone said, 'You can't deny that Indian men are misogynistic.'

'Of course I'm not denying that. I'm saying we're just as misogynistic as the rest of the planet. Hell, nature's misogynistic, or haven't you noticed yet?'

Seema said, 'But we're not talking about Nature, we're talking about something against nature. We're talking unnatural crime, right?'

'Yes, and the unnatural crimes in Kandewadi can't be equated with the misogyny we encounter on the street every day,' I said.

'Why not? The guy who cops a feel on the bus might rape the next woman, how are we to tell?'

'And that is really the question, isn't it—how are we to tell?' Seema wrapped up the discussion. 'Let's hear what our writers have to say. I would have loved to begin with a small piece written specially for this evening by none other than Suketa Das.'

Frenzied applause. I felt the dismay I usually did when Suketa's name was bandied about in public. Professor Suketa Das had been my mentor throughout my brief academic career. I had expected to hear her quoted everywhere ever since the Kandewadi story broke. Suketa's firebrand feminism had takers only when disaster struck. Otherwise, she was dismissed as batty. To me, conversely, her intelligence was worth most when she was not caught up in political harangue. It was five—no seven—years since we parted, but not a day passed without me thinking of her with admiration and gratitude. We were no longer mentor and student, but somehow better friends apart.

But Seema was still talking. 'Unfortunately, Professor Das—Suketa as she prefers to be called, isn't feeling too well today. But we will be meeting soon, and she has promised to participate in our next session of Writers for Change. She has also asked for transcripts of all the readings this evening. So writers, you will have one very critical and very eminent reader apart from this very discerning audience …'

The first writer had brought six typed sheets. She began to read.

'When I read about the rapes at Kandewadi, my vagina twitched. I felt that happen in my vagina …'

The second writer had a poem that she wrote in hospital while undergoing an abortion. She had made the decision to abort immediately after reading about Kandewadi. 'It was a gesture of protest I felt obliged to make,' she said. 'I felt the need to protest with my body.' In common with the others, she pronounced the word broadly, bhaahdy, accompanying it with gestures that seem to detach and set on view her breasts and pelvis.

She began to read; 'Blood clot, water blot, placental membrane, membraneous placenta, blotted water, clotted blood, blame. Blame, blame, blame. No shame. I rise up in pride of refusal, I rise up in pride of rejection, in pride of blame I rise. I kill you to protect you, child of my marrow, I kill you, I kill you, for the world is no longer the same.'

Many women in the audience were sobbing by now.

'I reject shame!' the poet shouted. 'I reject trauma! I reject rape!'

It seemed to me that all she had rejected was her fetus, but her proclamation was taken up enthusiastically by the house.

'Yes, let's talk trauma,' somebody urged. 'Why do we consider rape to be traumatic? I mean why should there be any psychological trauma?'

This was too much to bear.

'Are you seriously suggesting a rape victim is not traumatized?' I asked.

There was a collective gasp. Glances were exchanged. Eyes rolled. Seema took the mike and said with very deliberate gentleness, 'I must request you, Seeta—Sita, not to use the word *victim*. Please say *survivor* instead. We must honour her courage. We should congratulate her, celebrate her, not shame her by calling her a victim.'

Celebrate? Congratulate? What was rape, an exam to be passed? Tamely, I nodded. 'Survivor, then. I'll repeat my question. Do you really think a courageous survivor of rape has suffered no psychological trauma?'

'Why should she? Nothing's happened to her mind. It's just sex, after all.'

'Personally, I'd rather be raped than, say, fracture my leg or even sprain my shoulder.'

'Frozen shoulder, eew. Yeah, that's like really painful.'

The collective opinion seemed to be that courageous survivors were not traumatized by rape.

'But I'll tell you one thing,' a woman stood up. 'After this, I'm all for sex determination, na? Who wants a daughter if she's going to get raped before she's what—six or seven?'

I stuck it out for half an hour more, then left. I walked mindlessly though the bright streets, torn and ashamed at what we had become.

At what I had become.

I had lacked the courage I might have had five years ago to tell those women what a misogynistic bunch of voyeurs they were, what pathetic human beings they were, if their only response to the pain of others was to trot out sorry tales of their own. I wondered what they would have said, or done, if they had seen Tara in her empty hut.

Worst of all, I wondered if by sharing their air, I had not tacitly become one of them.

Lalli took one look at my face as I entered the house, and held back questions.

Dinner was simple and delicious, and we watched an old movie as we ate. I asked about Savio.

Lalli grimaced, 'You don't want to know, Sita.'

'But what's he doing with Dr Q?'

She shook her head, refusing to be drawn. She had other news.

'A middle-aged man came to the store looking for Daya. He knew Mangesh was Daya's friend. He asked for Mangesh. When Mangesh told him of Daya's death, he reacted strongly. The police stand-ins were useless. They got no information about him from Mangesh, all they had to report was that the man 'became emotional.' They aren't even certain what that emotion was. Was he sad? Angry? Baffled? Shocked? They did tell me he vomited. That's it.'

'No great harm. Probably just a customer.'

'He vomited.'

'His reasons may have been gastric.'

'Probably. Sita, get an early night. When are you leaving?'

'Leaving for what? Good God, it's Friday!'

I had completely forgotten the weekend.

Was it on? Was it off? I hadn't heard from Arun for forty-eight hours—the longest silence since we met.

As if on cue, the phone rang.

He'd pick me up at eleven, he said. We should get there just in time for a breathtaking sunset.

'Great. I'll pack a picnic—'

'Absolutely not. Let's just cut free.'

Hit the road and cut free—suddenly that was all I wanted.

Lalli was intent on her laptop, and I went to pack for my romantic weekend.

I didn't feel particularly romantic, but I supposed it would be all right on the night. I was frowning over a choice of leggings—red or black—when Lalli came in.

'Red.'

I tossed the red pair into the bag. Certainly red was more-ish, and I have very little leg to begin with. Black's not my color. Is it anybody's, on the subcontinent? Just how did it get so *de* bloody *rigeur*?

At Vasu's parties—at one of which, incidentally, I met Arun—the crème de la crème is easily spotted. The women are always in black. It isn't all black black, of course—it's charcoal, anthracite, graphite—but *black*. Ramona, my guide in all things sartorial, assures me everything's safe in black except umbrellas, and a black umbrella makes you, like, totally dead.

The only accessory I have in black is a darn umbrella.

'Don't you have a redder red?' Lalli asked. 'Or maybe, shocking pink?'

'I wish.'

'I'm going out, Sita. Thought I'd tell you I might be late getting back.'

'Can I come?'

'If you aren't too tired—no come along, anyway, you can fall asleep in the car.'

Sleep was the last thing on my mind just now, but I was glad she'd chosen to drive. It's a zen thing, sitting next to her when she's driving. I can either completely switch off, or be on red alert. Either way, it's restful. And if you're wondering how a red alert can be restful—I told you, it's a zen thing.

Tonight, I switched off till we stopped.

Lalli had pulled over and driven off the road into the shadows. We seemed to be in a socket of darkness, the only one in the neon-lit night.

I made a move and Lalli's hand restrained me.

We were staying in. A stakeout, then.

Traffic zipped past us in an unreal glare of fluorescence that dismissed the night. I had to crane my neck to catch a glimpse of the sky—a pallid fume above the neon dazzle.

'Where are we?'

'Not too far from Kandewadi.'

'What are we waiting for?'

'Late night traffic. It's nearly midnight. We got here too early, but I didn't want to miss them.'

'Them?'

'The cars I'm waiting for.'

'You mean the people you're waiting for.'

'No. No. The cars. Or, maybe just one. No—that isn't right. One, but with followers.'

'How do you know they'll come this way? And who are they?'

'We'll find out. I know they'll come because the road repairs are done. Two days ago when Shukla was on the beat he noticed some road-work on this stretch. Curious, because this highway's barely a year old and well maintained. But they were working by night, powerful lighting, machinery borrowed from the Metro site—it all looked very urgent and important, so Shukla hung around to see what was happening. They were leveling down speed bumps. They had been ordered to get the job done by morning. Shukla took some time tracking down answers, but he told me this morning—the orders were from the politician who won the last election from this area. That was predictable, but I would never have guessed the reason. He wanted the speed bumps leveled in order to try out a new car.'

'What the hell!'

'Evidently this is his personal fiefdom—and that includes Miravli Chowki.'

'Oh. So you think the order to hush up the murders came from the same guy?'

'Likely, don't you think?'

'So we're here just to see what his new car looks like?'

'More or less.'

I could, perhaps understand how a tinpot dictator could twist the arm of the Municipality to alter a stretch of road—but to hush up such horrific murders? Who would want to do that?

Who, except the murderer?

I didn't know what this guy looked like, but he couldn't be any different from the faces on political posters—bloated with greed and arrogance, ingratiating with evil servility the janata he has looted, so that they could wearily vote him in and get looted all over again. And without exception, every one of those faces had a sleazy scandal behind it. What was it about power that pushed for depravity?

'Greed,' Lallis said. 'The need for excess. There's no limit.'

'There's no limit to outrage, either, judging from Kandewadi,' I retorted angrily.

'Strange that you should say that.'

'Why?'

'It may be the key to the case ... but it's too soon to tell.'

We relapsed into a pensive silence. The day's events unspooled in my brain.

I remembered how excited Lalli had been over Shukla's exposition. I didn't think for a moment that she bought into his theory, yet there had been something ...

She had been holding the flacon of perfume when he said, 'Perfume also may be stolen.'

'So you think Daya stole the ylang-ylang?' I asked. 'He may have been a kleptomaniac. All those pretty things Anita said he had. The chocolate, the doll.'

'Really, Sita! The surgical blade? The carpet? Where did he pinch those? The others could have been shoplifted. But not these.'

'He could have pinched them when he made home deliveries. He could have got talking over the carpet and offered to get it cleaned. Maybe he even meant to—after he was done with it. The surgical blade? From any hospital. He's a compulsive thief, but I don't think he's Shukla's Jekyll and Hyde.'

'No? I don't think so, either. But I don't think he was a compulsive thief, I think these pretty things were gifts.'

'Payment?'

'Oh no, no. Daya wouldn't accept payment!'

'Rewards, then?'

'No. These were gifts.'

She seemed very certain of that, very certain of her understanding of Daya.

'Who would gift him a carpet, Lalli?'

She made a moue. So she hadn't worked that out yet. But there were other puzzles she had solved.

'And how did you find Lilavati? Tambe?'

'Yep.'

'Funny, she didn't tell Tambe what she'd seen.'

'Tambe didn't ask. He didn't want to know. It made him feel less guilty.'

'But he did talk to the press.'

'Eventually.'

Which brought me back full circle to my principal worry. 'How did Seema Aggarwal know all those details? You think Lilavati lied about not talking to her?'

'No, I don't think it was Lilavati. Seema has another source.'

So then I said it. 'Right. I'll ask Arun.'

'How would he know?'

'Seema and Arun were close. Maybe they still are. She set him to pump Savio about Daya.'

'What!'

'Yeah. I was shocked too. Savio told me. Lalli, where is Savio? I miss him.'

'He'll turn up. Why Savio? Why didn't Arun ask you?'

'Because he'd kind of blotted his copybook the day before.'

'Ah. The sordid life dig. He couldn't very well ask you after that.'

'Why would he even be interested in knowing about Daya, unless Seema wanted information?'

'That's a very astute observation, Sita.'

'Astute? It's obvious, isn't it?'

'Not entirely. Hush now. They're coming.'

I could hear nothing.

It was a little past two.

Over the last hour, the traffic had thinned to the occasional cab or car. The night murmured in restless protest against the rise and fall of rhythms not its own—the hot flashes of neon, the rumble of lorries and now a high sweet drone like an approaching swarm. It came in like the tide, with a sudden lunge of speed out of the horizon.

A startled yelp, and a thud—and the car was past us.

I ran out on the road, grabbing Lalli's flashlight. The car had hit a stray dog, flung it and then run over it, leaving a mangled mess of blood, guts and brain.

The flashlight wavered in my hand. It was not the dog I saw, but Lilavati's memory. Was this Pinky? Was it Mary? Jamila? Sindhu? It was all of them, it was none of them. It was the lost children before them, and the ones to come. It was—

Something—a hoop of steel—grabbed my waist. I staggered, trying to find my feet as I was pinioned and dragged, I was conscious of a tremendous rush of heat just a hairsbreadth away. A brightness zoomed past and became the tail lights of a retreating car.

The hold on me loosened and I realized I was encircled by Lalli's arms.

I looked up. Her eyes were dilated with fear. But only for an instant. She let me go.

'Get back into the car, Sita. Quickly.'

The speeding car had vanished, with nothing but my terror to tell me it had very nearly taken my life.

We ran across the road, into our car. Lalli started the engine.

'I nearly lost you, Sita. I nearly got you killed.' Her voice shook.

'What are you going to do?'

'Get them.'

'Them? I thought there was only one car.'

'There were two. One is a Lamborghini, the other's a Ferrari, I think. They'll be back. The dog was first, you were next, I don't want a third.'

'Lalli, how are you going to stop them—they're doing what, 120, 150?'

'Watch.'

We stayed camouflaged by shadow till the cars reappeared in brilliant haze of speed.

Lalli waited till they had just passed us, then plunged forward. She had killed the lights, and keeping just outside the trail of brightness, we tailed them amazingly close. I realised both drivers were completely oblivious of us. Lalli's old Fiat couldn't possibly take on those two racers—but somehow, it did.

Just ahead was one of the bottlenecks usual to this city in midecdysis—our four-lane highway crossed a bridge over a nallah, and narrowed into a one lane connection with the next highway. A nightmare at peak hours, but now a barely noticeable transition.

We were still behind them, still unseen and about a minute away from the bridge when Lalli put on a burst of speed.

We zoomed past them, shot across the bridge and then, in a terrifying torque, Lalli turned abruptly and parked crosswise, blocking the road.

Our headlights blazed. The Lamborghini's brakes squealed and the Ferrari slammed into it with a satisfying crunch.

'Stay here.'

Lalli walked over to the Lamborghini.

'You crazy bitch!' A tall guy jumped out and rushed at Lalli. She waited till he was within an inch of her, then let fly with her left fist and knocked him out cold.

There was something in her right hand. She stood there, waiting.

'What the—'

The driver of the Ferrari came out yelling. His flood of abuse dwindled to a whimper as Lalli raised her right hand. I saw something flash. It was a knife. I recognized it as the Rampuri an old enemy had sent her a while ago. She tossed it carelessly in the air. I couldn't take my eyes off its thin edge of light. It twirled and winged its way towards Driver No 2.

Lalli caught it when it was seconds away from his neck. 'You! Get your friend out of the car. Now!'

Ferrari obeyed mindlessly. He yanked out a short fat kid who looked about sixteen and ready to mess his pants any second.

'Cell phones, car keys, wallets. Now!'

The knife twirled again.

Ferrari gibbered.

'Now.'

With cold deliberation, Lalli placed the point of her knife beneath his chin.

The fat kid had dropped his goods on the ground. Ferrari fumbled at his jeans in terror. He howled suddenly as Lalli withdrew the knife and

I realized she had cut him. He grabbed his chin and stared disbelievingly at his hand.

Back came the knife, and keys, phone, wallet, all tumbled out.

'Good. Now get Lamborghini's stuff. Go on!'

Lamborghini was still out cold.

'Is he dead?' the fat boy screamed. 'Gaurav's dead!'

Lalli laughed. 'No such luck. Dead is what you will be, if you don't have his stuff here at the count of three.'

They plundered Lamborghini.

'Now take off your clothes. You heard me. Do it! You can keep your underwear and spare me a sorry sight. Right. Now pick up your stuff and bundle it in your clothes—keys, wallets, phones—I'm watching. Pick up the bundle and walk to the railing of the bridge. Now drop the bundle over the railing into the nallah.'

They did it.

Lalli walked over to the fallen boy and prodded him with her foot.

'So this one's the geek? Which one of you is the medical student?'

'I'm a doctor,' Lamborghini growled.

Lalli laughed. I always thought this laugh of hers dangerous, but I had never before heard it in context.

'Don't you dare call yourself a doctor,' she hissed. 'I'm not finished with you yet.'

She turned away.

'Wait!' the fat kid had found his voice.

'What?'

'Who are you?'

'Shut up Rajiv,' Ferrari muttered.

'Yeah. You do that Rajiv,' Lalli stuck out her fist at him and the knife blade dropped within an inch of his face. 'Just shut the fuck up.'

Lalli then did something that made me cringe. She drew her head back and spat full in the face of the Lamborghini guy.

She got into the car and we drove off in a hard bitter silence.

When we got home, she stalked off to her room and shut the door.

Saturday, 26 March

I was trembling. I got myself a glass of water and sat down miserably at the kitchen table. I'd seen Lalli get tough before, I'd seen her enraged. But never before had I seen her express contempt towards another human being. Spitting on the face of the unconscious boy was more than an expression of contempt. It was a gesture of utter revulsion, a mindless rejection like crushing a cockroach with a broom. And Lalli was never mindless.

She came in and drew up a chair.

'I'm sorry I upset you.'

'Why did you have to spit on him, Lalli?' I burst out.

She looked surprised.

'That upset you? Too bad. It was my visceral response to his ugliness. I couldn't scare him, he was out cold. I couldn't bring myself to pee on him as Italian women did on Mussolini's corpse. But I couldn't just leave him unpunished. He nearly killed you. Forget it, Sita, it never happened. Let's get the coffee started, and I'll bake a cake, a babka for breakfast.'

There are times when I have to get really severe with Lalli.

'It had nothing to do with me, Lalli, and you know it.'

'Okay.'

'No, it's not okay. You threatened those boys, you assaulted them and you want me to say it never happened?'

'Yes. That's exactly what you're going to do. You're not to breathe a word of this.'

'We'll tell Savio, of course.'

'I will not and neither will you. Savio is the last person who should know.'

'And what if the police tracks you down? What will you do then? Deny it?'

'Definitely. But the police won't track me down because they'll never hear of this.'

'The boys will make a complaint—they have to, for insurance. If they don't, their godfather, the speed bump leveler, he isn't going to stay quiet, is he?'

'He won't buy their story. Think of it, Sita. Three strapping young men stopped at 2 a.m. by an old lady who overtook a Lamborghini and a Ferrari in a beat up Fiat and then stripped them and threatened them with a knife—who'd believe that?'

I couldn't help giggling and soon we were both laughing helplessly.

I got the coffee started and we passed up the babka in favor of gingerbread although Lalli said she doubted if Savio would be in for breakfast.

The air sang with cinnamon and cardamom and a cool breeze teased. It promised to be a wonderful day. We were waiting for the cake to cool when I asked Lalli the question that had eluded me for the last two hours.

'Lalli you knew those boys, didn't you?'

'No.'

'You did! You told me you were waiting for the cars, but you knew these boys would be driving them.'

'No. I thought boys like these might be driving them.'

'Oh no. You knew one of these boys was a geek, another a medical student—'

'Oh that!' Lalli chuckled. 'Shot in the dark.'

But it hadn't been, not entirely.

'Okay, look, it wasn't a random shot in the dark, those were just pieces in the jigsaw and I wanted to try them out.'

'You think these boys have something to do with Kandewadi?'

'I don't know. At this stage I think everybody suspicious has something to do with Kandewadi.'

She was stonewalling, and Savio was missing in action. Right. I did have a sordid life, but the gingerbread improved it quite a lot.

Shukla turned up just as I caved in for a sliver more of the cinnamony caramelly crust.

'Bread is smelling of elaichi. Elaichi is for digestion,' he reproved. 'Nobody is putting it in black bread.'

'It's brown, not black. Don't fuss, Shukla. Have a slice.'

'Sita, I cannot risk, just now I am full of vada pao.'

'Then the elaichi can digest that.'

'Good idea. But I will require large dose. I had two vada pao.'

'Why?'

He looked injured. 'It was party.'

'At 7 a.m.?' Lalli called from the kitchen. 'Sita, will you watch the stove, please?'

There was nothing on the stove. She wanted me out of the room. I obeyed and made some random noises above which I could hear them quite clearly.

Lalli set down Shukla's mug of Nescafe and waited till he had taken an appreciative sip.

'So what was the party for?'

'You are making perfect coffee, Lalli, why don't you teach Sita? Sometimes she forgets to put milk.'

'She has too much on her mind just now, Shukla.'

His voice dropped an octave. 'Ek Do Teen Char?'

Lalli didn't reply.

'Yesterday he phoned me, asking details of Kandewadi. So many questions. Who is this Daya? What did we find out about him? So many questions, leave me with a question I cannot ask him. So I will ask you. Why he is asking Shukla and not Sita?'

Lalli, unlike me, disregarded that. 'But tell me about this party, Shukla.'

'One minute. Digestion is very quick with this bread. Small slice, very small. Thank you. Party was in Traffic Chowki. You remember that speed bump repair I told you about? This morning 6 a.m. patrol found two cars crashed near that road. Never before Chowki has such tiptop cars. One red Lamborghini, one black Ferrari. Calls for celebration, no?'

'Absolutely!'

'Lamborghini was complete 377! Ferrari ghusawed through and through. Cars could not be separated.'

'No injuries, I hope?'

'Not visible, but may be internal. Whole matter very strange. One minor, two older boys. Two older boys were fighting, one was wearing only underwear. Minor was hiding. Also in underwear, but excuse me, Lalli, uska goo nikal gaya tha, he was unable to control. There is a fountain outside Plaza Hotel, Traffic fellows pushed him into it, smell was too bad. Boys are in lockup now.'

'Suspicion of loitering, public indecency?'

'Rich boys. Phone call will get them out in one hour.'

'Maybe you should let Savio know right away. Any suspicious behaviour might be a link to the case.'

'Already done. After yesterday, he is not in mood for vada pao, so he said he would go straight to the Chowki.'

What had Savio been doing all of yesterday? And why was Arun being such a schmuck, digging for Seema Agarwal? Which reminded me, the paper would have come. I was about to get it when the doorbell rang.

A young guy in grimy overalls grinned shyly and looked over my shoulder.

'It's Abdul,' he called out.

Lalli came to the door, and propelled both Abdul and me into the lift.

'I've brought Chakram,' Abdul protested. 'He needs to—'

'Yes, yes.'

'But madam—'

'Abdul, I have Inspector Shukla in there with me. We don't want him to see Chakram, do we?' Lalli said in a low voice.

Abdul, it turned out, had a job to do on the car. I didn't have the keys, but Abdul assured me Chakram didn't need keys.

Indeed, the bonnet was open and a small boy was fiddling with the entrails. To my horror he had dismantled the engine.

'Relax, Lalli Madam said it's okay to do it today,' Abdul assured me.

'Do what?'

'Replace the engine.'

Replace it? Whatever for? The Fiat had given the Lamborghini a run for its money last night—

'Ran like water, eh? Listen up, Chakram.'

Chakram was a skinny kid with more teeth than his mouth could accommodate. He greeted me with a kind of regal disdain.

'How much did you do? One twenty, one fifty?'

'I wasn't driving, but yes, around one fifty.'

'You could have done two hundred easy, I could show you.'

'Chakram—your name can't be Chakram?'

'Chakrapani.'

'But we call him Chakram,' Abdul put in. 'It suits him.'

'Right. Chakrapani, you fixed the engine wonderfully well. But why are you dismantling it now?'

'Lalli Madam wanted the old engine put back before eight o'clock.'

'The old engine?'

'Fiat.'

'So what's this one, then?'

'Honda Civic.'

Chakram was certainly a wizard at his job. He had the Fiat's original engine fitted back and running in fifteen minutes.

Shukla looked in on his way out. 'Car trouble?'

Chakram slid like a lizard beneath the car.

'Starting trouble,' I said. 'Abdul's fixing it.'

Shukla gave Abdul his predatory grin. 'Mind you fix it tip-top or you'll be hearing from me.'

'Anything I can do for you, Sahib?'

'Not for me, but, there's a big denting-penting job waiting at the Traffic Chowki. Any of your buddies are upto foreign cars? Ever seen a Lamborghini? Go take a look. Get educated.'

They waited till Shukla's bike sputtered off, then Chakram emerged.

'Let's go get the Lamborghini,' he said.

'Think you can manage it?'

'Sure.'

They suddenly remembered me, but I was listening to the engine purr.

'Sounds sweet now,' Chakram said. 'Tuned it better.'

'How much do I owe you?'

'We've been paid.' They hoisted the engine into a hold-all and dragged it out to the rickshaw parked at the gate.

I couldn't help feeling hoodwinked—all this while, I'd put last night's driving down to Lalli's heroics.

Lalli laughed at my indignation. 'I knew what I'd be up against, I just went prepared.'

'Do you know Chakram's on his way to pinch the Lamborghini?'

Lalli didn't respond to that. Silently, she handed me the newspaper.

DEAD MAN WAS KANDEWADI
KILLER AVER POLICE

The accidental discovery of the corpse of a young man who appears to have died of natural causes has led the police to hold him responsible for the brutal murders of six children in Kandewadi. The body of Daya Velji Champaneria, 25, was discovered at the nallah a short distance from Kandewadi. The body was naked and the clothes were found abandoned in the nearby bushes. The clothes were heavily blood-stained, but reliable sources maintain that the blood was that of the dead man. The cause of death has been certified as a gastric bleed following an alcoholic binge.

Although there is no apparent connection between the death of this young man and the savage murders of children, the police are pursuing this line of enquiry in the belief that Champaneria, who was employed in a nearby store, was familiar with the dead children. When this reporter questioned Champaneria's co-workers, they were surprised to hear that the police suspected alcoholism. To their knowledge, Champaneria had never touched alcohol in his life.

'He was a simple boy,' said a co-worker who did not wish to be named. 'I cannot believe that he could have committed such terrible crimes.'

Meanwhile the police have lost no time in assuring the residents of Kandewadi that their children are safe.

'If this boy is the murderer, we are happy he is dead,' said Kulsum Begum, 34, mother of one of the victims. But it will be a very long time before children feel safe in Kandewadi, averred Begum.

The mood in Kandewadi continues to be skeptic and vigilant. Questions are not encouraged and residents refuse to talk to the press. A television crew was met with a hostile reception: local youth armed with cricket bats and hockey sticks opposed filming. The police refused to intervene.

Inspector Savio D'Sa, reportedly in charge of the case, was unavailable for comment. Reliable sources within the police state that D'Sa, who was deputed to the case, has not been available for the past 48 hours.

A candlelit vigil was held outside Kandewadi on Thursday night. The mohalla residents were prevented from attending by the police.

Follow us at Twitter@kandewadi.com.

'Where is Savio?' I asked. 'This is beginning to look very bad for him.'

Lalli looked upset, but said nothing.

A little later, I heard her singing in the shower. She only does that when she wants to block off a problem in order to grapple with another.

The phone rang. It was Seema Aggarwal. 'Hey, thanks a million for being there last evening!'

'Sure.'

'Listen, I wonder if you read my story this morning—'

'Yes, I did.'

'And?'

One can't shrug over the phone.

'What's up with this Inspector D'Sa? Arun said he's a pal of yours.'

'Yes, we're friends.'

'Great! Look, I need the inside story on this dead guy. Any chance of setting up an interview?'

'Sorry, I'm not in the loop. What about your reliable source?'

'He's out of the loop too.'

'Touché.'

'Hey, I meant to tell you yesterday, Suketa asked about you. I didn't know you were her student.'

'Seven years ago.'

'She still thinks the world of you. I told her how I met you and your aunt. She wanted to know all about your aunt. Lalli, right? The moment I mentioned the name, she said she knew her too.'

'Small world.'

'Yeah. She sounded a bit J, actually. You know how Suketa gets. Mother hen! She said your aunt's famous. Is she?'

'You're the journalist.'

'Yeah but all I know about her is that she carried the corpse into the morgue. In her arms. As if it was her child. As if it *mattered*. People don't do that kind of thing. That was certainly peculiar, but she couldn't possibly be famous for that. So what is she famous for?'

'You tell me,' I rang off.

Lalli was at the door, dressed in a delectable purple cotton sari. A fresh fragrance enveloped her—lily but with a brief sparkle to it. I breathed in appreciatively.

'Too much?'

'No. It's just lovely.'

'I've put the bottle in your bag.'

'Thanks! Where are you off to? You're dressed to kill.'

'It's armour. I'm going to meet an old friend.'

'Someone you don't like?'

'I haven't thought about that in a long while. But I did develop a ferocious dislike to her about … say … twenty years ago. Now suddenly she has something important she must talk to me about, at once. Today. I have no idea why I'm going. Perhaps because I dislike her.'

I understood that apparent antithesis. Dislike has heavy responsibilities—we go to great lengths to be just to the people we dislike. It's hard living with yourself if you don't.

'Arun's picking you up at eleven? I'll see you Monday, then?'

I nodded.

She touched my cheek briefly and left.

Arun called at five minutes to 11. He'd be at the gate in five.

I was a few minutes hesitating over which notebook to take. Finally I decided on a pristine blue one, chucked it in my bag and clattered madly down the stairs.

I was surprised to find Shukla at the gate. Arun was holding forth with the car bonnet open.

'Car trouble?'

'No worries. Just showing HK the ejector.'

'Happy journey! Shubh yatra! Bone voyages!' Shukla flashed all thirty-two lightbulbs and kicked off before I could answer.

Arun grinned. 'Funny guy, HK. Still, I'd take him any day over that muscle-bound halfwit D'Sa.'

Which was, you'll agree, an unpropitious start to our romantic weekend.

I tossed in my backpack. He winced. A little later, he informed me my backpack was pink. I pointed out my handbag, spanking new, was definitely grey, but that didn't console him. He kept on till I could feel its incandescent pinkness singe the nape of my neck.

He was a bad driver. Or perhaps I was just used to Lalli and Savio.

By the time we left city limits, I was exhausted.

At the toll gate, he quarreled over the change. He wouldn't stop for lunch. He said he wasn't hungry. When I suggested a vada pao on the fly, he said, 'What don't you get about the statement that I'm not hungry?'

At 3 p.m. I took out my notebook. The blank page seduced me quickly and the next five minutes were deliciously sane.

'What are you doing?'

After weeks of hanging out with me, surely my notebook was no surprise?

'We should talk about this, Sita.'

'Now?'

'Yeah. Now. Focus, please. What are you writing for, Sita?'

'It's what I do.'

'Only because you do nothing else. It's not as if you can't. You just won't.'

'Should I?'

'Shouldn't you? This is just an ego trip, and it's time you faced it. Who reads your books, Sita? Who's even heard of them? How much do they pay?'

'Not much, but I live in hope.'

'But is there hope?'

'Cosmic question.'

'Someone's got to ask it. Your aunt's too batty to bother, Vasu's an irresponsible idiot. Your parents are too wrapped up in themselves. Who else is there? Savio? HK?'

I took a really deep breath. 'Nobody calls Shukla HK, not even Shukla. And yes, I talk over most things with Savio. Please don't call Lalli batty, or we'll quarrel. And you know better than anyone else that my brother is not an idiot. My parents know their daughter can take care of herself. Now that I've answered all your anxieties, can we please get something to eat?'

'Your aunt's sweet, but what is she?'

'She's a famous detective.' It sounded silly even to me.

He laughed.

'Yeah, like you're a famous writer and I'm a famous math man and Savio's a famous policeman.'

'Why do you dislike him so much?'

'He's just so dumb.'

'Savio? *Dumb*?'

'Does he even talk? And what's this thing between him and your aunt? Look I have an open mind, but your aunt's simply infested with men—'

'I hadn't noticed.'

'What about the Man in White—he really is intolerable.'

'Dr Q? Why?'

'Why does he wear white all the time?'

'Does it matter?'

'It doesn't seem to matter to your aunt. And HK! Hari Kumar Shukla is really pedestrian. So what are all these guys buzzing around her for?'

'Murder.'

'Sorry?'

'Lalli's in the murder business.'

'Of course, you've told me, but you're not serious are you?'

'No, but she is. Would you like to hear about some of her cases?'

'Please! Spare me your corpses. Here, I'll be kind and stop for a snack. Your treat.'

The break got us a half hour truce.

He ate his way through the menu, and of course, afterwards things improved. First he turned nice, and then he turned mushy, and towards dusk, nature tuned up for romance.

At the hotel, Arun reached for his wallet—and found it missing.

We turned the car inside out, but it wasn't there. He swore he'd put it in his pocket after he'd paid up at the petrol pump just before he picked me up. But it was just—gone.

I had enough cash on me to cover for now—but not for the whole weekend.

'Haven't you heard of plastic?' Arun snarled.

I was surprised by the grim sense of duty that made me stay. Any pretense of pleasure had long since fled, but my bloody-minded insistence on seeing things through made it impossible to renege.

Sunday, 27 March

I woke up at five, trapped in an unfamiliar room with a stranger.

He slept on his perfect back (*waxed*, I kid you not) in elegant repose, supremely unconscious of what a disaster it had all been.

I suppose I had to find out, but it was just too awful, even in culinary terms. He hadn't considered aperitif or hors d'oeuvres. The entrée was sloppy, the main botched, stodgy and underdone. I passed up dessert.

But he was the kind of man who heard applause in his dreams, and might wake up expecting an encore.

It would be smart to leave now.

I went out into the balcony. The cool air soothed me. The beach was a mile off, but I kidded myself into hearing the sea. I sank into the only piece of furniture there, a cruel metal chair, perversely glad of its cold shoulder, its iron embrace.

For an instant I slid into the perfect ease of solitude—and then realised what I had been missing for a while.

Me.

For nearly two months I had worn myself out, trying to be quite another woman, anxious to make the grade, and never quite getting there.

But did I want to?

Not if it meant the rest of my life would be last night, extended to eternity.

I had almost metamorphosed into the woman Arun saw me as. What if I couldn't go back to being me?

Perhaps Arun's carping was compelled by something I had failed to acknowledge or notice? Some hurt I had thoughtlessly caused, some warning I had refused to heed?

But for the life of me, I couldn't discover what.

I must have dozed off.

The next thing I knew the sun was in my eyes. I got out of that punishing chair cramped and aching, and was about to go in when a sharp current of scent gave me pause.

Rose has about a hundred different notes of odour, and this was the lightest. It was the lemony, tea-like perfume that roses reveal when still bedewed, the fragrance that's only a nuance away from wet grass and petrichor.

And there she was, the perfect pink rose, a satin frou frou, a pirouette of silk in a thorny tangle. Wild, impudent, alone.

Just one flower, a briar rose. She would droop by evening. Not even a bee would notice her stay. And yet here she was, reckless with scent, having her solitary say.

We were having breakfast in the empty floodlit restaurant downstairs when someone switched on the TV.

I jumped up, spilling my coffee.

No, it wasn't Kandewadi.

The face on the screen was someone I knew. It was someone I loved. It was my teacher, my mentor, Suketa Das, and she was dead.

The reporter shouting on the mike outside a building in Santa Cruz kept calling her a feminist icon. The banner beneath read **DEATH OF A FEMINIST**.

The reporter was swiftly replaced by activists, social workers, lawyers. Every woman in the human resources racket had her two seconds on TV.

They kept flashing a picture of Suketa in the background. It was an awful photograph. She looked elegant and snooty, very different from the forthright woman I adored.

She had taught me everything I knew about feminism. I had spent half our time together fiercely combating her ideas. We had parted because I rejected her ideologies. I told her I might arrive at a philosophy if I wrote enough—or I might not. I needed to write free.

And now she was dead.

She had hanged herself.

She had left no family.

'What do you expect?' Arun shrugged. 'A predictable end. Be warned, Sita.'

'Meaning you might do it too?'

'I? I'm not a feminist.'

'Death by hanging is a predictable end for a feminist?'

'It should be, if it isn't.'

I looked closely at him. He was just as madly perfect as he had been yesterday. He hadn't developed warts, or a squint, or even halitosis. The impish glint in his eye was the same, his lip had the same sardonic droop. Nothing had changed.

What made him so irredeemably loathsome?

'We should go,' I said.

We did, without too much bloodshed till we were on the State Highway, well past Mahad. That was when I took out my notebook.

My pencil was still hovering when Arun grabbed the notebook and pitched it out of the window.

'Stop the car!'

He kept driving.

The pulse at his temple did a quickstep.

'Arun, stop the car!'

'And if I do, what do you plan on doing? Trudge back a mile to find your notebook?'

'No. I won't, you will.'

'Why should I?'

'Because you lost it just now, but you're basically decent?'

'I'll show you just how decent I am.' As he spoke, he picked my handbag off my lap and chucked it out.

I froze.

It dawned on me there was nothing really that I could do, except jump out when he next slowed.

'I never liked that bag anyway,' he said.

I concentrated on staying very still.

He switched on music, some mind-numbing repetitive thump and squeak.

I kept my eyes on the blurring scenery.

'Okay, I'll stop the car. Happy?'

We pulled up at a small roadside café. By my reckoning we were miles from civilization. This was probably a pit stop for tourist buses. The sign said: *Meals Ready, Toilet Avlable.*

I got out warily and walked into the shadowy barn. Flies buzzed cheerily on the sticky tabletops. Red and yellow plastic chairs were stacked against the wall. A disgruntled man walked in, waving a towel at the flies.

Arun was at his charming best. 'Something to eat? Something cold for the lady. Kadak chai for me,'

I wasn't hungry or thirsty, but I didn't want to rock the boat.

I sipped the lemonade and listened to Arun explain that there was something intrinsically wrong with people who winced at kadak chai.

It took all my self-control to keep from hurling the kadak chai at his handsome face. I would have done it too, if only I had any money on me.

My new, incomparably elegant soft pearl-grey bag was nestled somewhere in the brambles along the highway, complete with wallet, phone, and a hundred other necessities that make for survival. The only reason why I could endure the thought was because its only important content—my notebook—was several miles further away.

'Excuse me for a moment,' Arun got up, flashed a brilliant smile and walked towards the car.

I think I knew, the moment he got up.

I think the waiter knew, too.

Both of us waited passively to see if Arun would do what we thought he would.

He did.

Arun got into the car, and drove away.

I suppose I waited for about half an hour for him to have a change of heart and return.

The waiter took away the chai and the lemonade. He plonked a bottle of mineral water and a glass before me.

Then he stood there, waiting to be noticed.

'I don't want the water,' I said. 'I'm sorry, but I can't pay. I don't have any money on me.'

'You left your hand bag in the car?'

'He threw it out.' What a relief it was, just saying that aloud.

'He's not coming back, is he?'

'No. I don't think so.'

He pulled up a chair and sat down.

'I have to get home,' I said.

'Don't go back to him. Go to your parents first. You have parents in Bombay?'

'Yes.' In a crisis, Lalli was my only parent.

'How are you going to get to Bombay? A bus stops here at about one o'clock.'

'Could you lend me money for the ticket? I'll pay you back immediately.'

'No cash. Look at me. How do you think I look?'

I examined him. Despite the gelled hair and pirate earring, this was a miserable man.

'Gloomy?' I ventured.

'Gloomy is right. You think you're in a mess? What about me?'

'What's wrong with you?'

'I have that bus coming at one o'clock. Tourist bus, double decker. Seventy-five passengers plus driver and two staff. First time I've pulled off a contract for lunch, and what happens? Today of all days?'

'What?'

'Cook's gone. Left last night. He cleaned out the cash, not a paisa left on me. What am I going to do?'

'Get the kitchen going.'

'How? I can't cook.'

'I can,' I told him.

His name was Punto Singh. He had come from Ludhiana as a teenager and stuck on doing garage work along the highway. Last year he'd finally bought this spot and started off the dhaba.

Business was good in fits and starts.

The problem, always, was the cook. None of them stayed long. Couldn't blame them, the place was in a wilderness, but he had TV, and it was only an hour's ride to Mahad. Finally he'd managed to land this deal with a bus route. He was thinking of going to Punjab for a bride this Diwali, but what's a man to do about destiny?

The kitchen was bare, but surprisingly clean. It was also ambitious. My luck was in. There was gas and an electric grinder, and a big pressure cooker. The utensils were all ogre-sized and the stove lit up a supernova on each of its four barrel-like burners.

Rice, dals, oil, ghee, atta were all present and correct, but not a fresh vegetable was in sight. I discovered a hill of potatoes and onions. I opened the gigantic fridge. Milk cartons, ice cream, cold drinks, mineral water. No food.

'What are we going to cook with?' I asked. 'We need vegetables, fruit, condiments.'

'I'll see what I can get.'

'I'll need help, I can't have you disappearing, so get back soon. What do you want? Home food or fancy?'

'Home food.'

'Your home or mine?'

'Which is quicker?'

'Mine.'

'Do that, then.'

'You're clear about my ticket on that bus.'

'Leave that to me.'

Punto whirred off on his motorbike, leaving me to get started—but what could I start with?

I walked out of the back door.

There was the usual kitchen garden one finds in a small town. Papaya, banana, drumsticks—these spring up everywhere.

I harvested four fair-sized green papayas. There were drumsticks high up on the tree, and I left those for Punto to garner.

If I could find seasoning, I could have the menu planned before Punto returned.

I soaked dal for vadai, kneaded dough for poori, and pressure-cooked a ton of potatoes before Punto staggered in with a sack of assorted vegetables. Most of them were wrinkled or squelchy. We spent the next ten minutes on salvage and came up with a modest, but definitely edible, selection.

I sent Punto out for drumsticks and when he returned, set him to peel onions.

From then on, it was fierce and fast, and about half way through, I caught myself laughing madly at Punto's asinine jokes.

We had earsplitting bhangra rap to keep us going, and Punto opened a giant bag of potato chips.

He really was a nice guy. He cracked coconuts, peeled, ground and washed up with manic energy. He drew the line at knife work, though.

I found the grater and set him to work on the papayas, and got serious over slicing, julienning, dicing, chopping.

By half past twelve, we were done.

Punto had discovered the joys of the rolling pin, so even the poori was ready for the ogre's kadhai.

As one o'clock approached, Punto grew morose.

'What's the matter, isn't it good enough?' I demanded.

'Sweet dish. They always want sweet dish.'

'But the fridge is full of ice cream, Punto!'

'Ice cream is not sweet dish. It's separate from the menu.'

'Today it's *on* the menu.'

But nothing would convince him.

Sweet dish in these parts meant sheera. Take it or leave it.

I needed that bus ticket, so I took it.

All that ghee and cardamom made for an aromatic welcome as seventy-five ravenous passengers spilt out of the bus.

Punto had whistled up four lads to help with the service.

Once the stampede to the bathroom was over, we sent the boys out with buttermilk fragrant with the vaguest hint of asafoetida and the coolth of curry leaves.

I showed the boys how to fill the katoris on the thali and got the pooris started.

The first thalis went out with all six katoris brimming. Maybe after the fortieth or so we'd have to dilute the sambar.

I had a couple of dishes on standby in case we ran out half way.

We did.

Punto took over the poori frying. He charred the first batch—and I got to making not two, but four, entirely new dishes.

Out in the barn, the passengers were polishing off their thalis and getting them refilled at Formula One velocity. It was incredible, the way they kept those boys on their toes, demanding more pooris, more rice, more everything.

'I told you not to put hing in their lassi!' Punto grumbled. 'Now they'll never be satisfied. We'll need more rice.'

We cooked more rice. The pace had slackened a bit, but they still wanted more.

'Make more sheera,' Punto said.

But I was done. I yanked open the fridge and dug out the ice cream. That was it.

'What about you and me?' Punto asked.

'What about us?'

'We make a great team, don't you think?'

'Yes, we did.'

'Think of staying on?' Punto looked away, terrified by his nerve.

'Actually, Punto, I'd like that, but you know I can't.'

'Because of him?'

'Who? Oh him? He isn't important. No, I have to get back to my job.'

'You have a restaurant?'

'No. I write books.'

'Cook books?'

'No.'

'You should. Only today's menu, please write down for me.'

'How about we eat first?'

Punto had a long talk with the driver. It ended with me getting a seat in the driver's cabin.

The passengers were in no hurry to leave.

The driver kept honking, but they lingered over adrak chai (brewed by Punto himself). They bought chips and cold drinks recklessly in case famine overtook them by nightfall.

It was 5 p.m. when I waved goodbye to Punto. My brief career as chef was done.

It was nearly midnight when the bus dropped me on Nehru Road. I hadn't realized how tired I was till I set off walking towards home. The knapsack felt like lead.

Scraps of conversation chased around my brain, compounding my misery. Everything had gone so terribly wrong. Even the darn knapsack had been wrong.

'Trust you to have a pink knapsack, Sita. What are you, twelve?'

What was he expecting? Louis Vuitton?

But he wouldn't let up.

'Why pink?' And the more he persisted, the pinker, more glaring, more vulgar grew my trusty companion of a million adventures and escapades. By the time we got to the hotel, I was ashamed of it.

That memory almost had me doubled in cringe. I hugged the knapsack close now, burying my face in its familiar burnt rubber smell. I was back in my world now, one where nobody bothered about what my baggage looked like—unless it was the baggage on my soul.

Darn—I'd have to wake Lalli, the keys were caught in the undergrowth somewhere along that highway. But as I reached our lane, I noticed the lights were on.

Lalli opened the door, took one look at me and gathered me up in a bear hug, knapsack and all. Over her shoulder, I caught sight of Savio. He looked lost.

A brief incredulous silence greeted me as I stepped in.

Dr Q was the first to recover. 'You're just in time, Sita. I'll give you five minutes—'

'Let her rest, Dr Q, she's tired,' Shukla protested, surprising me.

'No, I'll be back.' I rushed to wash. A shower could wait till I found out what was going on.

Savio looked in with a mug of hot chocolate and coconut biscuits. His usual comfort food—not mine.

'Lalli said you needed a meal, but I thought not.'

'Not.'

He perched on the bed and we nibbled biscuits companionably.

'I didn't hear the car, or I would have come to the gate.'

'I took the bus.'

That sank in slowly.

'You're okay?'

I waited till he put his arms around me—and then I was.

I burst in on them with the news I'd almost forgotten in the relief of coming home.

'Lalli, there's some terrible news. Suketa Das committed suicide. Maybe you didn't know her. She was my mentor. I caught a glimpse of it on TV, all the usual suspects rounded up for Death of a Feminist—what?'

Incredulous silence again, the second time in half an hour.

'What do you think we're here for?' Savio asked.

'Kandewadi?'

'And Suketa,' Lalli said quietly. 'I knew her too, Sita. She was my friend.'

Suddenly it all fell in place. The friend she had appointed to meet on Saturday—gosh, was that only yesterday?—was Suketa Das.

'You met her yesterday?'

'No. She never turned up. I waited an hour. When I got home I found a message on the answering machine. Just three words: *Too late, Lalli*. I panicked. I didn't have an address. I had them trace the number. That took some time. It was terrible, that wait—'

It was an address in Santa Cruz. The police went around.

Suketa didn't answer the door.

The neighbours said they had seen her the previous day. Nobody bothered much about her, they passed her occasionally on the stairs, exchanged a smile, but that was about all.

The police got back to Lalli. There was nothing suspicious. Suketa Das was probably out, shopping.

Lalli was at Suketa's flat in ten minutes. She asked the constable to look the other way, and opened the door.

It was too late.

Suketa's body was hanging from the ceiling.

She had hanged herself with a skipping rope.

She was long past reviving.

There was a note on the table:

At high noon, quietus.

She had signed it, with the date and the time, 11 a.m.

'The police has accepted it as suicide. I have reason to think otherwise,' Lalli said. 'There were features I can only call grotesque, having known her. That was a long time ago, she might have had a change of heart. But you, Sita, you knew her more recently—'

'Till about seven years ago, I knew her pretty well. She was an amazing teacher, challenging, iconoclastic, demanding—but very just. She—' Suddenly Suketa's intelligent face overtook the moment.

Tears welled out at last, the tears I had contained all day.

'She didn't deserve to die like that,' I cried, 'and I didn't even know she was so alone. She always had disciples trailing her. Where are they now?'

'On TV, apparently,' Dr Q said drily.

Lalli said, 'I've spoken to some of them, but nobody seems to have seen much of Suketa for the last five years. None of them knew where she lived, she'd dropped out of the academic circuit.'

'The library. They'd know her there.'

'That'll have to wait till morning. Sita, as your mentor was she still the radical feminist I knew twenty years ago?'

'Oh yes. Strictly speaking, more misandrist than feminist, I'd say.'

'Then you will agree this is grotesque. Suketa's body was dressed in a red and gold Benaras sari. There was sindoor on her forehead, and in the parting. I didn't examine the body—' Lalli turned her face away.

Sindoor! I could almost hear Suketa's outrage. What bitter irony had led up to this?

'Lalli, that's impossible. She loathed the emblems of marriage. Shackles and chains, she called them. She never married, as far as I know. And as for sindoor, she once gave us a brilliant lecture on

Apotropaiacs Against the Inevitable Rot. I can't think of her dressing up for an exit, honestly. But then, I can't think of her hanging herself. She would have chosen something grand, something classical. Hemlock. Opening her veins. Spontaneous self-combustion. Gone out in a blaze.'

Lalli nodded thoughtfully. 'I thought it terribly out of character too. I didn't examine her body. The Juhu guys took over. Now Dr Q, please tell us.'

'Suicide note is high funda,' Shukla interrupted. 'What it means? Handwriting is definitely her own?'

'Yes.'

Lalli went to the bookcase. She was some time finding the book she wanted—it was on the highest shelf, close to the ceiling. Savio reached up for it. Andrea Dworkin's *Life and Death*. It was inscribed in the spidery scrawl I knew so well: *To Lalli, for enlightenment.*

'I stayed unenlightened, I'm afraid,' Lalli remarked. 'But the handwriting's pretty distinctive. The note was written with the same fountain pen with a scratchy nib, in the same uncertain blue right across an A4 sheet of Executive Bond.'

'I know that pen, I know that writing. She would never use a ballpoint pen,' I said.

'But why such high funda words?' Shukla objected. 'At high noon, quietus—what it means?'

I sighed. 'That's what she was like, Shukla. Her words matched the moment.'

Suketa had—aplomb.

'Dr Q, please.'

'Lalli, you didn't examine the body, but tell me what you noted,' Dr Q said.

Lalli was slow in replying. 'The face was suffused, terribly so, more in keeping with suffocation than death by hangman's fracture. There were petechiae in the conjunctivae, the tongue protruded. I called her appearance grotesque because the dressing up was so arbitrary. There was sindoor in the parting, but the hair was a mess. The sari was gorgeous, the blouse faded and worn. No earrings, no jewellery of any sort. It didn't fit. '

'Exactly.'

Dr Q and Lalli exchanged the look of swift intelligence that passes between them for a smile.

With something of a flourish, Dr Q tossed a small object on the table.

It spun, unrolling as a pale blue sinuous strip.

A hair ribbon.

It was stained and creased and streaked with grime.

I picked it up with a shudder.

It smelt musty as if it had slid off a little girl's plait and had been put away unwashed a very long time ago. The ends were frayed. I recognized that sort of fraying. All my school ribbons had been frayed in exactly the same way. This ribbon had been chewed, by a meditative little girl. A very little girl, no older than six or seven.

And suddenly—I knew.

So did the rest of the company, judging from the heavy silence.

'This was the ligature, Lalli,' Dr Q said quietly. 'She was a fat woman. This was buried in her short thick neck. Concealed completely.'

'That doesn't console me, Dr Q. I should have examined the body. I couldn't bring myself to do that. There was too much I couldn't forgive myself for.'

Lalli left the table and wandered off into the balcony.

'Baby's ribbon. Wedding sari. Lady had history,' Shukla said.

'She also had a diaper,' Dr Q said, a surprising non sequitor.

'Some ladies are having that problem,' Shukla offered.

'Some gentlemen also,' Dr Q countered. 'But such was not the case here. The diaper was put on over her, er, underclothes.'

'Like Phantom,' Shukla explained, in case we hadn't got it.

Lalli pulled up a chair and sat down. Savio poured her a glass of water.

She drained it in a gulp and began to speak in so low a voice that I had to strain to hear her words.

'I disliked Suketa Das when I knew her twenty years ago. We were never friends. I thought her worthy—intelligent, witty, kind. But she forced her cynicism on the young, and I disliked that. As a teacher, she was in a position to do that. That angered me. Suketa's philosophy was angry and bitter, clearly based on her own experience. It served her well, but it was not a universal truth. When I told her so, she was furious. She accused me of taunting her with her past. The truth was, I knew nothing about her past. That was twenty years ago. We never spoke again.

'Then, out of the blue, she telephoned me last Friday, saying it had taken her a week to track me down. She wanted to meet. I didn't. She said—her exact words –'These murders make it imperative that we overlook our differences'. Unwillingly, I invited her over, but she wanted to

meet in a coffee shop. We planned to meet the next day at twelve. I left
home early, at 11, because I had things to do on the way. I think if she'd
planned even at 10.30 to commit suicide, she would have called and can-
celled our appointment. She was meticulous and considerate by nature.
She wrote that note at eleven, of that I have no doubt. But I think suicide
was very far from her intent. And then, she called here at 11.15 a.m.—'

'I left at 11,' I interrupted. 'If only I'd waited—'

'I think she just about managed to sneak that call. Her murderer was
already in the house with her. Perhaps she called when she was dressing—'

'In that sari? She never would have worn it,' I objected.

'No. She did. She had to. He made her do it.'

'What was motive? Marriage or murder?' Shukla asked.

'Both,' Savio said. 'Like you said, the lady had a history. Lalli, why did
he make it look like suicide? It couldn't have been easy to hang the body
after she was dead. Perhaps he had an accomplice.'

'Oh he did, he did,' Lalli leaned forward earnestly. '*She* was his accomplice. He had brought the skipping rope with him. I noticed it was
an old rope, recently cut at one end to loop it through the hook on the
ceiling. Like the ribbon, it was a memento.'

'Revenge!' Shukla yelled. 'He was taking revenge for death of be-
loved daughter. He was ex-husband. Mother neglects child. High fever,
meningitis, death. Couple is immediately divorced. Mother becomes famous professor. Father becomes drunk. Finally, it is too much, and he
gets revenge.'

'Write for the films, Shukla,' Dr Q urged.

'I don't think Shukla's very wide off the mark,' Lalli said. 'I want
you to consider what she told me on the phone. *All these murders make it
imperative we talk.* I can only assume she meant Kandewadi. There's nothing else in the news. Was she killed because she knew something about
Kandewadi? Or did her murderer know she was about to talk to me about
Kandewadi?'

'We can push it further,' Savio said. 'We can assume three facts. A.
The murderer knew that Suketa knew you. B. He knew that you're looking into Kandewadi. C. He knew what Suketa knew about Kandewadi. So
whom did you and Suketa know in common?'

'Me,' I said.

Monday, 28 March

The meeting broke up soon after that.

I fell asleep on the sofa while Lalli and Savio were talking in the balcony, and the next I knew, it was morning.

I heard Lalli in the kitchen.

It was late, past seven. I staggered to the bathroom and showered. The icy needles of water pierced the fog finally, and I emerged, if not yet human, at least not quite the zombie I had been half an hour ago.

I suctioned up coffee without quite tasting it. I hate it when I miss my morning cup with Lalli. She faced me across the table with the look she reserves for really hard cases when they don't fess up.

'Will you tell or should I ask?'

I was dying to tell, actually, but coming from her, the very soul of discretion, the question was unexpected.

Then she put my bag—my cherished, pearl grey squashy, flung-out of-the-window-on-NH17-treasure—on the table.

To say I threw myself on it would be an exaggeration, but only a very mild one.

I emptied it on the table, and except for my notebook, everything was present and correct.

'How did you find it?'

'Serendipity. A constable found it last evening, started looking around for a body, then thought to open it. He called Savio on your phone and was pleasantly surprised to find you alive. He was on his way to Dadar on assignment, so he dropped it here at six. So what happened? You're not a woman who leaves her bag behind. And your notebook's missing.'

'Right.'

'So there was a quarrel?''

'Yep. No, actually I manufactured one, I think.'

'Because you wanted out?'

'I had this brilliant post-coital flash of clarity.'

'Ah.'

So then I told her the rest of it.

'You left something out, Sita. Did you have enough to pay the hotel bill?'

She slid a wallet on the table. I recognized it instantly. It was the posh black number Arun was presently mourning.

Lalli laughed heartily at my amazement.

'What, the constable found this too?'

'No, Shukla did. That's why everybody looked so uncomfortable when you turned up last night. He'd just told us the story. I was wondering how to keep it from you—you won't mind hearing it now, I'm sure.'

'As long as I don't have to be the person who returns it.'

'No fear. Apparently, Shukla discovered Arun's Siachen story was a bit shaky.'

'What do you mean?'

'It was all puff. Shukla's been to Siachen, he knows the ground. His brother was posted there, so he asked around, and Arun's story didn't jell. So on Saturday he had the mad idea of blurting it all out to you. But on his way here, he met Arun.'

'I know. They were chatting at the gate when I came down.'

'Right. Shukla found out you were weekending on the beach, and panicked. So one mad idea replaced another. He got Arun out of the car on some pretext, and swiped his wallet.'

'What!'

'In the dumb hope that when Arun found his wallet missing, you'd head back home, virtue intact.'

'What an idiot, why didn't he think I'd pay?'

'Women don't, in Shukla's world.'

I remembered Arun's look of fury when he found the wallet missing—and the smug grin with which he had pitched my bag out of the window. Lalli's mouth quivered, dangerously close to laughter, and I dissolved helplessly into giggles.

I hadn't laughed this hard since I left school. It was even funnier than the prank Lalli had played on those rich brats.

'Lalli what happened to those boys?'

'I thought you'd never ask. We're going after them as soon as we're dressed.'

'We're dressed.'

'Not suitably. Wear that muddy sari of yours,' she called over her shoulder as she hurried to her room.

My muddy sari is actually a sophisticated terracotta and perfectly decent, but Lalli loathes it.

She returned transformed. Shorter and thicker somehow, in a blowsy shalwar qameez. She was wearing a pair of spectacles that gave her a peering inquisitive look and her hair had been tortured into a bun. She was heavy on mangalsutra and kumkum and red and green glass bangles. Her face had mysteriously developed dark circles and pouches. Her gait was ponderous.

'Try and look bullied, Sita,' she sighed.

'All this to examine Suketa's flat?'

'Oh, we're not going there right now.'

'Any other instructions for me?'

'No. Just look bullied, and afterwards let's go get those shocking pink tights.'

Which just about left me to my own devices—and no questions. I did try going over the weekend to get good and miserable, but it left me practically buoyant with relief.

Lalli didn't take the car. This was to be in character, then.

As usual, the neighbours we passed greeted me and gave her a curious look. I've never fully understood how my aunt can become totally unrecognisable with very few props to pull it off.

We took a rickshaw along the road where Lalli had crashed two cars. The address we were headed for was a posh high rise, just about a year old, one of those luxury enclaves that spring up overnight on the amputation scars of flattened hills. They always seem to have Italian names and this one was no exception.

After a complicated body-check by a security guard, our rickshaw was permitted to sputter up the landscaped drive of L'Allegra.

The coin dropped. I remembered one of the bereaved mothers at Kandewadi had told me she worked in Lala Gram. It was Pinky's mother, Shanta. Lala Gram had sounded like a local charity or NGO, and I hadn't pursued the matter.

Visitors to L'Allegra didn't arrive in rickshaws, apparently. We might have been Martians for all the next security guard could tell.

After name, provenance, and purpose of visit had been entered in the register (Lalli leaves these details to me as I invent quicker), we were reluctantly permitted into the foyer.

Lalli shot me a warning look and I relapsed into muddy misery.

In time a maid with Orphanage written all over her escorted us in a claustrophobic lift to the fifth floor. It was the service lift, and the maid pushed open a nondescript door saying Madam would be with us in five minutes.

We were led into a latter day Diwan-e-Aam—four plastic stools lined up against a laminate partition. There was also a cushioned chair for the interrogator. I thought Lalli should take that, but she settled herself humbly on a stool.

The woman who entered looked a little taken aback by us.

'Mrs Khatri?' Lalli 's voice was even more unrecognisable than her appearance. It was high pitched and quavering. 'We are from Crime Branch, about domestic theft. I think you have received information already?'

'Yes, yes, the Building Secretary said you would be coming—you wanted a list of stolen goods?'

'Yes. What was your servant's name and address?'

'I don't know, they're all alike, so hard to tell one from the other. Security has all the names and I-cards. Despite all that care, they still loot us!'

'Valuables were stolen? Money? Jewellery?'

'Not exactly. But expensive things!'

'Watch? Computer? Electronics?'

'No, luckily not. Some trinkets. My sister was visiting with her little girl, and the child's doll was stolen. That was unbearable! I knew immediately it must be the servant because she was always boasting about her little girl. And then I missed a bottle of perfume from my dressing table. Very expensive French perfume. So have the police recovered the stolen goods? Have you arrested the woman?'

'That is why we are here,' Lalli said quietly.

For the first time the woman noticed me. I cowered in my muddy vestments.

'Many women work in the police nowadays,' she observed.

'She is only trainee,' Lalli dismissed me with contempt.

'When can I have my things back?'

'Make out receipt,' Lalli ordered.

I obediently rummaged in my bag.

'This is your perfume, I think?' Lalli held out the bottle of ylang-ylang.

'Oh yes!' Mrs Khatri made a grab for it, but it evaded her grasp. 'Careful, it's very expensive,' she yammered.

Lalli slipped it back in her purse and held out the powder puff.

'This also belongs to you?'

'Yes.'

'And this?'

She held up the doll.

Mrs Khatri gasped. 'I told them she'd taken it, I told them! Nobody would believe me except my son. Get out, he told her, get out or I'll call the police.'

'Your son? Is he at home now?'

'I—I'm not sure. He's always at the computer—'

'But he also suspected the servant of these thefts?'

'Yes, in fact, he's the one who discovered she'd taken all these things. Things kept disappearing, you see.'

'Can we talk to him? Every bit of information we get is important. You see these people operate as a gang.'

'A gang! I'll just see if I can disturb him. He may be resting. He's just recovering from an accident. Gaurav beta—'

Gaurav beta hadn't recovered all that well.

Lalli smiled richly when he entered, exclaiming over the large purple bruise with pardonable pride. 'Oh you're badly hurt!'

Lamborghini scowled and interrogated his mother with his eyebrows. Mrs Khatri gushed happily. 'They're from the police, they've recovered all the stolen goods, imagine! Tell them, beta, you were the first to suspect that woman.'

Gaurav shook his head, spaced out. 'What woman?'

'Recognize this?' Lalli held up the bottle of perfume.

Gaurav backed away.

'What's the matter, beta? Feeling dizzy?' Lalli asked.

'Yes, yes, go lie down, Gaurav. Please excuse him.'

'Yes, yes of course. Thank you for identifying the things. Trainee has forgotten receipt book again. We will deliver package by courier along proper channel,' Lalli smiled.

'Can't I have them back now?'

'Through proper channel, I have to follow procedure, madam.'

I stayed in character till we were in the lift.

'You think Pinki's mother gave Daya all those things?' I asked incredulously. 'And he used them to lure her own daughter?'

'What? No, no, Sita, that's crazy. That poor woman should never learn of this visit. It would kill her. You'll have to wait till tonight, we should know the whole story by then.'

Lalli confronted the Security guard at the entrance with Daya's photograph.

'Why did you let this man in without ID?' she demanded. 'I'm going to report you. This will cost you your job.' Of course she flashed that illegal badge she carries in her bag.

'He has ID,' the man protested. 'Signed and stamped.'

'Nonsense. I'm letting the Inspector know, you can answer his questions at the Chowki.'

'Wait, wait, no need to do all that. I'll show you the ID.'

He unlocked a small cupboard in his cabin and returned with a plastic ID card.

'There. What did I say?'

The card had Daya's photograph, name and the A-1 General Stores address.

'So when was the last time he made a delivery here?' Lalli asked.

'He doesn't deliver groceries. He only comes on special work for Gamadia Sahib.'

'Carpet cleaning?'

'Yes.'

'He takes the carpet up to Gamadia's flat?'

'No, I make the call on the house-phone. Usually Baba comes down, this guy puts it in the lift and takes off.'

'When did you last see him?'

'A week ago, maybe two weeks ago.'

'Make up your mind!'

'Two weeks. No, it was nearly twenty days ago. I made the mistake because three or four days ago he brought the carpet at night. I wasn't on duty, but the night guy mentioned it.'

'And when does he come to collect the carpet for cleaning?'

'Oh that's very early in the morning. He told the night guy he starts his run at four o'clock. Often comes here at 5 a.m.'

'So how many carpets do these Gamadias have that they have to get them cleaned so frequently?'

'Rich people, what can we say? Actually, they have a cat. Every time the cat throws up, pisses and shits, that carpet gets cleaned. Cheaper to get rid of the cat, but even the cat is imported. What can I say?'

'I'm sure their car is imported, right?'

'Imported? Racing car! Ferrari. Got slammed yesterday, too bad.' There was a big grin on his face.

'And these Gamadias have a flat on the sixth floor?'

'Seventh. But they own two flats on the ninth. They open those up for parties.'

Lalli shrugged. 'Rich people. What can one say?'

When we were out of L'Allegra she called Savio.

'Go right ahead,' she said.

Wait till tonight, Lalli said. I knew from experience it was no use asking her anything till then. She was silent all the way home, and then isolated herself with the laptop.

What had the Khatris and the Gamadias to do with Daya? True, the doll, the puff and the ylang-ylang had come from the Khatris, and the Gamadias had sent their carpets to Daya. These things were props in five terrifying murders. Did their owners know that?

When I called Lalli for lunch, she said she wasn't hungry.

I swallowed a gloomy meal in the kitchen, cleared up and was wondering if I deserved a nap when the doorbell rang.

It was Arun.

We stared at each other for an angry moment, then I let him in.

'Go away,' said Lalli without looking up.

'I need your help.'

'Leave.'

'Seema is missing.'

Lalli looked up.

'She hasn't been seen since Saturday night.'

'And this worries you because?'

'Her parents are certain something's wrong.'

'She lives with them?'

'Yes.'

'You think there's something wrong too?'

'Yes. It's about Kandewadi. Seema was desperate for information on that man who was found dead. When I asked her why, she said she'd email the story she was about to file. She didn't file it. But here it is.'

He placed a pen drive on the table.

'Thank you.'

Lalli copied the contents and returned the pen drive.

'You may leave now.'

'But—'

I left the room.

I was unprepared for—everything. I felt neither pain nor anger. Just revulsion.

I heard the front door shut.

In a few minutes, Lalli came in and sat on the edge of the bed. She had the laptop with her. She threw a cushion across and I sat up, obligingly.

'Get comfortable. This will take a while. I'm going to read you a story.'

Here is what she read out:

THE FINAL FRONTIER
By
Seema Aggarwal

Star Trek all over again? NewAge Sci-Fi? Not a chance. The Final Frontier is the edge beyond good or evil. Do you have it in you to dare it?

Daya Champaneria, an unlettered orphan from a small town in Gujarat, had never heard of Star Trek or Sci-Fi. Though he may not have known the English words 'Final Frontier,' he was very well aware of the concept. And he dared to explore it in a criminal way.

There is no longer any doubt that Daya Champaneria raped and killed five innocent children in the Andheri slum of Kandewadi, although the police continue to be tight-lipped about his mysterious death.

This reporter, who has been following the story since it broke, had been reliably informed by an eyewitness of the details of the first four murders. The reliable source, who does not wish to be named, described the horrific injuries inflicted on the victims (editorial discretion has withheld some of those details).

When the body of Champaneria was recovered, the medico-legal examination concluded death was due to hypovolemic shock following a gastric bleed consequent to consumption of alcohol.

The last fact prompted this reporter to investigate further.

Champaneria was employed in a general store in Kandewadi. His co-workers describe him as 'bhola,' innocent. When asked if that did not seem the wrong word to describe the monster who preyed upon the children of Kandewadi, the general response was bewilderment. They could not understand how a man who never smoked or drank or ran after women could have committed such evil. He disliked vice of any kind and discouraged several of his co-workers from consuming alcohol. Furthermore, he was undergoing some training in yogic meditation that he said was the ultimate reward, beyond pleasure or pain.

One of his co-workers spoke of him as a Sanyasi, although nobody had heard him mention any guru or place of instruction.

It is possible that Champaneria may have committed these violent acts in a yogic trance state?

The police have dismissed the idea, according to inside sources. They have yet to explain how a man who detested alcohol could die of alcohol-induced bleeding.

The Kandewadi case is very far from being solved.

Why did Daya Champaneria rape and murder five innocent children? What caused his death?

Are the children of Kandewadi truly safe now?

The police have no answers to these questions.

Inspector Savio D'Sa, in charge of the case was, as usual, unavailable for comment.

It was just blather. There was nothing new in it.

'Except for the fact that Seema was prevented from filing it,' Lalli said.

'Maybe she just changed her mind. Maybe she's out following another lead.'

'I wish I could believe that, Sita,' Lalli grimaced.

'Don't tell me you think she's dead.'

'Of course she is. This murderer takes no prisoners. I called Savio and he's got those store boys in protective custody by now. I just hope my call wasn't too late.'

We fell silent, each in our own turmoil. To say I was stricken was to put it mildly. I had been jealous of Seema, and now she was dead, and I would never be able to make up for that meanness. Worse, I had been jealous over Arun. That was really bad judgment.

I hadn't expected him to show up after his dramatic exit. The visit must have been as distasteful to him as it was for me. He had braved it out of concern for his friend. He couldn't be all bad, although I'd loathe him for the rest of my life.

'Are you okay to go?' Lalli shook off her reverie. 'We should take a look at Suketa's flat now.'

Suketa's flat had a havaldar guarding it. He greeted Lalli like an old friend. He was the officer who had discovered the body, Lalli told me. He assured her nothing had been touched, he had sent away several visitors.

'Neighbours?'

He scowled. 'Now her neighbors all claim they never knew her. No, these visitors were tourists. Students, college professors, all wanting to offer condolences. To whom? Nobody in there, I told them. Locked up.'

It was a small one-bedroom flat. We stood in the room of death and gazed at the ceiling fan. Her noose had depended from the hook. A chair lay overturned, grim reminder of the murderer's final step—not hers.

The rest of the furniture was sparse but comfortable. A bookshelf overflowed on to the floor. A cushioned armchair. A desk, with the portable typewriter I knew so well. There were a few sheets left in the box of Bond paper next to the open typewriter.

The wastebasket was empty.

Her fountain pen, a grey Schaeffer, had been laid down on the paper with an air of finality.

'Lalli, I know what she was doing,' I barely recognised the voice as my own. 'That wasn't a suicide note.'

'No, it wasn't.'

Lalli put an arm around me and led me to the armchair.

It felt strange sitting there, knowing the usual occupant was dead.

But it was right too. It matched her sense of occasion that I should make my pronouncement from her chair.

'That was not a suicide note. It was the title page of her manuscript. She had just finished typing the book. She looked at the clock as she wrote the title. *At High Noon, Quietus.*'

'I thought you'd find out the moment you saw her desk,' Lalli smiled.

The box of paper, nearly empty, and the open typewriter. Above all the pen, resting obliquely on the blank sheet.

How could anyone have mistaken that for a suicide note?

'The Juhu guys decided it was. I didn't disabuse them.'

'Where's the manuscript?'

The desk was bare but for the typewriter. Perhaps she had taken it into the bedroom to package it—

'The murderer took it. That's what he came here for. He wouldn't have murdered her if he hadn't found it.'

'Why—why would he want the manuscript? From the title, it sounds like a novel.'

'Really? I think it was a life. Her own, probably. He didn't want the world to know the story.'

'He knew her, then?'

'Intimately. Suketa had a PhD from Jadhavpur University, 1985. She would have been around thirty-five then. What was she doing before that? Let's find out.'

I trailed Lalli into the bedroom—it hardly deserved the descriptive. The narrow cot was heaped over with clothes in various stages of laundry—dirty, just off the line, folded and ironed. There was a cupboard crammed with clothes.

The bathroom was disgusting.

The kitchen bristled with cockroaches. The fridge had bad breath.

Here was nothing, really, that made up a life.

To my knowledge, Suketa was more of a reader and a thinker. She was not much of a writer. The books on her shelf were mostly old favorites. Nothing revealed the tenor of her recent life.

If this had been her life, she must have welcomed escape.

But this hadn't been her life, had it?

Her life had been the book she was writing.

'What are you looking for, Lalli?'

She shrugged. 'I don't know. Except that I can't find it.'

'It being?'

'An oasis of solace. Something she would return to when life became unbearable. Everybody has one. A still point. One retreats there. And then one can begin over.'

'Donne.'

'Eh?"

'John Donne. He was her solace.'

'*Then since I may know,*

As liberally as to a midwife show

Thyself; Cast all, yea this white linen hence.

Here is no penance, much less innocence. Ha. Strange choice for a misandrist.'

'You're unfair. His *Devotions Upon Emergent Occasions* is profoundly moving.'

'Oh, so is this one. See if you can find the volume. If it continued to serve, you'll find it within easy reach.'

She found it before I could.

She opened the window, and angled the armchair towards it. She sat down and let the book drop on her lap. It fell open at a bookmark—

I heard Lalli gasp.

A minute later, she held out the picture of a young boy. It was an old photograph, frequently handled, the gloss smudged with fingerprints.

The kid in the picture had a crooked eleven-year old grin. The sun was in his eyes. His jug ears stuck out like flags. The left side of his face was mottled with a curious map-like stain.

Lalli had fallen into a reverie. She stared out of the window, her hands clenched.

I picked up the book again and examined it curiously. Apart from Suketa's name on the flyleaf, it was unmarked.

I began reading. I read the poems she had treasured, savouring the paradoxes and ironies, thinking how they distanced the poet's griefs and despairs. For the first time I saw Donne as a man darting into the crevice of a poem for shelter from a severely inclement life. Perhaps these were all the conversations that mattered. They stayed, when the rest had drifted away.

'Let's go.'

'But aren't you—'

'No. I'm done here. We need to make a stop on the way home.'

I noticed she had slipped the photograph into her bag.

I was about to put the book back when Lalli said, 'Keep it, Sita. Suketa would have liked you to have it.'

I was surprised to hear the break in her voice. She wept unashamedly all the way to the car.

At Kalina Chowki we halted for a moment. Then in depressed silence, we went home.

I thought we could use some coffee and while I was in the kitchen, I heard Lalli answer the phone. She came in and sat down at the table with a gesture of defeat.

Seema Aggarwal's white Ritz had been found in an abandoned lot. Her body was slumped over the wheel. She had been strangled.

We left the house shortly after ten. As yet, Lalli had told me nothing, so I was surprised when she handed me the car keys. 'Kandewadi.'

It was a tense, silent drive. I expected to park along the main road, but just short of Kandewadi, Lalli asked me to make a left turn.

I drove into a narrow lane that ended in a bank of tamped garbage. It was evidently used as a parking lot for heavy vehicles. There were a couple of trucks. And a tempo.

It looked frighteningly like Daya's tempo.

It *was* Daya's tempo.

We got out of the car.

To my surprise, Lalli didn't approach the tempo. She made instead for the wall skirting the lane. She leapt over it lightly and held out her hand to help me over. I jumped down and was surprised to find myself inside Kandewadi.

The place was deserted.

Lalli held a cautionary finger to her lip.

I followed her silently. She darted into a gali between two walls. Luckily, out came her flash to show me the ground, or I would have stepped into the broad gutter at my feet.

She took a few steps forward, then stopped and crouched down, sinking on her haunches, gesturing me to do the same.

'Watch.'

There was nothing to see, just a blank wall of night.

Then suddenly—there it was!

I would have cried out if Lalli hadn't gagged me with her hand.

There it was, a green flash.

Asif's green light.

It hovered in the darkness, first one flash, then another, and yet another.

I couldn't see the rest of Asif's painting. There was no moon tonight to see it by.

But here was the light, in the mathematical center of my memory of Asif's picture, a green scintilla flashing on and on.

It would catch a child standing at the gutter slap in the eye and leave him bedazzled. Like Asif said he was.

Lalli rose and we turned back.

I realized now that we had been looking up at the raised ground of the parking lot. As I looked over the wall, the green light flashed up close, blinding me.

Lalli directed my attention away from the light. I followed her pointing finger.

Way up in the darkness, a green light flashed sky high.

I had been blinded by its reflection in a mirror.

The side-mirror on Daya's tempo. *That* was what Asif had seen.

But who was flashing the light?

And from where?

It seemed very high up, there were a few lighted windows below it, but—

'That's L'Allegra,' Lalli said. 'And that's Savio flashing a green light from the ninth floor.'

'That was what Asif saw reflected in the mirror –'

'It was the signal meant for Daya. He was parked here, waiting. When he saw the green light it was time to drive up to L'Allegra and collect the parcel.'

I gasped.

'Are you sure? Couldn't the signal have come from elsewhere?'

'Where? There aren't any other high-rise buildings around. It had to come from pretty high up to hit the side-mirror at this angle. This is Asif's case, really! I relied on his accuracy because he has an artist's eye for geometry. He had placed the light close to the ground. A truck or bus would have reflected it higher. It could be a tempo or a bicycle or a rickshaw or a scooter or a motorbike. A lot of choices—unless you refused to ignore Asif's statement that the next morning brought a dead child back to Kandewadi.'

'Lalli, did it happen there?' I asked, terrified.

'Yeah. I think so, on the ninth floor. Savio will tell us soon enough. Drive please, Sita. I've work to do.'

'Take a look at this,' Lalli held out the laptop.

It was open at a Twitter page, @GreenLight

Disagree #kw; not unique.
She clicked on the hash tag and six other Tweets appeared.

@Glider tweeted:
Pigs kill #kw messenger.

@BGOE tweeted:
Rise beyond #kw.

@Blade tweeted
#kw needs to settle down first

@BGOE:
#kw is over.

@Glider:
Right. Lets nix #kw. Start anew.

@BGOE:
#kw was unique. Start different.

GreenLight's Tweet **Disagree.#kw;not unique.**
had a reply from @BGOE.
Really? Tell me.

Lalli typed in a Direct Message:
Only 2005 was beyond good or evil

@BGOE replied almost instantaneously
Tell me more

GreenLight wrote:
I don't know more. Do you?

BGOE answered :
Yes

GreenLight wrote:
I aspire to know

BGOE:
Many do. Few make the grade.

GreenLight:
Like the clumsy bunglers of kw? They're pathetic

BGOE
True. The pigs will get them.

GreenLight
That will make me laugh. What about you?

BGOE
It's got nothing to do with me.

GreenLight
So you imagine you're BGOE. But you're not even halfway there.

BGOE
Then who is?

GreenLight
If you must ask, you're lying. You know nothing about 2005

BGOE
And you do?

GreenLight
#kw is finished. What next?

BGOE
That depends on you.

GreenLight
I'll be in touch.

BGOE
I look forward to it

I noticed Lalli was sweating. Her hands trembled as she put away the laptop.

'What's all this about, Lalli?' I demanded. 'I had no idea you were socially wired.'

'I opened a Twitter account soon after Seema's first article. I started following Twitter @Kandewadi. It was trending by the next day, and I found the Tweets arbitrary at first, but soon a pattern emerged. There were always a few that seemed curious about curiosity.'

'What do you mean?'

'Most Tweeters wanted details of the crimes. But a small group was interested in the reactions to these details. For instance, you remember Seema's article mentioned that one of the bodies had the intestines looped around it? There were a lot of horrified Tweets on that. But look at this small group—'

She opened a file, and I read:

@BGOE:
Horrified? You should feel pity, not revulsion.

@Glider:
Too childish! Why focus on trivia and ignore the main event

@Blade:
Too distracting. Shouldn't be repeated.

@Chocolate:
Scary, huh?

'And now look at this one.' Lalli scrolled down and I read:

@chocolate:
Reminds me of an old song:raindrops on roses, whiskers on kittens

@sexygirl;
Duh what's sound of music got to do with it?

@chocolate@reply
Don't you know the last line?

@sexygirl:
You're a perv, @Chocolate, these are some of your favorite things?

@chocolate@reply
No, the line before

@sexygirl @reply
YAWN

'Brown paper packages tied up with string,' I gasped. 'He meant *newspaper*.'

'Exactly. The newspaper packages were never made public. Even Seema didn't know about them. Of course, the information could have come from someone in Kandewadi itself. There may be many social media users in Kandewadi, but look at the reference, Sita. It doesn't seem likely that a Kandewadi resident would refer to *The Sound of Music*.'

I nodded, horrified.

'Also, note the tone of responsibility which is inescapable in BGOE, Chocolate, Glider and Blade's tweets. BGOE, Glider, Blade, Chocolate. I started following these people. Then I began tweeting. I had to create a following, so I set up as @GDAD, and explained the acronym in my first tweet: *Great Deeds Against the Dead are always scary until you learn how they can move you Beyond Good Or Evil.* That also clued BGOE that I thought on similar lines.'

'Did it work?'

'Oh yes. I kept tweeting in that vein, feeding them tidbits of True Crime, and these four kept following. Soon it was Direct Messaging. I got all sorts of detail out of them that they couldn't have known unless they had actually seen those children raped and murdered. Blade told me about the missing liver long before we heard Lilavati. I also know what happened to the liver. I got the feeling BGOE was the guiding spirit. The rest followed him slavishly.'

'How many followers did GDAD have in all?'

'Twelve. After we met Lilavati, I tweeted that I was dying of cancer. That got me a gush of tweets from Blade. He wanted to know if I could tweet him in my last moments. He wanted to share my suffering, he said. I closed GDAD and got out. By that time, I had opened a new account as GreenLight. On this I Tweeted about Daya. I told them about his last hour. Predictably that got me all GDAD's old disciples. Meanwhile I set Vinay to hack into their accounts.'

'And?'

'They're all very fiercely protected and it's taking Vinay forever. He told me yesterday that he expects to be done in a day or two. I don't know anything about how this works, but apparently BGOE is the master brain, with Glider trailing close.'

I'm leery of social media myself and it seemed a little naïve to expect anybody to bare their soul in a Tweet, but then, as Lalli pointed out, I overlooked the motive force of crime: the need for attention.

Social media, Lalli said, was murderer heaven. You could tell the world all your exploits—

'And never get found out?'

'Oh no. Every murderer wants to be found out. The criminal mind, if there's such a thing, thrives on adulation. Anonymity can only get you so far. Murderers need more.'

'Maybe it was all just a game to them, Lalli. Maybe it's a fantasy.'

Lalli was pensive for a long while. Then she said, 'Perhaps they always had that fantasy, Sita—Glider, Blade and Chocolate. BGOE dared them to make it real. That's what makes the net such a scary place. How many more disciples did BGOE have? We'll never know.'

I couldn't afford that morbid reverie. I needed practical details. There was a lot I didn't yet know.

'Granted, you knew about Glider, Chocolate and Blade on Twitter, but how did you trace them? You knew who they were before we went to L'Allegra! When you stopped the cars, you knew Lamborghini was a geek and Ferrari a medical student, don't deny it, Lalli!'

'Oh that was easy, Sita. Asif solved that for me! The green light was the signal for Daya to collect the bodies. Glider and Blade had to be close to Kandewadi—the crime scene was nearby, judging from Asif's observation. But even before that—this case had privilege written all over it. The murderers were quite confident they were protected. Miravli police was effectively gagged.'

She didn't think these were lust murders. They were crimes of arrogance, I remembered her saying, and yes, Miravli Chowki had orders to bury the case.

'The speed bump story was serendipity, and I had to check on that,' Lalli continued. 'Without that I would never have found those boys. So when the Ferrari and the Lamborghini came roaring up, the moment I saw them, I realised who they were. Lamborghini was wearing a T-shirt with the hacker's glider emblem—he had to be a geek. I already knew there was a medical student involved—Daya's blade was a No 11 surgical knife. That's only used for small stuff, like draining abscesses. It's the blade a medical student or intern uses.'

'It wasn't used for the mutilations?'

'No, that was probably a big kitchen knife. So I guessed one of the Ferrari guys was a medical student. I was sure of Glider, so this one might be Blade. Also it was evident from Daya's gifts that he was dealing with wealthy people—' she shrugged. Very quickly the animation faded from her face. She shut off the laptop and grew inward.

I said, 'Your username—GreenLight—surely that must have warned them.'

She shook her head. 'They're too self absorbed to notice. The only way I can get them to respond is to praise them or dare them. You know what scares me the most? Ever since Twitter @kandewadi took off, Chowkis all over the city have reported child rapes and abuse. Some cases may be hindsight, but many did happen. Acting out can often be a mirror response, without intent. It's the delinquent's response to the excitement of the forbidden. The dare.'

'That sounds as if the Kandewadi reportage has disinhibited more rapists,' I said angrily.

'I shudder to think what will happen once Blade and Glider talk to the press. And they will. They'll be all over TV. There will be other Kandewadis very soon.'

'No!'

'Oh yes. More candlelight vigils, more public confessions of childhood trauma, more public prurience—and definitely more rapes. Except with sadists, rape is a bravado crime. It feeds on attention.'

'You don't think these rapes were sadistic?'

'Not in the true sense of the word.'

Lalli's phone pinged with a text message.

Get here.

It was Savio

Lalli was out of the flat already. She had the car revving up at the gate by the time I joined her.

'Maybe you shouldn't,' she muttered. 'It's going to be ugly.'

'It hasn't been pretty so far. Where are we going?'

'L'Allegra.'

I wouldn't have guessed. This was a new road we snaked through, a tarred parting through disheveled hutments drowsing restlessly in the glare of streetlights. Lalli parked at a deadend. We'd gone uphill to the building the last time, but there was no elevation in sight here. Not unless you counted the embankment of garbage.

And that, apparently, was to be our route.

I tried not to think, as we squelched our way up over slithery plastic bags, ignoring movements underfoot. Miraculously, there was a tree ahead. The next moment, Lalli's hand hauled me up to solid ground.

Daylight would explain the peculiar geography. The blasted face of the hillside had become a gigantic dump. In time it would acquire strata and narrate a new geology. A million years later we might be mining right here for plastic.

While I was working that out, Lalli busied herself noiselessly clipping out a hole in the wire fence. She has a clever Swiss knife, but that's just for fun. On the job she carries a mean pair of dikes.

She oozed in through the hole, and then pulled me through. We padded across a grassy mound littered with the detritus of high living. Lalli entered a shed of sorts. It was shadowy, but not exactly dark. Pushing past a door, we emerged into bright light, and Lalli walked with assured step into a passage that led to the back of L'Allegra.

The service lift was unattended. We rode up and stepped out on the 9th floor.

Savio loomed at the window, his massive frame a black intaglio against the soft grey sky.

'Commissioner's refused the search warrant,' he said in a low voice.

'Did you tell him about the green light?'

'No use. Not enough evidence.'

'So?'

'So I found the evidence.'

'Ah. Tricky.'

They fell silent. I understood the problem. Savio had broken into the flats on this floor—the flats belonging to the Gamadias. He had found what he was looking for, but he could hardly present that as evidence now after an illegal break and entry.

'Let's see it,' Lalli said. Her voice sounded strained.

I put a hand on Savio's arm. He was trembling. 'I don't want you coming in here, Sita.'

'Stick with Savio, Sita,' Lalli said and disappeared into the door to my left. It had the number 910 on it. The ornate brass numbers reflected a spectral light.

I plunged in after her, dragging Savio with me.

The dark room we entered smelt as if nobody had breathed in here for years. Savio's flash lit up a cylinder propped against the wall. It was a rolled up carpet. It could have been the twin of the one in Daya's tempo, but that was just from the size.

Lalli had disappeared into the adjoining room, and I dived into the one diametrically opposite. It was the kitchen, fitted with the latest appliances that nobody would ever use. There was a stale reek in the air, but here too was a sense of desolation.

Savio touched my arm, and swung his torch beam. It lit up a corridor. Lalli was at the far end, staring at a blank wall. Savio's fingers tightened on my arm. When I looked up, I was surprised to find his face animated. His eyes, fixed on Lalli, sparkled with laughter. He stopped my question with a warning glance.

Lalli was still staring at that blank wall, and then, she walked right into it and disappeared.

Savio's low laugh told me he'd done the same. 'Come on, Sita.'

There was a door in that wall, of course, but I couldn't have found it. Nothing betrayed its presence, no change of texture or cast of light. It was seamless, a part of the wall. But it was a door, and we were through.

Savio was trembling again, and now, so was I.

Past that door, everything changed.

We were inside a mortuary.

There was no mistaking the smell.

Strong bleach, with an undertow of decay.

Savio's torch showed another long corridor ahead, and stopped at a door. There was something written on its blindingly white surface.

My feet refused to move.

Verboten.

The unfamiliar German word burned like hot pink neon in my brain.

What was forbidden?

This.

This was forbidden.

And this.

And this.

And this, this, this.

Five dates scrawled on the door.

Five dates, beginning 3rd March, the day Pinki's body was delivered at her doorstep, and ending 22 March, the day Deepika's body was found.

The dates were written with a broad nibbed black marker.

The M of March was distinctive, with a jaunty flourish to the finial.

Five dates for five deaths.

Or five dates for five killings?

Lalli had gone ahead. Savio waited for me to move. 'We can go back,' he murmured.

I went through.

The stench grew stronger. I gagged.

Lalli stopped abruptly, arrested midstride in rock-like immobility.

I couldn't see what petrified her, but I stared, infected by her horror. Savio propelled me forward, and I saw it.

It was a large bed.

A carpet was flung over it.

It looked exactly like the one in Daya's tempo.

The stench rose from that carpet.

It exhaled a foulness so intense, I heard Lalli retch.

But I smelt something beyond that feral stink.

Bleach.

The flat clean waft of chlorine beneath that foulness was so terrifying and unreal that I clung desperately to the familiar solidity of Savio's arm. His skin was clammy with sweat.

His torch lit up a row of large lamps lined up against the wall, and a photographer's umbrella.

Lalli broke her trance and moved towards another piece of furniture.

An ironing table, covered with a rubber sheet.

In the torch's glare the stains on the sheet looked like black encrustations. By daylight there would be no mistaking them. Dried blood.

The door to our left probably led to a bathroom. Lalli pushed it, but it would open only to a small angle. She threw a questioning look at Savio.

'I left everything as is,' he said.

The smell of bleach was suddenly very strong—why? Nothing in view had been scrubbed clean.

Lalli squeezed past the jammed door into the bathroom.

I stole a look at Savio. He was holding his breath, intent on that door.

There was a dragging sound, and then Lalli came out. She pushed the door wide open. 'Show her, Savio.'

'No, Lalli.'

'*Show her.*'

My aunt's voice was as stony as her face.

I walked into the bathroom.

The first thing I saw was a large plastic drum that had earlier obstructed the door. Lalli had now dragged it aside.

The smell of bleach was overpowering.

Savio lifted the lid off the drum and held his torch over it. I peered in.

The beam cut through a column of murky fluid.

Crouched in its wavering depths, was a child.

For a long time I felt nothing, heard nothing. Life, as I knew it, had stopped. There was only this moment and this grotesque parody of innocence.

I would stay here, watching, as it was leached out of existence. I wouldn't move until it bared its bones.

The child's face and gender had been erased. But from the size, it had known at least ten years of life before its body got into this drum, slowly dissolving in alkali that would eventually macerate it down to the bone.

I thought nothing could be worse, but there was.

Savio showed me the closet.

It was next to the bathroom, a little space, no more than two feet deep and two wide.

Airless.

Unlit.

It was coated with dried blood and shit. It reeked of urine. There were spools of hair everywhere.

But it wasn't over yet.

Savio's torch beam hit the inside of the closet door.

About a foot off the floor the door had two red blotches.

The bloody palm prints of two small desperate hands.

We found Lalli at the bedside, staring at a glass jar on a small table. It was a large jar with a screw-top lid, the kind you see on windowsills and terraces in summer when people put pickles out to sun. The contents were different, but this one too served the same purpose.

Within this jar, pickling in formalin, floated a lobe of liver.

Savio had one more exhibit.

He opened the door to the balcony.

'I'd brought along a bit of green cellophane for my torch, Lalli, but I needn't have bothered.' He pointed to a lantern on the chair. He switched it on. It flared bright green.

Half an hour later, we were home, sitting glumly at the kitchen table, waiting for the coffee to brew. We were profoundly distressed, but anxiety overtook even that. Lalli's stony face made us abandon any thought of conversation. Savio ate biscuits absentmindedly till I took away the tin. It was nearly 2 a.m.

'Call Shukla,' Lalli said abruptly. 'Ask him to get here now.' She rose just as I poured out the coffee.

'Where are you off to?'

'I need the laptop.'

'I'll get it.'

When I got back, they both looked a shade better. The coffee was hot, wet and sweet, but nothing else registered.

'Savio, let's smoke them out,' Lalli said.

'How?'

'I'll just tweet.'

Savio looked shocked, then broke into a grin. 'Hooked are you?'

'You have no idea. Tell him, Sita, while I tune up.'

I told Savio about GreenLight and GDAD. About BGOE, Glider and Chocolate.

'You're not serious?' Savio asked.

Lalli looked up, 'I've got Vinay working on their emails, but no show yet. They're all triple firewall protected, whatever that means, so it's all upto #kw. Here, take a look.'

@GreenLight had tweeted:
A little bird's been asking what's on the 9th floor #kw?

@GreenLight also sent a DM to @Chocolate
They'll be asking about the rest of that liver by 8 a.m.

'What if they don't read their tweets?' I ventured. 'They're probably asleep.'

'No, they don't sleep till eight. They tweet all night. They have a thing that pings. Vinay rigged it up for me, but it was too annoying. Now, Savio, fill us in, please.'

Savio's response was to push his mobile towards her. 'See that picture? And the next? Something looks familiar, eh?'

Each photo had a date and time written in broad-tipped felt marker:

15 March 3.30 p.m. — 18 March 2 a.m.
20 March 2 p.m. — 23 March 4 a.m.

In both cases, the writing was the same. The letter M carried a distinctive flourish.

The background was dingy, grey-brown, flaky. Certainly not the sharp white paint against which we had seen those dates a few hours earlier.

'Written on the bodies,' Lalli said in a low voice.

'Over the spine. The first is Jamila's, the second Mary's.'

'Wait—how?' I couldn't get the words out fast enough.

'Yeah, that's where I was Friday,' Savio said heavily. 'All that time your journo pal said I was missing. I was with Dr Q, exhuming those kids.'

On Friday morning, Dr Q had managed to get an exhumation order from the magistrate. Then began the slow and painful business of getting two bereaved fathers to agree.

Dr Q and Savio knew these men would not mention the matter to their wives. They expected rage, anguish, refusal. They found only resignation.

Neither parent seemed to connect the contents of the grave with the laughing daughter he cherished. Yes, they had buried their children, but the pathetic bundles they had carried to the graveside had nothing to do with the children they missed.

With irony, they heard out Dr Q's assurance that the remains would be treated respectfully.

'What's the use of treating the dead with respect when the living didn't get any?' Mary's father asked. 'Do whatever you must and get the man who did this to my baby.'

Jamila's father said nothing. He waited outside the Qabristan and watched them load the stretcher into the jeep. When they returned, he was still rooted to the spot, as if he had never turned away.

The law required the presence of three medico-legal experts at the autopsy, so Dr Q had summoned two of his colleagues.

The first body they examined was Mary's.

Mary was seven, a year away from her Confirmation. But her parents had got her that coveted dress, and buried her in it. When Savio lifted the body from the coffin, the white swathe of lace seemed an added cruelty over the decay beneath.

Dr Q was used to death's more malefic insults, but nothing had prepared him for what he saw when the white dress was removed.

A bulge of putrefying viscera confronted him through a gaping wound. Dr Q staggered, overcome. Savio had to steady him.

Dr Q's colleagues stood in earnest conference at the far window, their backs to the remains. There was no help to be had from that quarter.

Dr Q recovered with some irritation and examined the organs.

The liver was missing. It had been hacked away. From the tear in the blood vessels, Dr Q concluded that it had been done with a broad bladed knife.

The child's hip joints had been torn and avulsed long before her death, The joint cavities were filled with blood clots.

Jamila's body was just as mutilated, except that there was no abdominal wound. Her pelvic injuries were horrific. Her torso was covered with bite marks.

Dr Q was able to retrieve dental impressions from the back where the skin was intact.

Jamila had also been injured in the chest. Several ribs were broken and punched in. The fragments had punctured the lung. Blood had pooled in the chest cavity. Dr Q concluded the stove-in chest was sufficient cause of death even without the strangulating ligature on the throat.

Both bodies had one peculiarity.

A time-line, scored in black marker pen, inscribed over the spine.

Jamila's read: 15 March 3.30 p.m. — 18 March 2 a.m.
Mary's read: 20 March 2 p.m. — 23 March 4 a.m.

Lalli broke into Savio's narrative, 'Dr Q must have had something to say about that.'

Savio, taken aback, said, 'How did you know?'

Lalli shrugged. 'If only they had bothered to examine the back at Miravli Chowki. But they never do. They never turn the body over. Not the police, not Lilavati, none of them did. They washed, dressed, delivered, without actually lifting up and examining those corpses.'

'Dr Q said we could have saved at least one child if only they had turned the bodies over. All of them probably had this time-line on their spines.'

Dr Q and Savio had to work fast to get the bodies buried before sundown. Afterwards came the most difficult part—explaining their findings to the two fathers, Kamran and Daniel.

Savio could not remember, even an hour later, how they had found words that concealed even as they described. They made no mention of the writing or the bite marks. Nothing they said conveyed that the children had been tortured for the three days they had been missing.

They had to end the day without completely shattering the sanity of these two men. Savio was silent for the most part, but somehow Dr Q managed it.

That night, when Savio returned to his post in Kandewadi, four men sat up through the night with him in angry silence.

Kamran and Daniel had not spoken of the exhumation, but Dagdu and Mahesh, whose daughters had escaped this last indignity, understood their reticence.

'What made Daya do these things?' Dagdu mused. 'Even a rakshas could not have dreamed up these evils, and this boy was so innocent. He never retaliated with a harsh word even when the Tower boys got at him.'

'What Tower boys?' Savio asked.

'Rich kids from LalaGram whizzing in and out in their fast cars all night. Once they caught hold of Daya and made fun of him, calling him mental. No other boy would have stood for such antics. But Daya only smiled.'

'He was mental,' Mahesh spat. 'Couldn't read or write, but he could count well enough. Never made a mistake when it came to adding up the store bill. Must have been mental. Why else did he do this?'

Savio sighed. There was little sense in keeping the truth from these men. Nobody had greater right to it.

'Daya didn't do it,' he said. "Daya didn't kill your children.'

When Savio related that bit of the story, Lalli said, 'Tell us what the boys seemed like when you questioned them. That's how we got their names. Sita,' she turned to me. Her eyes held a kind of warning I couldn't understand. She continued impatiently, 'Don't you remember Shukla's vada pao party? Savio questioned those boys. That's how we learned they were from L'Allegra.'

Of course. I was being warned to hold my tongue about the car chase.

So I nodded and urged Savio to tell us about the boys.

At six that morning, Savio got a call from Shukla.

Two rich kids had crashed their cars approaching the highway. The Traffic guys were celebrating a Lamborghini and a Ferrari for the first time in towing history. The kids had been apprehended in their underwear and had no convincing explanation. One of them had to be cleaned up at the fountain before they could let him into the jeep.

'I'll talk to them,' Savio said.

Three young men awaited Savio in the Chowki. Two of them were in their underwear, the third, fully dressed, had a growing black eye.

They gave their names as Gaurav Khatri, Varun Gamadia and Rajiv Chawla. Their address was L'Allegra. They had no driving licenses, no wallets, no mobiles.

They also had no explanation apart from saying that Gaurav Khatri had braked his Ferrari abruptly and Varun Gamadia's Lamborghini had crashed into it and they had got into a fight afterwards.

'What happened to your clothes?' Savio asked. They looked foolish, but said nothing.

Savio showed them Daya's photograph.

Rajiv Chawla vomited. A lurch of bilious slime shot across the desk, distracting them.

'Rajiv's sick,' Gaurav announced. 'He needs a doctor.'

'We'll get him one,' Savio said. 'As soon as you tell me if you know this man.'

Both Gaurav and Varun denied knowing Daya. Rajiv vomited some more.

'Who's he? Why are you asking us if we know him?' Gaurav demanded.

'He knew some boys from your building.'

'Not us.'

'But you know who he is, don't you?'

'We just told you we didn't know him.'

'But you know of him. He's the Kandewadi killer.' Savio had no idea why he said that.

Gaurav greeted this with a guffaw of incredulity. 'Him!'

'What's Kandewadi?' Varun interrupted. 'Where is it? What's been happening there?'

'Shut up Varun,' Rajiv broke in. 'Shut up, just shut up both of you. Keep your traps shut till my dad gets here.'

'Relax, it's just a routine question,' Savio smiled. 'We're asking just about everybody about this guy.'

'Is he missing?' Varun asked.

'He's dead.'

The room went very quiet.

Savio heard his heart pace deliberately.

'I thought you said he was the murderer, not that he had been murdered,' Gaurav said.

'That's right. That's exactly what I said.'

'Slum kids,' Varun said, 'what can you expect. These things are always happening in slums.'

Savio let them go. They could have walked home, but they waited till Rajiv's dad roared up in his Pajero to fetch them.

Savio's face was suffused as he finished his narrative. 'Their arrogance upset me, Lalli. They were sitting there half naked, covered in vomit, unashamed, as if they owned the place. As if they owned me!' Savio was almost incoherent with rage. 'I don't know what came over me, but I was damned if they could just walk out. So I set them to fill forms, making them write out personal information—to what end I had no idea. Fill it up in capitals, I told them. I was just being bloody-minded. But when I looked at those forms, I found something. Varun Gamadia's M was identical to the M inscribed on those dead girls. Here, see for yourself.'

Savio showed us another picture on his mobile, this time a photograph of a page in the police register.

Varun Gamadia had written his name in capitals, and the M stood out with its peculiar hook.

'Coincidence, serendipity, or the devil's own luck sent them my way,' Savio said. 'If they hadn't crashed their fancy cars, who knows, we might never have learned of their existence.'

Savio set about investigating the three boys. He knew that Kandewadi had a connection with L'Allegra.

Every highrise is powered by the nearest slum. All the work force is sourced from there. Two of the dead children of Kandewadi had mothers who worked in L'Allegra—Pinki's mother Shanta and Mary's mother Flossie. Shanta had been fired from her job at L'Allegra a week before Pinki went missing. She had indignantly told Lalli that she left when the memsahib accused her of theft.

Savio let L'Allegra know that the police were looking into robberies and small thefts that could be the basis for large-scale burglary. Had any of the residents recently missed small items, knick-knacks, cosmetics? He asked the Secretary of the building to make enquiries.

The first residents to report were the Khatris. They had recently fired their maid for theft, and would be very happy to see her arrested.

Savio assured them the police would send around one of their lady officers.

And that was how Lalli learned that the ylang-ylang, the puff, and the doll came from the Khatri household.

Savio followed up on the watchman's account of Daya's carpet cleaning visits. There was no longer any doubt.

The carpet recovered from Daya's tempo had blood on it. The tempo had been used to ferry the children. The children had been doped with the drugged fruit juice found in the tempo—the drug was a commonly prescribed anti-allergic syrup. The drug and Daya's blade pointed to a doctor or medical student—Varun Gamadia. The carpet too, belonged to his family.

A havaldar did the rounds, asking about the carpets.

Mrs Gamadia flatly denied having her carpets cleaned, but by now the story had got around, and her son came out with the statement that food had spilled on them during a party. He had got them cleaned before his mother noticed. He told the havaldar that one carpet was still at the cleaner's.

The havaldar showed him Daya's photograph. Was this the carpet cleaner?

The watchman was present too, and he agreed before Varun Gamadia could say a word. Varun could only echo the watchman, quite forgetting that he had not recognised the photograph at Miravli Chowki, just a day ago.

With all this evidence, it should have been easy to get a search warrant—but it was refused.

Daya was the murderer. The case was closed. Savio was powerless against the order.

Time was running out.

Savio expected the three boys to abscond. Lalli suggested he appeal directly to the Comissioner. It only remained to test if Asif's green light had come from L'Allegra.

Brought upto date, the story still had one missing element: Seema Aggarwal.

There was no doubt she had spoken with the boys from the Store, though none of them had owned up to that when Shukla took them into custody that afternoon. But Shukla had a way of getting people to deny their own names, speaking of which, what was taking him this long?

I'd just voiced that when I heard his bike at the gate.

Shukla's dazzling smile dimmed at bit as he met my eye. There was still Arun's wallet between us. 'Mother serious, all forgiven?'

'Actually, Shukla—thanks!'

'Mention not, anything for my friend.'

I was touched, but he quickly explained, 'Not you. Savio.'

I led him to the kitchen and left him with Lalli and Savio. I carried the laptop to the sofa and checked #kw.

Chocolate had answered GreenLight.
Kababs for breakfast?

I rushed to the bathroom and lost the coffee.

Relieved, my brain could focus on the question that had been bothering me. 'Why didn't they clean up, Lalli?' I demanded. 'How could they leave those horrors—'

'Because, as I told you earlier, it's a crime of arrogance. They don't *need* to clean up. They're above the law, completely unaccountable. And as for disgust—they probably don't feel any. They've reached a paranoid plane of power. Even now, in the next hour when we've compelled them to clean up, I can bet they'll send their sweeper to do the job and tip him well, confident he won't talk.'

'That's impossible,' I said flatly. 'Nobody can be that brazen.'

'Let's see. It's all upto Shukla now.'

'What's the plan?'

'Let's go.'

Tuesday, 29 March

It was nearly five o'clock as we parked at the foot of the hill and walked up to L'Allegra. Savio had phoned ahead, and the Security guy let us in quietly. The night watchman joined us, and led us to his cabin. His street clothes hung on a hook. Shukla appropriated them and vanished. When he returned, the only thing familiar about him was his grin. He prinked a bit at the mirror on the wall and slicked his hair down with a bright blue comb. Lalli reached up impatiently and tousled his hair, yanked back the shirt collar and threw him a grimy kerchief she found balled on the table. A pair of rubber chappals completed the ensemble. All we had to do was wait.

On the 9th floor it was still lights out.

Half past five.

Quarter to.

'What if it doesn't work, Lalli?' Savio asked.

'Then I'll take over, Savio. I promised those parents. Either the police bring them the murderer alive, or I bring him in dead. When I made that promise, I didn't know there would be three of them. But I'll keep my word.'

A little after six, the lights blazed on the 9th floor.

Ten minutes later, the watchman's intercom buzzed. The nightwatchman nodded to Shukla. 'Ninth floor.'

When the night watchman and his companion reached the ninth floor, Varun Gamadia was waiting outside 911.

'I need the flat cleaned up,' he said casually. 'Visitors are expected by the early morning flight and I just discovered what a mess it is. Can you find someone to clean it at once? Just take away the kachra and scrub down the place.'

The night watchman shrugged. 'You won't find anyone at this hour, Sahib. It's just gone six.'

'It's six-thirty, you idiot. Listen, do it yourself! I'll pay you.'

'Sahib, I cannot do such work. I have no experience.'

'What about this fellow with you, who is he?'

'This bechara, Sahib, has just come from my village. Poor boy, he can neither hear nor talk—'

'Excellent. Five hundred bucks. Get rid of the kachra and scrub the place out.'

'Some party-warty Sahib?' The watchman had been instructed to make it easy for Varun, and he posed the question delicately.

Varun shrugged. 'Can't control your guests can you?' And he flashed a vulpine grin meant to ingratiate.

The watchman's deaf mute pal made a few gestures.

'He's asking about bucket and broom.'

'Oh, everything's in the bathroom. There's a plastic drum full of kachra in the bathroom. Save yourself some trouble, throw it out, drum and all. There's a nice tight lid, no need to open it. Just throw it out as is. I don't want to stink up the place.'

'Whatever you say, Sahib. I'll come down and call you, shall I, when it's cleaned up? I'll stay in case he needs anything. Whom else can he ask, bechara?'

Varun nodded and ran down the stairs.

Ten minutes later, the watchman phoned Savio. 'Inspector Sahib, ghazab ho gaya! There's a dead body in the bathroom.'

Savio put down the phone, relief in every feature.

'Drop me at Kandewadi, Sita,' Lalli said. 'Drive fast, or all hell will break loose.'

It was eight when Lalli came home.

Already, the police had swarmed L'Allegra. An hour later, warrants were issued for the arrest of Varun Gamadia, Gaurav Khatri and Rajiv Chawla for the rape and murder of the five children of Kandewadi.

Savio had two phone calls that morning, within minutes of the arrest. The first was from the Commissioner, congratulating him. The second was anonymous: 'Touch one hair of those boys and Kandewadi will burn tonight.'

Lalli laughed when she heard that. 'Don't worry, arrangements have already been made,' she said. 'L'Allegra should have made a deal by now. It's either that, or Kandewadi will torch the building. Sita, don't you want to go watch? I'll wait for prime time.'

I was already at the door.

The lane that led up to L'Allegra was jammed. The press was trying to muscle in without success.

The crowd was all male. Silent. Waiting.

I spotted the watchman in the foyer. He looked ill. After a moment, a havaldar emerged to keep him company.

Two men from the crowd went up to the havaldar. The havaldar made a phone call.

In a few minutes a fat man in a crumpled kurta pyjama emerged from the lift. The watchman saalamed him. Evidently, the Building Secretary.

He went up to the two waiting men and spoke with a kind of earnest desperation. The two men turned to the crowd and made a sign. A murmur passed through the crowd, a riff of anger that didn't need words.

It was agreed, that was the news. It was agreed. I heard the words over and over again.

It was agreed, and they were coming out.

The lift opened.

Savio and Shukla stepped out.

Three handcuffed men followed, all three I remembered from that wild car chase. They wore the customary hoods to hide their features— towels or tablecloths, flung on hastily. They had been marched out in crumpled nightwear.

The moment they stepped out, Savio and Shukla found they had something urgent to say to the Secretary. That functionary, eager to please, ducked back into the lift with them.

The watchman took off and merged with the crowd.

The four havaldars accompanying the prisoners too had an urgent appointment elsewhere. They marched their charges to the fancy rock garden at the corner of the foyer and handcuffed them to the metal railing. Then they stepped away.

The three captives struggled, and the towels slipped from their faces.

The crowd murmured again. It parted to permit three men to walk up into the foyer. Each man carried a bucket. A sickening stench filled the hot air as the buckets poured down a brown stream of excrement over the prisoners.

The last man hurled the bucket with great force at Gaurav Khatri. It caught him on the head. Blood spurted out through the ochre coating of shit, and the crowd exploded with laughter. It was the most mirthless sound in the world.

The laughter stopped.

The crowd waited.

Savio and Shukla returned with the Secretary who now burst into wails at the spectacle, shaking his fist feebly.

'We have an agreement,' the first man from the crowd said.

'Yes, yes, but this is—'

'Disgusting, no? Here, start cleaning up.'

The watchman threw a mop at the shocked Secretary.

Shukla now addressed the crowd. 'You can see it's impossible to take these men to the Chowki in a police jeep in this filthy state, but don't worry, they have cars. Traffic Police will tow them to the Chowki. You are requested to clear the road. The cars will be towed very slowly.'

Two havaldars brought around the Lamborghini and the Ferrari. The prisoners were prodded in with lathis and handcuffed to the wheels. The towing truck hooked on to the Ferrari and the Lamborghini was attached with a chain. I couldn't be certain, but I thought I caught a glimpse of Chakram in the van.

The crowd moved alongside the cars.

When the cars had cleared the lane, the crowd started pelting stones. The windows cracked, and glass shards flew against the terrified faces within. Plastic bags full of filth followed the stones. It was a silent concourse, broken by occasional screams as a splinter of glass or a stone hit its mark.

'Why were there no women, Lalli?' I demanded as I burst into the house.

I stopped when I noticed Lalli's companion. It was Arun.

He rose. 'Can I speak with you, Sita? Please?'

I could have refused, but what the hell, I was curious.

Lalli wandered off.

'It was a silly quarrel. Let's get over it, Sita.'

'It's over.'

'No. I'm sorry. There, I've apologised. Your turn now.'

The man was vile. 'I'm sorry too,' I said. 'I'm sorry I don't like you.'

'You don't like me? What's that supposed to mean?'

'That I don't like you.'

He backed off.

Lalli came in. 'Please tell Seema's parents I'll be in touch. Now get the hell out of my house before I throw you out.'

Seema!

Guilt whipped my insides to a soufflé. I had forgotten all about her. I didn't feel even a twinge of misery—what was wrong with me? All I could think was that she had missed the scoop of a lifetime.

The memory of our last encounter returned with clarity. Seema knew Suketa. Suketa was dead and now Seema was, too. Who, or what, connected the two women?

I collapsed heavily next to Lalli on the sofa. 'Where were all the women, Lalli? Why were none of the Kandewadi women there at L'Allegra?'

'I kept them away. I wanted to see those rapists and murderers publicly shamed by *men*. I wanted the press to show that. So that young men who think of rape as an act of daring can see it for what it really is—a loser's crime. I want them to see the rapist as the ultimate failure, the universal target of scorn and contempt. In our enlightened times we can no longer cut off a rapist's nose—'

'Or his genitals?'

'Oh, that doesn't count. Who'd notice? No, I don't hold with the brutality of cutting off a rapist's nose or his penis, but I do want to show up his baseness. When a rape takes place, every woman on the planet is a victim and every man stands accused. The cry, *How can I bear that someone should use my body like this?* Is usually read as a woman's outrage. But isn't it equally a man's? It is men who should protest against rape, not women.'

I agreed with the truth of that. What rational man can think of his penis as a weapon of hate?

'I have seen enough to know that a prospective rapist will take no account of a woman's outrage. It will only excite him more, increase the dare and spur him on to rape. It's exactly the attention he craves. But a rejection that's so completely male—that might make him stop and think.'

Lalli drew me close. I needed that comfort because I was crying in harsh bitter sobs, without quite knowing why.

We had a visitor at six. It was Vinay Dasgupta.

I hadn't seen him in a while. After the noise over the Monochrome Madonna had abated, Lalli had got him into the CyberCrimes Division where he had his small but devoted geekdom.

His divorce had finally come through. Sitara was in Yerawada, serving out her sentence in solitary after she had knifed a cellmate and seduced the guard in her earlier prison.

Vinay quickly suppressed a wince when he caught sight of me.

Perhaps I reflected that too. We couldn't help thinking of the day when I first saw the Monochrome Madonna.

But he was here to see Lalli.

She could barely contain her eagerness. 'Sita, you remember Vinay's computer skills? I asked him to magic the photograph we found in Suketa's book. That child was about ten or eleven, if you remember.'

'And here he is now,' Vinay placed a print on the table.

It was the little boy, grown up now, about as old as me. The ears were the same, but the stain on the left side of his face had faded to a faint memory.

'I might have left the birthmark if you hadn't told me it fades with age.'

'Yes. A portwine stain pales, but seldom vanishes. In his case it persisted perhaps a shade or two darker than what it appears in your picture. Now I have something to show you.'

Lalli went into her room and returned with a photograph. It was a group portrait, Lalli seated among uniforms.

The grown up little boy stood grinning behind her. He looked a little younger than Vinay had made him—but it was the same man.

'Pretty accurate,' Lalli sighed. 'I wish I could feel happy about this, but it only makes everything worse.'

For a fleeting moment, she looked frail and helpless. Vinay didn't ask questions—he didn't want to know the story.

To stay any longer might reopen old wounds, and his anxiety was palpable.

'I won't keep you, Vinay,' Lalli said. 'Meanwhile how's the other thing coming along?'

'No good. Sorry.'

'Well, we have three of them in the lockup now, and you can have their computers by tomorrow. Will that help?'

'Yeah, that's great. That should do it.' He left, cheered.

Wednesday, 30 March

The next morning Savio called to say Rajiv Chawla was prepared to give a statement. Savio would be recording it. Lalli could read it later in the day. Vinay Dasgupta had the computers and would be working through the day. He'd let Savio know when he was through.

'For Savio, this will be evidence against those three boys, but for me it's something bigger, Sita. There are two murders more to solve, and many more to prevent.'

Suketa Das. Seema Aggarwal. But their murders were so different from the Kandewadi crimes. How could these boys have killed those women? How could they even know them?

The boy in Suketa's treasured photograph was probably a son or a nephew. No--considering she had been put to death bedecked as a bride-- definitely, her son.

And Lalli knew him grown up, as a *policeman*. She hadn't known he was Suketa's son. What of him now?

Surely by now Lalli had let the police know he was Suketa's son. The news must have reached him already. Soon, then, we would know the rest of Suketa's story. Perhaps even the story that she told in *At High Noon, Quietus*. And that, surely, would explain her bizarre murder.

Despite the horrors of L'Allegra, it was Suketa's death that shook me the most. I wanted her restored. I wanted her free to write and say the outrageous truths that had inspired me. I was irritated with Lalli's admission that Suketa's philosophy was shaped by her experience. Isn't everybody's?

And then there was Seema. Brutally killed—for what? Daring to write about Kandewadi?

'Lalli, it's that politician,' I said. 'The speed bump leveler. He backed out of L'Allegra, but he silenced Seema. Perhaps he even killed Suketa.'

'Why should he ritualize Suketa's murder with a mock marriage? No, he didn't have anything to do with her death. And as for Seema, we need to find her source.'

I remembered I hadn't told Lalli about the last conversation I had had with Seema. 'Seema's source didn't know anything about Daya's death,' I said.

'Yes, I remember you said that earlier too. The reason why she got Arun to ask about Daya was because her usual source didn't know about his death. Or else because he needed to know the details of Daya's death.'

'That almost presumes that he knew Daya.'

'Didn't he?'

Throwing that question at me, Lalli left the room. She didn't show up till lunch. Her eyes had a look of defeat I had never seen before.

Vinay might have something for us by evening, I mentioned, trying to cheer her.

'The computers will have all the details,' Lalli said. 'Every assault, and every indecency. They can't get away with this evidence. But you know what, they still might.'

'Lalli!'

'I'm perfectly serious. Justice depends neither on the police nor on the prosecutor. It rests entirely with the judge. Our courts are full of ignorant, inept, corrupt and shamelessly sexist judges. How many rapists who come to trial are convicted? How many child molestors? How many murderers?'

'In small courts maybe, but surely—'

'The Supreme Court? Don't make me laugh. They're good at setting up Commissions. That I'll agree to. But what do those old farts come up with? A lot of platitudes and a lot of blame. Do they ever even mention the judiciary and how it makes a mockery of justice? They tell us we Indians have to be sensitized to crime, that our moral compass has gone awry. What about theirs? I won't be surprised if these criminals walk. There must be a judge or a minister who will ensure that, for the right price.'

'Lalli, that's really cynical.'

'It's the truth. Certainly, blame the police. They're as corrupt and as biased as the judiciary, but that's not the policeman on the beat, not the honest inspector who does his or her best to keep their area clean—until they buckle under pressure from their superiors. Look at the extent to which the Miravli people went to kill this case.'

'But then they called in Savio.'

'Yes. Savio's done his job. Now let me do mine.'

Savio and Shukla came in an hour later. Rajiv Chawla's statement tallied with what Lalli had deduced from Twitter. By his account the three of them, Glider, Blade and he himself as Chocolate, had been guided and inspired by a guru they knew only as BGOE. Glider had met BGOE in a chat room. Chawla had also given the police the url for the site at which he had posted photographs for sale. Several of the photographs had gone viral on Facebook.

Savio had two of those photographs on his mobile. I screamed when I saw the second.

'I am not going to sleep for the rest of my life after seeing just two photographs,' I shuddered. 'How can people want to buy them?

'You are simple-minded writer only, Sita. Your world is more safe,' Shukla said.

'The average guy or gal is insatiable when it comes to violent porn,' Savio said. 'Remember that case in Ranchi where this boy beheaded his girlfriend in college? His friends ringed the body with their mobile cameras. They felt compelled to photograph it. That's what the police found when they arrived on the scene. The body twitching at their feet wasn't real to those kids. The picture on their mobiles was.'

'This boy also, he kept saying it was only a game,' Shukla muttered. 'To them it was all happening on their computer screen.'

'Not to them, Shukla,' I protested. 'To the people who buy those photographs, yes, it might be some kind of cyber-fantasy. But these boys committed brutal acts, deeds no sane mind can even contemplate.'

'They did not think their acts were brutal,' Savio growled. 'This boy said in his statement: "It's not as if they were real children from good families, they were only from the slums, they were used to it." These boys aren't even remotely human. Hanging's too good for them.'

'Oh, it will never come to that,' Lalli said. 'They'll walk, or else get killed in prison.'

'Not this time,' Savio and Shukla spoke together.

'My blessing on that,' Lalli said. 'Pull that off and I'll die a happy woman.'

'Dr Q will be here any moment,' Savio said. 'He was waiting for some reports.'

Lalli nodded absently.

We were all reticent, in the same reverie of pain, yet apart in our privacy of thought.

Despite the gloom, I felt a lightness I couldn't explain—and then I realised it was relief that Savio had a watertight case.

'Vinay can't trace BGOE, Lalli,' Savio said. 'The moment he tracks down the IP address, BGOE's no longer there.'

'I'll get him,' Lalli said quietly.

'How? Where will you look for him?'

'He'll find me,' Lalli said.

'Good God, Lalli, what have you done?' Savio gasped.

'I'm doing this alone, Savio,' Lalli said. 'This is my case.'

Dr Q walked into the uncomfortable silence that followed. He placed a file on the table.

'Everything you wanted. Sambalpur, 2005. It's Kandewadi raised to the power of ten.'

'Same MO?'

'Very likely. The girls followed him trustingly. But with one difference. He concealed the bodies.'

'Naturally,' Lalli sounded a trifle smug, and reached for her laptop.

GreenLight on DM to BGOE:
Only Sambalpur 2005 was beyond good or evil.

BGOE answered at once:
What do you know about Sambalpur 2005?

GreenLight:
Not enough. Can you tell me more?

BGOE didn't answer.

'Lalli, explain,' I said sternly.

But just then, the doorbell rang. A middle-aged couple stood outside.

'We're looking for a lady called Lalli—I'm sorry, we don't know her full name.'

'That is her full name. Please come in. You are?'

'Aggarwal.'

'Seema's parents? I'm so sorry—'

'You knew Seema?'

'Yes, yes, she was my friend.'

What possessed me to say that?

The next few minutes passed in getting them comfortable. The force moved off to the table, leaving Lalli and me with the Aggarwals.

'Seema was a brave woman,' Lalli said. 'Trapping her murderer is my responsibility. I asked you to meet me so that I could learn the details of the last time you saw her. I know how painful it is—'

'No, it isn't,' Seema's mother said decisively. 'Anything we can do to find Seema's murderer gives us a reason to continue living. We were so proud of Seema. Now she's gone, we must take pride in giving her justice.'

Her husband was not so vocal. He wept noiselessly, the tears ploughing down his creased face, his hands helplessly twisting and untwisting themselves.

'She was going to meet Uncle,' he said suddenly.

'Now you remember?' his wife asked incredulously.

'It's true, I'm telling you. Friday night, just as she was getting into the car, "I'll be back for dinner," she told me. "I'm only going to meet Uncle in the usual place." That's what she said.'

'What uncle? Whose uncle?' his wife demanded.

'Nobody's uncle. Just Uncle. She used to call that man Uncle out of respect. He was a retired police officer. You may be knowing him, madam, but I don't know his name. She used to meet him daily when the Kandewadi story was on. He gave her many details. She always met him there.'

'Where?' his exasperated wife yelled.

'In that Irani, Noble Café, opposite Hindmata.'

'In Dadar? She went all that way?' Seema's mother sounded puzzled.

'I thought you knew. She always met him there, between 7 and 8. Maybe he's waiting for her, today too. Maybe he doesn't know. Hurry, Kaushalya, if we hurry we'll get there by 9, he might still be there—'

'Calm down, Mr Aggarwal, we'll find him in time. Seema relied on him for information about Kandewadi?'

'Give and take.'

'What? Seema paid him for information?' Mrs Agarwal asked.

'No, no, nothing like that. He gave her information, but he also wanted information, didn't he? When that boy's body was found, he put pressure on Seema to find out details.'

'Why?'

'He was writing a book about the case. Will he say now in his book that my Seema solved the case? He told her he would, if she got all the details. But then he got upset when that suicide lady phoned Seema.

Professor Das. She was writing a book too, but not about Kandewadi. About how Kandewadi started. That's what she told Seema.'

'Kandewadi, the place?' Lalli asked.

'No! The reason for the murders! About how the murders began. She told Seema she was going to show the manuscript to her friend. That friend was you, Madam. She said your name and Seema answered that she knew you. She told Uncle this. He was upset. He was jealous, Seema said. So she told him, if she got the manuscript from Professor Das, she would let him read it.'

'Did Seema get it?'

'No. But she had another piece of news. She was going to file her story, and she wanted to show it to Uncle first, that's why she wanted to meet him Friday night. But she never got there—' Sobs overcame him.

Lalli waited till he was calm before she stumped him with a question: 'How do you know she never got there?'

Mr Aggarwal stared at her, speechless.

His wife took over. 'If he had met her that night, surely he would have contacted us. He would have felt bad, no? Even if for some reason he didn't want to contact police, he himself being retired police and all? He knew how things work. No offence, please excuse, but it is the truth.'

Lalli winced. 'It is the truth.'

'And even if he didn't come forward, the Irani owner would have said something, no? He knew her very well, she never left without a package of pau for breakfast. He would have remembered if she had been there that night.'

Savio and Shukla joined us.

'Would you recognise this Uncle if you saw him?' Savio asked Mr Aggarwal.

'I think so, from Seema's description.'

'Let's go then. Perhaps he's still there. He's a regular, you said.'

'Oh yes. Stays till closing time.'

'You knew all this and you never said anything,' Mrs Aggarwal's voice began to rise dangerously.

Shukla took charge. 'But, Mrs Aggarwalji, it is you only who can tell us about Seema herself. From a mother's point of view, what do you think she did that evening? If she didn't meet Uncle, where else could she have gone?'

He talked her out of the door and we watched them get into the jeep and drive away.

Dr Q, who had been in the balcony all this while said suddenly, 'You're not doing this alone, Lalli. I'm coming with you.'

'What are you talking about, Dr Q?' Lalli asked.

'They won't find Uncle at the café, will they, Lalli?'

Lalli sighed and threw her hands up helplessly.

'If the Aggarwals hadn't turned up, would you have taken Savio along?'

'No.'

'I thought not. Savio will solve Seema Aggarwal's murder. But you have something else to do, don't you?'

'Yes.'

Lalli's voice was so low, I had to strain to hear it.

'You'll do it, too. Tonight?'

'I hope so. I don't know yet.'

'Right.'

'You're not coming with me.'

'This is going to be one of those deadlock arguments—you say no and I say yes.'

'It might be dangerous.'

'I'm all for danger.'

I had to laugh, then.

Dr Q ducks paper darts, cowers at thunder and shudders at motorbikes and fast cars. Knives and guns make him physically sick. I adore him, but I can't deny he's a wimp.

'Danger's not your style, Dr Q,' I said.

'You're wrong, Sita.' Lalli's voice had an unusual asperity. 'It's Dr Q's case too. We go together then, Ali Haidar.'

I've known my aunt to do many mad things, but nothing so utterly demented. She had sent away two tough guys and chosen monkish Dr Q for backup. I wasn't going to let this bit of insanity pass.

'Don't fret, Sita. I'll take care of Lalli,' Dr Q had the nerve to tell me.

'Sure, and I'll take care of you. You're not leaving me home, Lalli. I'm coming too.'

To my surprise, Lalli agreed meekly.

'Whom are we going to meet, Lalli?' I asked.

In answer, she picked up the laptop. After a few minutes, she showed me the exchange.

@GreenLight on DM to BGOE:

Shocking events #kw

@BGOE:
Why are you shocked? They got what they deserved.

@GreenLight:
The motive was unworthy, the plan flawed, the execution unintelligent.

@BGOE:
How so?

@GreenLight:
Motive was self-serving. Daya was the flaw. He failed his Master.

@BGOE:
You understand. But what shocked you?

@GreenLight:
The insult to you. They did not deserve your tutelage.

@BGOE:
Do you?

@GreenLight:
Only you can tell. Let me show you.

@BGOE:
What do you have to show me?

@GreenLight:
Tonight, as kw sleeps secure, I will show you something worthy of Cattle Island.

@BGOE:
What do you know of Cattle Island?

@GreenLight:
I look to you for enlightenment. Judge my worthiness tonight.

@BGOE:
Time and place?

@GreenLight:
Turn L at the store, walk for five minutes, turn R. The gate will open. 2 a.m.

@BGOE:
I will be there.

'What's Cattle Island?' I asked, mystified.

Lalli had left the room, but Dr Q replied. 'It's an island in Sambalpur. Used to be a hill before the Hirakud dam was constructed in 1957, flooding the village. People fled, abandoning their cattle. As the waters rose, the cattle hurried to the hilltop. When the waters receded, they found themselves on an island. They've lived and bred there ever since. It's a curious story. Another scam, like our own Gilbert Hill. A man-made disaster being touted as a natural wonder.'

'What does Lalli have to do with cattle? You knew about BGOE and GreenLight, Dr Q?'

'Only since I found the file Lalli's reading just now. She filled me in. Now, Sita, I'm hungry. Can I help you get dinner?'

It was a quiet meal.

Dr Q's vaunted appetite didn't stand up to more than one paratha.

Lalli ate absently.

They both refused coffee later, and I switched off the kitchen lights long before ten.

All we had to do now was wait, and my company seemed resolved on silence.

Savio called to say Mr Aggarwal had failed to spot Uncle.

Uncle hadn't been at the cafe for the last two days. Uncle was a regular, good for omlet pau and chai, but that was the extent of their knowledge.

'I'm turning in, Savio,' Lalli lied. 'It's been a long day.'

When she put down the phone, she turned to me.

'I hope you'll understand later, Sita, why I must do this alone. You'll have to change, Dr Q. I've laid out your clothes. Black, Sita.'

All of us were in black when we left. Dr Q was almost unrecognizable. I wondered if the metamorphosis was significant—his usual immaculate white vestments had clothed the gentle soul I knew. Would the black Tshirt unleash ferocity?

On Lalli's instructions I parked where Daya's tempo had caught the green light. We let ourselves over the wall, into Kandewadi.

Dr Q and I followed Lalli intently. Her movements were barely discernable in that dim light.

She slid into a hut and we followed.

We walked right through it and emerged in a yard. Lalli shut the door behind us.

We stood in a quadrangle covered with awning. There was bamboo scaffolding along one side. Shadowy recesses formed pockets of darkness. The centre was dimly lit by a concealed bulb. A wrought iron gate in a whitewashed wall opened on the street.

'Wait here.'

Lalli went forward. Dr Q breathed in light and quick gasps like an elderly bird. I began worrying about him. He wasn't used to the tough life. What if he buckled just as things heated up? Would I have to make the choice between reviving him and rescuing Lalli? I was no good at either.

'We aren't armed,' I muttered.

'I have my iPhone!'

A giggle welled up in me, but the man was dead serious. He usually viewed the gizmo at arm's length. It had an App for osteology. That, and GPS, were all he ever used, but he clutched it now like a Glock.

A figure oozed out of the shadows, and met Lalli.

2 a.m., I thought she'd said. It was only half past one.

This couldn't be BGOE, surely?

It wasn't.

Lalli and the man stepped into a recess. I caught a glimpse of a half opened door.

Presently, Lalli returned. She led us to the recess adjacent to the door.

'Stand well back, and no matter what, don't move. Dr Q, I have this in hand, don't plunge after me. Use your camera.'

To my surprise, after this she stayed right next to us.

The man we'd seen earlier came out carrying a chair. He set it at the entrance of the bightly lit room, took out a book and settled down to read. At first he appeared stiff and ill at ease, but after about ten minutes he looked as if he had been reading there a long while.

'What if he doesn't come, Lalli?'

Lalli placed a finger on my lip. I felt her hold her breath.

The gate opened slowly, about an inch, then stopped.

There was no sound at all.

It opened further and a man entered quickly, and slipped aside into the shadows.

Then he stepped out, and I caught my first impression of BGOE.

A slight man with a stoop, dressed quietly in a pale bush shirt and dark pants. His bald head caught a gleam from the lamp.

My heart thudded as he turned in our direction and I looked him full in the face.

It was an ageing face, late fifties, early sixties. He wore spectacles, square black frames.

It was a mean face, tightening as I watched, with suppressed energy.

He glanced once more all around him. Then he walked with quick light steps, almost on tiptoe with a ballet dancer's gait, towards the man reading at the door.

The man kept on reading.

BGOE was near him now. I felt Lalli strain forward.

BGOE raised his arms over the reader's head. There was a streak of light between his hands, and then they came down sharply over the reader's head.

Lalli flew like a black-winged bird and hurled herself on BGOE.

A yowl of rage—and then I heard a bone crack.

It was indescribable, that simple definite sound that punctuated the silence.

A long scream rent the air.

Lalli was holding BGOE's hand in a pleasant kind of way. Every time she shook it, he screamed.

The reader had got up by now. He felt his neck and stared at his hand as it came away bloody. He looked familiar—then I remembered seeing him at the mortuary waiting for Deepika's body.

It was Pinki's father, Dagdu More. He stared malignantly for a moment, then leapt forward, aiming a punch at BGOE.

The next moment, BGOE had a knife at Dagdu's throat.

His fractured arm dangled uselessly, pain forgotten. His good hand was driving the knifepoint deeper every minute into Dagdu's neck.

'Walk.'

He turned to Lalli. 'You have no idea who I am. Don't even try to stop me.'

'I won't stop you, Professor.'

That stopped him. He waited.

'You're here because I invited you to see something, but I see you've made a mistake.'

'I don't make mistakes.'

'No? I set up a decoy. I'm sorry about your arm, but he would have made an inconvenient corpse.'

'On the other hand, I find him most convenient.'

'To get away? Why do you need to get away, Professor? Why not take care of him after you've seen what I promised you?'

'Are you GreenLight?'

'Surprised?'

'I didn't think it could be a woman.'

'Surely we are beyond gender, Professor.'

'Why do you call me that?'

'As your prospective student. Again, I'm sorry about your arm.'

He laughed.

He had a surprisingly pleasant laugh.

If he wasn't holding a knife at a man's throat, it would have sounded almost social. I realised he was enjoying himself. The meanness had gone out of his face. His animated features looked strangely familiar.

'You said something about Cattle Island.'

Lalli said sharply, 'Be precise. I said I would show you something worthy of Cattle Island.'

'What do you know about Cattle Island?'

'Very little. Only what awaits you there. You will have to fill in the blanks afterwards. Enter, please.'

Indicating the room, Lalli stepped aside.

Professor pushed Dagdu away contemptuously. Extracting a checked kerchief from his pocket, he wiped the knife fastidiously with it.

'That's seen a lot of life, I'll bet,' Lalli said admiringly, 'although I see you prefer the piano wire. I lean towards horsehair myself. Have you tried that?'

'The Turkish method.'

'Exactly. I enjoy the precision.'

'Yes.' His smile was warm and friendly. 'There is something of the mathematician about you. I'm curious about what you have in store for me—but what about this man? Why is he privy to our conversation?'

'Forget him. He is my disciple as Daya was yours.'

'Daya.' He uttered the name heavily. 'I had thought him worthy, but he betrayed me.'

'As you were betrayed before,' Lalli's voice had grown deep and powerful.

'What do you know about that?' he rasped.

In answer, Lalli flung open the door. Professor turned towards the light—and screamed.

His scream shattered the night. Wordless and primeval, it was the visceral cry of utter abandonment and despair.

As it died away, I heard laughter. Mirthless, hysterical, laughter from Pinki's father.

Professor rushed at him with the knife, bellowing with rage.

Lalli intercepted him, reaching swiftly for his fractured arm.

He howled with pain and retreated into the room.

Dr Q and I hurried forward.

Lalli stood on the threshold, arms outspread, barring the way out of the room.

Professor darted madly at her, knife in hand, snarling with manic rage.

She averted each attack without moving an inch. He gibbered and cringed and moved away whimpering, and at last I saw what had driven him crazy.

A smiling young man in police uniform. A tall man with jug ears and a red mark like a stain on the left side of the face.

'Didn't you leave him in Cattle Island, Professor?' Lalli asked pleasantly. 'Why don't you say hello to your son?'

Pasted on the wall was a life-size blowup of Vinay Dasgupta's wizardry on the picture from Suketa's book.

'That is your son, isn't it, Professor?'

He glared malignantly, but said nothing.

'Perhaps I didn't tell you that we were acquainted? I met Inspector Patnaik in 2006 when he was hot on the trail of the Sambalpur Killer.'

I was so intent on Lalli's words, I had looked away from Professor for a moment. He sprang like a cat at Lalli. His knife had almost grazed her when she twisted it out of his grasp. It fell with a clatter at my feet. Dr Q kicked it away.

Lalli had Professor by the fractured arm now. This time she twisted it with malice.

'Say it!' she hissed. 'Say his name.'

Professor snarled, but said nothing.

'*Say it!*"

'Sudhendu.' He screamed out the name, as if it named his pain.

'Sudhendu. Now say his mother's name.'

When he was silent, Lalli twisted his arm again. 'Say it!'

'Whore. She was a whore.'

'Say her name or I will break the other arm more easily than I broke this one.'

Lalli aimed a kick at his kneecap, connected and was rewarded with another scream.

I was appalled.

'*Say it!*'

'Suketa. Her name was Suketa.'

'Tell me what you did to Suketa.'

'I did nothing.'

'What did she do to you, then?'

'She left me!' The words came in a snarl of hate and ended in a scream. 'She left me. Is that what a wife does? She left her son. Was he not her child? Tell me, tell me, was he not her child?'

'You had a daughter too. What happened to her? What happened to Monica?'

Something changed in him at that. He sank down on his haunches and held his head in his hands. From then on, he never looked up, but answered all Lalli's questions in a monotone. But first he had one more question for her

'Who told you her name?' he asked.

'Your son did. Inspector Patnaik was hunting the Sambalpur Killer, but nobody else in the police knew his sister had been the first victim. On the day I was leaving Sambalpur, your son came to meet me. He said, "Please keep this confidential, this case is very personal to me. My sister Monica was one of his earliest victims—I can't track any cases beyond that. She was six years old. I owe her, you understand?" That is what your son told me. Now you tell me what happened to Monica.'

'She was my daughter. Was it wrong that I should enjoy her?'

'*Enjoy*?' Lalli's outrage was explosive—he silenced her with his next comment.

'Suketa responded just like you. Monica responded just like you. With anger. With disobedience! I taught my disobedient daughter a lesson. I silenced her with her ribbon. She had two ribbons. I saved the other one for her mother.'

'You saved both the ribbons.'

'Yes! I saved both the ribbons. I laid Monica in her bed after I had finished with her and told my wife she had been a bad child and grieved me. I expected her to understand. She did not.'

'What explanation did you give Suketa?'

'That I had to rise beyond good or evil. A man can only achieve that by killing the thing he loves. Next to my daughter, I loved my wife. I told her in time I would do the same by her. So she left me.'

'Were you not afraid she might go to the police?'

'No. She wouldn't do that to me. She was a good woman. But she was not evolved enough. I couldn't educate her. She had a crude mind.'

'What did you do with Monica's body? Your son told me it was never found.'

'I took it to Cattle Island, left it there. I did that every time. I am a fisherman, I had a boat.'

'What about your son? How did you raise him?'

'He was unworthy. I observed him. He had inherited all his mother's crudities. I left him alone. I pursued my own education.'

'And how did you educate yourself?'

'By lowering the barricades, one by one. Fear, horror, rage, disgust, I had to lose them all. Each one I sacrificed by expending them on innocents. Each deed was more terrible than the last. I could not hurry. I had to be slow. Sometimes that was not enough. Their pain was not pure enough. I had to raise the bar every time before I felt release. Sometimes I had to eat them. Sometimes I fed them to my son.'

'You told him that, didn't you?'

'Yes. He had to know. Without that knowledge, I doubt if he would have been purified.'

'I will ask you about that presently. Let us stick to the time-line. When did you kill your daughter?'

'I did not kill her. She was my sacrifice. You are ill-educated. Suketa would have pointed this out: it is an ancient truth that a father may possess and sacrifice his daughter.'

'Did she say that to you when you told her you had raped and strangled Monica?'

'No. She did not say it, although she knew. Agamemnon and Iphigenia. Brahma and Saraswati. Every culture has a myth to explain it.'

'So when did you rape and strangle your daughter Monica?'

'You persist in using foul words. No matter. 1983. She was six years old, a clever child, clever enough to understand my purpose, but she too was unworthy.'

'When did you murder your next victim? Your next sacrifice?'

'There were so many, but never enough.'

'They were all girls of six?'

'Yes. All of them. Just like Monica. Every time I took a step further, but how the horizon receded! How quickly it receded!'

'No doubt. What happened in 2005?'

'I lost my boat. I couldn't afford a new one. I could no longer make it to Cattle Island.'

'You could no longer hide the bodies.'

'Yes, it was inconvenient. They were found—most of them were successful, but some of them were found. Only about five, I think. But that made it useless. That made all of that year useless.'

'Your son joined the police. How did you feel about that?'

'Why should I feel anything? I was a teacher, his mother was a housewife. He chose his own career.'

'What did you teach?'

'Physics, mathematics, computer science.'

'Were any of your victims among your students?'

'No. How could they be? My students were all too old. I was looking for purity. Once hormones take over, where's the purity?'

'When did your son start investigating the murders?'

'Right away, when the first two bodies were found. Overnight I became the Sambalpur Killer. I asked my son once, "What do you think the Sambalpur killer looks like? Does he look like me?" And he laughed.'

'What was his profile of the killer?'

'A young man, shy, insecure, probably with a domineering mother. That was my turn to laugh!'

'What happened next?'

'My son insulted me.'

'How?'

'He made out the Sambalpur Killer to be subhuman, a brute with no sense of right or wrong, an unintelligent savage given to insatiable carnality. My own son thought this of me, of me!'

'And you decided to disabuse him?'

'I told him he was wrong, I told him I would prove him wrong if he would come with me to Cattle Island.'

'On what date did you go there?'

'You know that already.'

'The 10th of September 2006,' Lalli said. 'No, wait, I got that wrong. You went there the night before. 9 September.'

He looked up angrily. 'Who told you?'

Lalli didn't answer.

He began to speak in a low rumble that seemed forced out of him under great duress.

Perhaps it was his pressure that obliterated everything except his words. We were no longer here in this quadrangle, he was no longer trapped in that room. We were all on a boat, watching.

Watching, and listening, to two men, sailing towards Cattle Island.

'I could teach you,' the older man said, but the wind blew away the words.

His companion, still in his reverie, took no notice.

'I could teach you,' he repeated, louder this time.

'Teach me what?'

'Everything. If you'd only let me.'

'Of course. I've learnt from you all my life'. That should mollify the old man. He had been carping all evening.

And now this excursion! To the island, in the dead of night—he didn't see the point of it.

'Why not wait till daylight?' he had ventured.

That hadn't worked, had it? It just made the old man more bloodyminded. He'd been at his throat all evening.

The last thing he wanted now was a quarrel. So he'd hired a boat for the night.

And now here they were, lurching towards Cattle Island.

There was no moon, but he had a lantern.

He had no idea what his father meant him to discover. Perhaps this was his idea of adventure. They had a boat when he was younger, but he didn't remember the old man ever taking him out on it.

'You'll see when we get to the island,' the old man chuckled. 'You'll see, you'll see. All these years I never showed you, but now I want you to see.'

There was nothing to see on Cattle Island except cattle. Wild belligerent cattle.

Last year a tourist had been gored to death in broad daylight. Would they attack by night? He didn't feel like asking his father.

'Come along, then!'

His father scrambled up the shore and hurried up the slope. He fastened the painter and followed.

'Switch off the torch,' the old man said, 'time enough for that later.'

'What can you show me in the dark?'

'What you're looking for.'

He stumbled along blindly after his father. Without the moon, a pale haze of mist made everything deceptive: surfaces, depths, promontories. But his dad seemed to know the way.

He'd humour the old man tonight. He'd be back on the trail tomorrow. Funny, the way the old man kept coming back to the case.

'You don't know the half of it,' he'd said—as if he did! The young man dared a contemptuous smile in the dark.

'What are you smiling at?'

'Nothing.'

There was no hiding from his father.

Oppression settled like a tight collar at his throat.

'Come on, slow coach. We're nearly there.'

His father was a dense silhouette in the grey film of mist between trees.

He seemed to quiver, but that was just the wavering light. Or was it?

As he neared his father, he smelt excitement. Animalic. Feral. His father breathed fast and shallow, in hot puffs of foul air that made him draw back.

'It's here,' his father said in a voice he did not recognise. 'Give me the torch.'

At first, he saw nothing.

Only mulch and leaf meal, filling a hollow.

'Can you see it? Can you see them?'

And then—because a sudden movement caught the light, he saw.

The sudden movement was the slither of a small snake. It shimmered briefly between two holes.

Two symmetrical black holes.

And then the snake disappeared leaving behind a flash of white teeth.

Small perfect teeth in a small perfect skull.

And then he saw the next. And one more. And then another.

The pit was full of children.

'You see?' His father's breath singed Sudhendu's ears. 'They're all here.'

Sudhendu forced the words out somehow. 'You knew he'd killed before—'

'He?'

Sudhendu whirled around, the torch beam hitting his father square in the eyes.

'You know who he is then? You knew all this while? You know the Sambalpur Killer? Tell me his name.'

He advanced, torch poised like a weapon, blinding his father, making him stagger.

'Tell me his name.'

His father leapt on him, knocking the torch out of his hand, clawing his neck.

Sudhendu struggled but could not free himself from that relentless grip.

His father's eyes stared into his own.

There was a light in their depths he tried to read, but it escaped him.

The hands on his throat tightened, knocking the air out of him.

His father's hot mouth was talking into his lips, snarling words that sliced into his brain.

'You evil spawn of a slut! Must I tell you your father's name? Say my name! Say it!'

The hands sprang off his throat, but the eyes still glared into his.

'Say my name.' The order came in a calm voice.

'Bimalchandra Patnaik.'

'Bimalchandra Patnaik! That is his name. That is my name. This is my handiwork! Mine! Do you hear me? Mine!'

Sudhendu moved a step back.

What had sent his father over the edge?

This was insanity. No fancy psychiatric label could distract him from the truth. His father was mad.

He had to get him home somehow, and then he would deal with it.

He said, 'Let's go home.'

'Home? Is that all you have to say? You've been hunting the Killer of Sambalpur and here he stands before you, and all you can say is, let's go home?'

His father's words, sane, incredulous, put ice in his heart. But he repeated stubbornly, 'Come on, let's go.'

His father grabbed him by the shoulders and pushed him towards the pit.

'Not till I've shown you everything, not till you've understood. For years I strived, do you hear me? For years and years I strived to reach perfection, and you have nothing to say?'

'Perfection?' Sudhendu could only stammer at the word.

'Baffles you, does it? You never had the intellect for it. These are great deeds, Sudhendu. To break and possess innocence is to liberate the mind, to free it, to let it soar high above good or evil. Each one of these innocents was a sacrifice I made to rise to a higher plane, each one. I tried to educate you, but I knew you lacked the capacity to understand. Do you understand now?'

'I understand. You discovered this pit. The shock of that discovery has overwhelmed you. It's deluded you into thinking you killed these children.'

Bimalchandra laughed.

'The child thinks I'm mad!' he roared into the night. 'You will never know how sane I am, at this moment, when I tell you their names, each one of them. Names, dates, places where I found them, where I took them, what I did with them.'

Sudhendu was trembling so hard he couldn't reach for the torch at his feet. His hand hit his hip instead, and the comforting hardness of his holster.

'Do you believe me now?' his father asked again. 'Don't answer. I see you do. I know you, my child. I know I live in you. I know you will be, one day, what I am today.'

'No.'

'So sure?'

Sudhendu was fighting for reason, grasping for some straw of sanity, and the question broke from him. 'Did you do all this because of Monica?'

Only silence answered him.

'Did you kill these children out of grief for your own daughter? Because some madman strangled her, did you feel compelled to keep replaying that crime?'

Sudhendu felt very distant from this madman who stood snarling a few feet away. He was no longer his son now. He was detached, cold, clinical. He only wanted to understand.

'Did you?'

His father sighed. 'I have no hopes of you, Sudhendu. I was quite mistaken when I thought you had potential. If you insist on asking about your sister's death, I will answer you with the truth. She was my first, my purest sacrifice. She was what I loved more than anything on earth. I possessed her. That was my right.'

'You raped my sister!' Sudhendu pitched himself at his father, maddened with rage. He was shocked by the steely resistance that met him. His father peeled him off like a scab and threw him down.

There still was the gun.

He drew the revolver. 'Get into the boat quietly.'

His father laughed.

'Why do you confuse yourself with ugly words, Sudhendu? Monica was a disobedient daughter. You, on the other hand, have always been an obedient son.'

'I?'

'Have I not fed you, repeatedly, the fruits of my sacrifice? How many meals have you enjoyed that rightly belonged in that pit? You ate them, Sudhendu. You ate them with me. I looked after you well. I put meat on the table. I fed you. You are my son, my son!'

One word had to be said and somehow he got it out. 'Why?'

There was no answer.

Sudhendu could no longer see his father's face.

A terrible sternness possessed him.

Everything grew still.

In the silence he heard a sound that offended him, that offended everything he believed in, every truth he knew.

It was his heartbeat.

It thudded on, uncaring, ruthless, feigning ignorance, untouched by what he had seen and heard.

He could not allow that.

It could not continue to keep up its senseless chatter when all life had already been silenced, all thought erased, all breath choked.

It must be stopped.

Sudhendu raised the pistol to his temple and shot himself.

I heard Lalli ask, 'What happened next?'

'After he shot himself in the head, I got into the boat and went home. The next day his body was discovered. I mourned my son. A few months later, I left Sambalpur. I had a crisis.'

'What kind of crisis?'

'I couldn't do it anymore.'

'You could not rape or you could not kill?'

'You persist in using ugly words. No, the sacrifice was ineffectual. I realized I had transcended that phase and must reach higher. I must impart my knowledge and watch it spread. So I came to Bombay, set up in the tuition business—and waited.'

'How did you meet Glider, Blade and Chocolate?'

'In a chat room. Cyberspace is full of curious minds, some so drunk with arrogance that they fail to see the difference between the real and the virtual. These three were easy. They were seeking thrills. They had no higher motive—you were right about that. You would have made a good pupil.'

'You already had a good pupil.'

'Daya. Yes.'

'How did you meet Daya?'

'I met him last year, long before I met the three boys. Daya delivered my groceries—it was destined. I hardly buy much, but that one time I had decided to stock up for three months, oil, atta, dal, rice. I asked them to deliver it all home. I was finishing tuition when Daya arrived. I asked him to wait. Later, we got talking and I realised what Providence had sent me.'

'Which was?'

'A blank slate. He was an innocent. With Daya, I could deal in absolutes. He was the perfect pupil.'

'You promised him—what?'

'Nothing. Nothing except freedom from pain. The boy was tormented by ridicule. He put on a brave front, but he was miserable. I promised him freedom from that misery. I told him nothing could hurt him, no matter how terrible the injury. All he had to do that was practice obedience.'

'And Daya did that?'

'Unquestioningly. His trust was absolute.'

'So absolute that he thought nothing of luring children to a tormented and brutal death? Or, are you going to tell me he didn't know what was going on?'

'Of course he knew what was going on. I made sure of that. I knew the details because Chocolate sent me pictures. I showed them to Daya. It was the supreme test. Would he go back the next time? He did! He was the perfect student. But he too betrayed me.'

'You knew Seema Aggarwal.'

'Yes. The journalist. She could have understood, but she refused, too. After all I did for her. Ungrateful bitch.'

'What did you do for her, exactly?'

'Did you see the first press reports on Kandewadi? That came from the police. It was so—trivial. The world had to be told of these grand exploits. I contacted the paper, asked to meet the reporter. We used to meet at a café in Dadar between 7 and 8 every evening. I wanted her to get the impression I lived around there. I showed her pictures.'

'The pictures Chocolate sent you?'

'Yes. Some of them.'

'I refused to let her publish them, but she didn't have the guts, anyway.'

'You learned of Daya's death through her?'

'No, I went looking for him. I couldn't believe he died of drinking alcohol. I thought that was a lie. But later, Chocolate told me, Glider had forced him to drink that last time. Apparently, Daya's nerve failed him. His death was justified.'

'What happened next with Seema?'

'She was unhelpful. I told her I could make things tough for her if she didn't produce information about Daya.'

'Tough? In what way?'

'I didn't say. I merely frightened her. She was a fool. But my move was the right one, because she told me about Suketa. All these years without a word from her, and my wife was living right here, two miles away!'

'What did Seema tell you about Suketa?'

'She said Suketa Das was a famous personality, a feminist scholar and critic. So that was what she was upto! She hadn't even bothered to change her name. Seema told me Suketa Das had contacted her saying she had the complete story on Kandewadi. She was writing a book. She was going to show the manuscript to a knowledgeable friend the next day, and then she would discuss the matter with Seema.'

'What did you do next?'

'Nothing. I did nothing. But the next day, I paid Suketa a visit. I went equipped with every persuasion.'

'What did you want to persuade her into?'

'Back into our marriage, of course. We were man and wife. I loved her, I still do. We belonged together. I wanted her to return to me, I wanted to read her manuscript.'

'Was she frightened when you showed up?'

'No. I would have understood that. She was belligerent. She threatened me. She brandished the manuscript at me. She read aloud the chapter on Monica's death. *I found myself married to a monster who had fed on the flesh of his own child.* She had the audacity to write that!'

'Why, was it not the truth?'

'Am I a monster? Had I fed on the flesh of my child or had I transported her to salvation? Answer me.'

'What was Suketa's answer when you asked her that?'

'You're right, I did ask her that! She crumpled. Confronted with the truth, the fight went out of her. I had to act fast. I made her wear her wedding sari, put on sindoor. I had brought these things with me. I think she expected sex, but I denied her that pleasure. To tell the truth, she disgusted me, old and fat and quite dirty. I had carried along Monica's skipping rope. I gave it to her. She wept over it. I told her to fetch a chair. I looped the rope on the hook in the ceiling. I asked her to stand on the chair. I made a noose and asked her to settle it comfortably around her neck. She did everything I asked with wifely obedience. I asked her to stand still for a moment and recollect her life. While she was doing that, I reached up and strangled her with Monica's ribbon. It was quickly and neatly done, quite painless. I kicked away the chair. I had brought a diaper to keep her from soiling. I wrapped it around her. She was my wife, after all, I wanted no indignity. I stayed for a while, reading the manuscript. It made me very angry. The book had a pretentious title—classic Suketa. She had signed it, with the time and date. It made a good suicide note.'

'What did you do with the manuscript?'

'I burnt it.'

'There's a copy.'

'No.'

'I have it with me.'

He rose slowly, heavily, his eyes were dilated and empty.

'Is that how you knew? No, no, there's nothing about Cattle Island in the book. You. Who are you?'

'Lalli.'

'What does that mean?'

'It's my name.'

'Are you going to punish me?'

'No.

'Why are you here then?'

'I told you. To learn and understand. What happened with Seema?'

'Ah, Seema. Why do you want to know? She said she had some news of Daya. What news, I asked. She said she had discovered Daya had a guru. She was filing the story, but she wanted me to read it first. Where did you get this information, I asked. One of Daya's friends had told her. I agreed to meet, but ten minutes before the appointment, I asked her if we could meet in Parel instead, as I was there. She picked me up in her car. She gave me the story on her jump drive. I told her I too had a lead for her, and asked her to drive into a cul de sac. She was very trusting. It was over quickly.'

'With Monica's other hair ribbon.'

'Poetic justice. Another disobedient daughter.'

'Glider, Blade and Chocolate will hang.'

'They deserve it.'

'You're in favor of the death penalty?'

'Aren't you?'

'No. I find it repugnant.'

'Lucky me?'

'Who knows? I'm done with you.'

'Why?'

'You're an empty shell with a broken mind, incapable of any human thought or action. You've devolved into a subhuman creature of compulsions. I have no time to waste on you.'

'But I have, on you.'

His voice rose energetic, almost joyous, as he sprang on Lalli, and fastened his claws on her throat. He couldn't possibly succeed, he had a fractured wrist—but I was wrong. He was way beyond pain, if not yet beyond good or evil.

For a moment I helplessly watched my aunt's face suffuse, her eyes strain under the relentless pressure of his thumbs on her carotids.

The next moment he staggered back, flung by a superhuman force as Lalli broke free with a karate kick.

Dr Q, knife in hand, ran at the fallen man and brought the knife down yelling. 'Don't move or I will slice your heart in two.'

I had never suspected Dr Q had so much drama in him. I decided not to point out just then that his hand was curled around the blade while the hilt knocked politely at his quarry's ribs.

'Of course, I knew,' he retorted later. 'That was on purpose. I might have injured him, otherwise.'

Wednesday, 31 March

We were no longer alone. Lalli had handcuffed Professor (I couldn't think of him as anything else) to the door. He wasn't going anywhere in a hurry.

I had called Savio.

Meanwhile, Pinki's father had opened the gate, and a sullen procession of women streamed in.

The five mothers—no, only four—formed the vanguard. I missed Tara among them. They advanced a few paces, then stopped, waiting.

Lalli pointed to Professor: 'I have kept my promise to you. I have brought you the murderer. This is the man who made those three boys destroy your children. He did the same to his own daughter, and to many other little girls. He forced his son to commit suicide. He killed his wife. He killed the journalist who wrote about Kandewadi. Here he is. Look at him. Do not touch him, for if you do, he will escape.'

Lalli jerked Professor's fractured arm suddenly, drawing a yelp of pain.

'I have broken his arm to stop you from breaking his neck. Let the law do that for you.'

There was an angry murmur, but nobody moved. Hate emanated from them like heat. One by one they stepped forward and spat on him.

By now, all of Kandewadi was here, men and children too.

I caught sight of Asif, and he came running up to Lalli, dragging Anita with him.

All of a sudden there was a rush and a tall figure stormed through the crowd—a fury, a whirlwind, a serpent ready to strike.

It was Tara. She had a plastic keg of kerosene in her hand. In her other hand, she held a matchbox.

'You will burn,' she said.

With one swift throw she emptied the keg on the cowering prisoner.

'You will burn. Every inch of you will feel the pain you made my daughter feel. You will burn. You will scream with pain as our daughters screamed. You will burn.'

I saw Lalli whisper something to Asif and Anita.

Nobody moved.

Dr Q shifted restlessly. 'Stop her Lalli, you must stop her.'

Lalli didn't move a hair.

I saw Asif and Anita run up to Tara.

She didn't notice them. She kept saying, 'You will burn' with increasing fervor.

Asif prised the matchbox from her hand.

Anita turned around and beckoned.

A stream of little girls ran out of the crowd, and hugged Tara.

She stopped muttering and looked down bewildered at the little upturned faces, so serious with dread.

She dropped to her knees and let them surround her.

The girls forgot about her and just stood there, staring at the monster.

A terrible cry broke from the Professor as he twisted and contorted, trying to escape their level gaze.

Lalli and I found Vinay Dasgupta waiting when we got home. He had a thick folder with him. He had also brought a transcript of Chocolate's statement.

We read the statement first:

I, Rajiv Chawla, state that the following statement is true and accurate to the best of my belief. I make this statement of my own free will.

Over the last month I have witnessed and recorded certain criminal acts in which I did not participate. These acts were carried out by my neighbours Varun Gamadia and Gaurav Khatri at the instigation of a Guru who taught the three of us that greatness can only be achieved by transcending good or evil. We met the Guru in a chat room in January last year: we knew him only by his cyber id: BGOE. We also maintained our cyberidentities: I was Chocolate, Varun was Blade and Gaurav was Glider. Varun and Gaurav have fast cars that they race at night. I accompanied them occasionally. On the 9th of May last year at 4 a.m., Gaurav ran over a child on the pavement while racing his Mercedes on CST Road. We returned to the scene of accident because Varun and Gaurav were advised by BGOE to achieve more. We picked up the injured child and brought her to our building, L'Allegra. We used the service lift to take her up to the 9th floor where Varun's family has a couple of flats, 910 and 911. Varun and Gaurav used these two flats for all their activities. The child was bleeding profusely and I thought Varun would give her first aid or take her to hospital, as he is a doctor. But he said that she was here for a different purpose and I could either stay and learn or I could leave. But if I left, Varun's uncle's goondas would take care of me. So I stayed. They took the child into the bedroom. Gaurav raped her repeatedly until Varun told him he was having sex with a dead body. At that point Gaurav stopped and asked me to fetch my camera. I have a Nikon D800E. He made me take photographs of the child. Later, we sent BGOE those pictures. Gaurav and Varun admired my pictures and asked me to keep clicking through all their activities. Later, I uploaded most of my pictures on the Internet and as they were very artistic, they all sold well. I realized I was sitting on a gold mine. The next day, Varun said he had taken care of the body. Gaurav sold his Mercedes and his father gave him his Lexus. We did not return to the flat for a few weeks.

Around September last year, we started on a really large project because Varun's uncle (whose name he never mentioned) became interested in their activities. Actually, he was a customer for my pictures, especially the hot ones I shot at parties with my spycam. He had a deal with Gaurav's dad who was trying to acquire the land at Kandewadi for a building project. Gaurav felt he had to help his dad. Varun said his uncle would protect us if need be, so Gaurav tried the idea on BGOE.

I want to make it clear that at no point of time did I believe we would actually harm anyone. It was all about achieving higher and higher goals. I had no idea where the children came from, and where they were sent, until much later. After Diwali last year, BGOE sent us his disciple, Daya. The boy was an idiot, very soft-spoken and bhola. We teased and tormented him often, but he never got angry or upset. He was completely obedient, but he let us know that he was not our servant, but his Master's slave. We understood by Master he meant BGOE, and made many attempts to get him to reveal his name and address, but the boy would not. After we got a warning from BGOE we stopped tormenting Daya. Gaurav said we should respect BGOE's privacy if we wanted our project to get off the ground.

I was not told the details of this project. I was only told to keep my photographic equipment ready. In the first week of March, I was summoned by Gaurav at 3 in the afternoon, to the 9th floor. A child was lying unconscious on the bed. Gaurav wanted me to film his activities and I did so over the next three days. On the third day, at around 2 in the morning, Gaurav strangled her as she was in great pain. Varun said it was the most humane thing to do. They had a pile of newspaper ready. After I had finished my pictures, we wrapped the body in newspaper and made a neat bundle of it. My job at this point was to signal Daya from the window. I was to flash a lantern from the balcony and

Daya would set out when he saw it. We couldn't call Daya on the phone, he didn't have one.

The bundle was rolled up in a carpet and Varun took it down in the service lift door where Daya was waiting with his tempo. I later learnt that the bundle had been delivered at the child's home. Gaurav said that would show them. The idea was to make the slum people vacate Kandewadi. Gaurav said it was necessary to push things further. Varun's uncle took care of the police. We had nothing to fear. Although I did not participate in the rape or the torture, I waited eagerly for the next opportunity to make more money off my pictures. I had a growing market. The snuff film I made of the kid's last moments was amazing. The gore sites just lapped it up. A few days later, Daya got us one more kid. Gaurav had trained him well, teaching him how to lure the girls. Now and then he gave Daya gifts. The boy was a fool but he had a real feeling for luxury. Daya brought the kids wrapped in a carpet and Varun collected the 'cleaned' carpet at the service lift door. Nobody suspected the carpet roll brought in a doped kid and took away a dead one.

Varun's uncle had seen the pictures and the snuff film. He told Varun that we had to keep up the pressure or he would withdraw his protection. I was growing sick of it all, but it was too late for me to back away now.

The third kid we got from Kandewadi gave us a lot of trouble. We couldn't weaken her even after three days without food. We never fed any of them. Varun said starving them would change the way they felt pain, and make them feel pleasure instead. He did a lot of experiments to prove his point, but I was not convinced. The third girl was very stubborn, so Varun decided she had to be taught a lesson. He cut her open and took out her liver and intestines. The bleeding was so bad that we had to stuff a sheet inside her to make it stop. There was no need to strangle her, but by now they were just ... mechanical. It wasn't easy packaging this one.

This incident made me really scared. What if I caught some disease? That kid was from the slum and slum kids are crawling with all sorts of germs. When I told Varun that, he laughed and said, 'It's all digested now, don't worry.'

I think we expected to go on indefinitely, but after the 4th child, a police inspector spoke to the press and the story appeared in the papers. Varun's uncle hurriedly told us the case would be transferred to a different police unit, and he could no longer protect us.

When we learned of that at around 7 in the evening, Gaurav said BGOE had decided we had to do one more, just to show our guts. I went to the store and told Daya we'd need one more passenger that night. That's what we called them when we spoke to Daya. Passengers. That's all Daya did really. He ferried the passengers to and fro. I didn't think he'd manage one at such short notice, but the boy was a champion. He brought a girl at midnight.

It was no fun though. When we unrolled the carpet we noticed she wasn't breathing. Gaurav said there was no fun in that, and Varun strangled her quickly just in case she woke up crying. That depressed us, especially Gaurav, who lost interest in everything. I took a few art pictures, but in an hour or two we summoned Daya. I think we were all too depressed to do anything right. We didn't manage to wrap her up well. So Varun brought Daya up to the flat.

This was a mistake. Daya lost it. We were used to the smell, but he couldn't bear it. I don't blame him, we hardly ever cleaned the place, just let it all pile up. Daya tried to run away when he saw the girl's body. Varun got him to stay by threatening him with the knife. Gaurav told Varun to put the knife away. He was very nice to Daya and told him after this he would never be asked to bring girls up here again. He would speak to Master and tell him Daya had done his duty. Then he made Daya down a stiff whisky. Daya gagged on it, but we forced it down his throat. Then we made sure his tempo was loaded and watched him drive away. We had no idea he would die. He never asked questions. He was the perfect disciple. After this, we ended our project.

I was not aware that we had caused actual harm. I never thought those kids were real. They weren't from good families. Their parents didn't care if they lived or died and soon they would all be whores anyway, so I believed Gaurav when he told me we had saved them from a life of shame.

I was in it only for the money and I didn't believe in Gaurav and Varun's ideas of greatness. We had so many followers on Twitter, and though we didn't tweet details of all our projects, we were admired. I enjoyed that. One of our followers, GreenLight warned us about the police raid, but it was too late.

My parents are upset with what I have been involved in, and they have been humiliated by the way I was treated by the slum people. If I have done wrong, I am sorry for it, but I would like to state that the police should have protected me from being harassed and humiliated by slum people.

The transcripts Vinay had brought were voluminous. Lalli settled herself on the beige sofa, and asked me to start reading.

Vinay's Note:

BGOE has a protected IP address.
Glider, Blade and Chocolate share a LAN, triply protected.

The conversations began in January last year and the last recorded was three days ago. From all the confused detail I waded through in the next few hours, I've culled the bits that Lalli marked as vital.

2 January, 2 a.m.

BGOE:
You talk of greatness. What makes greatness?

Glider:
Money.

Blade:
Ruthlessness.

Chocolate:
I'm listening.

BGOE:
How much money?

Glider:
More than anyone else's. There's no limit.

BGOE:
What should it get you?

Glider:
There's no limit to that.

BGOE:
What about something that money can't buy?

Glider:
Doesn't exist.

BGOE:
It does.

Glider:
Where?

BGOE:
In your head. What blows your mind?

Glider:
Speed. Sex. Booze.

BGOE:
What's the aftermath like? High or Low?

Glider:
Low. Very low.

BGOE:
Why?

Glider:
You're the Guru. You tell me.

BGOE:
Because you aim too low. You can never aspire to greatness.

Glider:
What do you know about my aims?

BGOE:
Let me guess. What's the maximum speed you've done?

Glider:
Two hundred.

BGOE:
And what did you hit when you were doing two hundred?

Glider:
Hit? Are you crazy? I'm a careful driver.

BGOE:

Exactly why you can never aspire to greatness. When you're speeding, you're constrained by other concerns. Therefore true speed eludes you.

Glider:

So what should I do?

BGOE:

When you speed, nothing should matter but speed.

Glider:

What about sex?

BGOE:

Same thing.

Glider:

I already do that. I think of nothing but sex when I'm having sex.

BGOE:

Whom do you have sex with?

Glider:

I'm straight, man.

BGOE:

So who are these women? Girlfriends? Whores?

Glider:

Both.

BGOE:

There you are. These are people who expect to have sex with you. Try the other sort, why don't you?

Glider:

There isn't any other sort. Every woman I know expects to have sex with me.

BGOE:
Then find one who doesn't.

Glider:
The element of surprise?

BGOE:
That's something to begin with.

Blade:
What about me?

BGOE:
You said ruthlessnes makes for greatness. How ruthless can you be?

Blade:
Try me.

BGOE:
What's the most ruthless thing you've done?

Blade:
OK. I'll tell you, but not the others.

BGOE:
All my students are one to me. You tell me, I tell them.

Blade:
Forget it.

BGOE:
All right.

Blade:
I'm only keeping it from you because you won't believe me.

BGOE:
I'll believe you.

Blade:
How do you know I won't lie to you?

BGOE:
You might, but I'll find out.

Blade:
Okay, I'll tell you. I killed a guy. He had cancer, terminal cancer.

BGOE:
You're a medical student?

Blade:
Doctor.

BGOE:
Postgraduate?

Blade:
Next year.

BGOE:
Intern?

Blade:
Yes. What's that got to do with it?

BGOE:
Level of experience. I need to establish that if I am to help you.

Blade:
Ok. This guy had cancer. He was on a morphine drip. I didn't put morphine in the drip.

BGOE:
Why?

Blade:
His suffering wasn't pure. I had to purify his suffering.

BGOE:

I begin to have hopes of you. How did you feel when you did this?

Blade:

Great. But it didn't last.

BGOE:

Naturally. Acts of omission are cowardly. Greatness requires courage.

Blade:

You said you have hopes of me.

BGOE:

Yes. Think further about your motives.

Chocolate:

What about me?

BGOE:

You've been listening?

Chocolate:

Yeah. But I can't do any of those things.

BGOE:

What can you do?

Chocolate:

I can make money.

BGOE:

How old are you?

Chocolate:

Seventeen.

Blade:

We'll look after him.

BGOE:
That's good. Learn from your elders.

Two weeks later, Glider ran over a child who was asleep on the pavement.
He made the report at 4 a.m.

Glider:
An hour ago, I hit a kid asleep on the pavement.

BGOE:
What did you do then?

Glider:
I floored the accelerator and fled.

BGOE:
I am disappointed in you. You should have checked on the child.

Glider:
I'm not a social worker!

BGOE:
You are uneducable. You will never experience greatness.

Blade:
What can I do now?

BGOE:
**Return to the site of the accident. Make your plans on the way.
We will talk this over tomorrow at the same time.**

The following day, this conversation took place at 4 a.m.:

Glider:
I understand your comment now. I made some improvements.

BGOE:
What did you do?

Glider:
All 3 of us went out immediately, it was about 4.30 a.m. The kid I'd hit was bleeding. There was nobody with her.

Blade:
I brought her into the car and we drove home. I took her up to my den.

BGOE:
Did you treat her injury?

Blade:
No.

BGOE:
What did you do?

Blade:
Nothing.

BGOE:
Omission again?

Blade:
No. I took a step after Glider was done with her.

BGOE:
What did Glider do with her?

Glider:
I took your advice

Chocolate:
I took your advice too.

BGOE:
You took pictures, I suppose? Selling them on the net?

Chocolate:
Here goes.

Three photographs were attached to this conversation.

> BGOE:
> **What did you do with the body?**
>
> Blade:
> **I've always wanted to own a complete skeleton, ever since First M.B.,B.S. It's a slow process.**
>
> BGOE:
> **How did you get her into your house? Are you sure you won't be found out?**
>
> Blade:
> **We're our own masters here. Pay them enough, and people will look the other way.**
>
> BGOE:
> **This is your first lesson. You have all done well. I'd like you to think deeply on what you've done. We'll talk about it next week.**

'Lalli this can't be true,' I shuddered. 'Maybe they made it up.'

'The photographs? The child in the drum? There's no running away, Sita.'

The first mention of Kandewadi came at the end of January.

> Glider:
> **You asked me what next. All I have is a fantasy.**
>
> BGOE:
> **Let's hear it.**
>
> Glider:
> **You know the way you want to crush a cockroach?**
>
> BGOE:
> **Mindlessly?**

Glider:
No. Crush it! Step on it! Stamp it out of existence!

BGOE:
Because its existence offends you?

Glider:
Yes! That's what I want to do to Kandewadi.

BGOE:
Kandewadi?

Glider:
It's a slum I can see from my window. Simply crawling with vermin.

BGOE:
Rats?

Glider:
People. Really spoils the view from my window. I want to nuke the place.

BGOE:
Burn it?

Glider:
Nah. Too easy. My dad's been trying to buy that land.

BGOE:
So what's your fantasy?

Glider:
I stamp on its soul, crush it, stamp it out of existence and show them that's their destiny.

BGOE:
Big words.

Glider:
I told you it was a fantasy.

BGOE:
And where or what is the soul of this slum?

Glider:
Kids. They parade their kids as if they're wonders. Maid at my place, she has a daughter. You should hear her go on and on about her kid.

BGOE:
Now that's a practical point. Think further.

Blade:
Glider's nuts. These kids aren't pavement urchins. They're well cared for. We can't touch them.

BGOE:
That tells me you've thought of a plan already.

Glider:
Yeah. We've thought of what we want to do, but we can't get to them.

BGOE:
You have been good students. Now let me see how I can help you. Where is this place?

Glider:
Miravli, off the main road.

BGOE:
Give me two weeks.

Chocolate:
Why do you bother so much with us? Why teach us the path to greatness?

BGOE:
You are my sons.

Chocolate:
You have no kids of your own?

BGOE:
I had a son, but he is dead.

Chocolate:
I'm sorry.

BGOE:
Don't be. Just be a good student. I will be back with news in a fortnight.

A fortnight later, BGOE introduced Daya to the boys.

BGOE:
I'm sending you my disciple, Daya. He will be waiting for you outside A-1 General Stores at 6 p.m. He is a simple-minded fellow, but do not be fooled by his innocence. He is trained to obey me implicitly, and I have asked him to follow your orders. Make your plans, but do not make him privy to them. Just give him orders and he will follow them. Let me see now, with his assistance, how close you can get to your fantasy.

There were no other plans discussed over the next few weeks, merely a lot of metaphysical claptrap about greatness being above good or evil.

The boys didn't tell BGOE their plans.

They didn't tell him about their deeds either. But they sent him pictures.

Savio and Shukla came in soon after we finished reading the transcripts. The four of us sat in glum silence. Savio said, 'Dr Q is home, lying down with an ice bag on his head.'

'What did you think of Rajiv Chawla's statement?' Savio asked. 'I'm inclined to believe him when he says he didn't brutalize the kids.'

Shukla shook his head.

'What difference does that make? He was just as culpable as the other two,' I said. 'He was their stooge, just as Daya was Patnaik's.'

'He might have raped and tortured the children if the other two hadn't forced him to eat the liver,' Lalli said.

I thought I hadn't heard right. But the tense silence told me I had.

'You didn't ask him? I would have. Especially because he says Varun told him it was all digested. Here, read this.'

Lalli leafed through the transcripts and pointed to a conversation.

BGOE:
You were paid well for your labors.

Chocolate:
Paid?

BGOE:
You received the highest prize. It guarantees you immunity from all guilt. You have absorbed the sacrifice. The others don't understand, because their motives are base. You are above them now.

Chocolate:
I don't understand.

BGOE:
You ate the sacrifice.

Chocolate:
You're not telling me the kabab—

BGOE:
Yes. The left lobe of the liver. The right, I understand, has been preserved.

'Why Lalli?' Savio ground his hands into his eyes. I can never bear to watch when he does that. 'Why did BGOE do this to them?'

'He made them do it again when case was given to Savio?' Shukla muttered. 'Those boys knew complete inside working of Miravli Chowki.'

'They boasted about this to BGOE,' Lalli said.

I read the transcript further.

Glider:

Right under the new inspector's nose! What do you think of that?

BGOE:

Well done!

Blade:

Not that well. We got nothing out of it. The kid was dead already.

BGOE:

That's irrelevant. You took one step forward, one more. That's relevant.

'Now tell us about Sambalpur,' I begged. 'Were you called in to investigate?'

'No. I was invited there to hold a workshop for senior officers in Homicide. Naturally, the Sambalpur Killings were the focus. They had occurred sporadically through 2005. The bodies, all little girls of 5 or 6, were found hidden or buried in the same town where they went missing. All of them had been raped and mutilated before being strangled. I think there were seven children in all. There was one more the week I was in Sambalpur, a five year old girl. I witnessed the autopsy. It was horrifying. Sudhendu Patnaik was the investigating officer. We met briefly during the workshop. A pleasant young man, but, not exceptionally intelligent. He hadn't made much headway, but I could see he was terribly earnest. That last encounter was just as I was leaving, a very brief conversation. Poor boy—a month after that, I heard the news of his suicide. I thought at that time he had killed himself over the case. In a terrible way, I was right.' Lalli buried her face in her hands, unable to continue.

'He will be at peace today, Lalli,' Shukla said.

'Yes,' Lalli roused herself. 'I'm writing a report to Sambalpur stating that the credit for trapping the Sambalpur Killer goes to Inspector Sudhendu Patnaik. All we did was to follow his lead. His death was not suicide, but murder.'

'This was the truth Suketa had lived with all the years I knew her, *this!*' I burst out. 'What kept her from going to the police? And what kept her going?'

'I don't know,' Lalli said.

'According to me she is complete criminal herself,' Shukla declared. 'She is silent accomplice of rape and murder of own daughter.'

'Oh come on, Shukla!' I protested.

'Isn't she?' Savio demanded. 'This happened to her own child and she kept quiet about it? She left another child to the mercy of this mad man?'

Lalli sighed. 'I think she was in denial till she heard about the Sambalpur Killings in 2005. Her terror must have been extreme when she realized her husband had unleashed his madness on other children. She had a breakdown. She faced up to the truth. She became reclusive. She wrote her book. I don't know what she might have done if Kandewadi hadn't erupted. But I'll always blame myself for not caring to find out what made her so vengeful.'

Vengeful.

I hadn't thought of Suketa as vengeful. Perhaps she hadn't thought that herself, either.

'Pity we lost that manuscript,' I said.

Savio handed me a jump drive. 'It's evidence, but you can do what you want with it after.'

'Cui bono?' asked Lalli.

March at its incendiary finish, with murder behind us.

I was out of love—or was I?

Savio had kept his job.

Lalli had withdrawn into a silence that threatened to be permanent. She hadn't eaten or slept for four days, but sat leafing endlessly through the Sambalpur file.

I was still shaken. I couldn't get the memory of Lalli confronting BGOE out of my head. I could hear that bone crack every time I looked at Lalli. I had never before witnessed my aunt so totally reject a human being, never seen her so devoid of pity.

As he got into the police jeep, Bimalchandra Patnaik had asked Lalli his son's last question, 'Why?'

'Why you committed these crimes? I don't know why,' my aunt answered. 'And I don't care.'

Patnaik had retreated into a convenient madness—it would be up to the courts now to establish his guilt.

Savio had all the papers sent to him from Sambalpur. There was a long haul ahead.

Epilogue

'It's not over,' Lalli said, her first words in a week.

But I knew it was.

That morning I took her out on a drive.

Savio and Dr Q were waiting for us outside Kandewadi.

It was just eleven o'clock.

The factories were noisy as ever, the traffic thick on the street outside.

A-1 General Stores was crowded.

Then—everything paused.

Here came the children, dressed for school, bright as morning, solemn as night.

Here too were parents, uncles, aunts, friends, strangers.

And here too were we, Savio, Lalli, Dr Q and I, worshipping the children as they passed.

Bombay
22nd July 2013